SCHOOL OF SECRETS

SCHOOL OF SECRETS

Menucha Publishers

RUTHIE PEARLMAN

Menucha Publishers, Inc.
© 2013 by Menucha Publishers, Inc.
Typeset and designed by Beena Sklare
All rights reserved

ISBN 978-1-61465-084-3

No part of this publication may be translated, reproduced, stored in a retrieval system, or transmitted in any form or by any means, electronic, mechanical, photocopying, recording, or otherwise, without prior permission in writing from both the copyright holder and the publisher.

Published and distributed by:
Menucha Publishers, Inc.
250 44th Street
Brooklyn, NY 11232
Tel/Fax: 718-232-0856
www.menuchapublishers.com
sales@menuchapublishers.com

Printed in Israel by Chish

ACKNOWLEDGMENTS

I would like to thank Rechy Frankfurter, editor of *Ami* magazine, to whom I owe the resumption of my writing career after a very long dry spell. She e-mailed me out of the blue when *Ami* was about to be launched, and asked if I'd write fiction for it. As someone suffering from chronic writer's block, there is nothing like committing to writing a serial for force-curing of said writer's block. *School of Secrets* first appeared as a serial in *Ami*'s teen section known as *Aim*. So I thought it could stand being turned into a book, both for those who missed the serial version for whatever reason, and for those who don't like reading serials, but prefer curling up with a whole book and no interruptions. Thank you, Rechy and *Ami*, for kick-starting my writing.

I'd also like to thank Menucha Publishers for believing in *School of Secrets*.

As usual, I owe a lot to my dear husband, Joseph. He has always supported my writing and always reads what I write, and seems to be enjoying it even if it isn't the sort of fiction he'd normally enjoy.

CHAPTER ONE

The approach up the driveway made Rosie think they were walking towards some huge, oblong, glass spaceship that somehow hung suspended low on the windswept reed grasses on the cliff. The architecture of the building was jaw-dropping; it was futuristic and innovative, while at the same time managing to convey a standoffishness — a lack of warmth and welcome that made her shiver with apprehension. So this was her new school — her home for the next who knew-how-many years. How could all that glass actually have a homey feeling inside? How could there be privacy, doors to close out the world, and walls to shut out the light?

Rosie stood for a moment before continuing up the neat blacktop path that marched, straight and directional as an arrow, between manicured lawns and tended flowerbeds, towards the building. She was part of a large throng of new girls, and obviously some older girls too, making their way up that blacktop. Almost being pushed along by the force of the crowd.

And yet she had never felt so alone in her life.

Rosie had chosen to come to Ner Miriam boarding school. It had been an escape for her, a refuge from what was fast becoming an impossible home life, and only doomed to get worse. Since the cracks in her parents' marriage a year ago had turned into an ever-widening crevice that could not be filled in by therapy and counseling, she, as the eldest of the four siblings, had taken it the hardest. She had been the most astute, the most aware of what was happening around them. And even worse than that, noticing her mother's tears when she thought no one could hear.

When it came out in the open that her parents were actually separating — that this wasn't fixable like everything else in her life had been until that point — Rosie's most dominant feeling had been anger. Pure, white, and hot. Anger that two supposed adults could be so selfish as to go their separate ways leaving four young children floundering, then being passed from one parent to the other like a tennis ball in a never-ending volley. Weekdays with Mom, every second weekend with Dad, the kids were constantly packing and unpacking small, lonely looking suitcases that stood in the hallway, never quite needing to be put away. Rosie, at fourteen, had begged to go away to school. And now she stood at the gates of her future, wondering which indeed would have been worse.

"Dunno which would've been creepier," said a voice in her ear that made her jump, as she had been so deep inside her own head, "a Gothic Mansion straight out of a horror story, complete with cobwebs and stone gargoyles on the gates, or this monstrosity."

She turned around to look at the speaker. She was about Rosie's height, but blonde to her dark hair, slimmer and more delicate looking, and had a steely look in her gray eyes that belied her fragile appearance.

"Hi," Rosie said somewhat shyly.

"Hi. I'm Shuli. You new here too?"

"Yeah. Is it that obvious?"

"'Fraid so. Nice to meet you…?" Her voice rose at the end, a question, and Rosie realized she had not reciprocated in the name offering.

"I'm Rosie. Sorry. Nice to meet you too."

Shuli grinned. "There, that wasn't so hard! Now at least we each know one other person! Hey, maybe we'll room together; that would be cool!"

"Do we get to choose who we room with?" Rosie wondered. She had always attended the local school and gone home at the end of the day to a warm, loving family, with younger siblings to care for and love. But now her house felt like a hollow shell, not like the home it should be at all.

"You've not boarded before, I gather," Shuli surmised. "My parents are outreach workers. You wouldn't believe the places they've schlepped me to in the name of *kiruv*. All over the world. So I've always boarded. I'm an old hand at this, trust me. You can put in a request to room with someone, and I'm going to request you."

"But you don't even know me. We only just met!" Rosie said, surprised.

Shuli smiled. "I think we're going to be friends."

Rosie felt loved and wanted for the first time since she could remember. It was a warm, fuzzy feeling, and she clung onto it like the blankie she had carried around as a toddler, and which her youngest sister still did.

The girls entered the huge glass portal now and into a bright lobby with high, arched ceilings and polished floors. Their footsteps echoed and, incongruously, made Rosie want to tap dance — even though she had never tap danced in her life. The room was filled with a crowd of her soon-to-be fellow students.

The heavy-set woman who confronted them was such a stereotype of an old schoolmarm type that it made Rosie want to giggle. The woman's iron-gray hair pulled back into a tight, unbecoming bun at the nape of her neck. Her hair was so tightly scraped back it made Shuli whisper in Rosie's ear, "Instant facelift! Imagine, no surgery and the same effect!" Rosie almost laughed out loud but the stern look on the teacher's face stopped her in her tracks.

"Welcome to Ner Miriam, girls," the woman said in a deep, resonant voice that Rosie found attractive. "I am Miss Colton, the deputy head. I'm in charge of assigning you to rooms. Those of you who are not new girls, go to your rooms now and unpack."

The crowd surged, bustled, surged again, and divided like a swarm of bees. Most of the girls disappeared down various glass and steel corridors towards, Rosie presumed, the bedrooms. About forty girls remained. They eyed each other warily, sizing each other up.

"New girls, follow me." Miss Colton started off down one of the corridors that fanned out from the central lobby like legs on a spider. The lobby itself seemed to glower like a spider. Rosie shuddered. Then she noticed another girl — short, curly-haired, a little plump but cute looking — dancing behind Miss Colton, mimicking her unusual rocking gait. Rosie couldn't believe anyone would have that much chutzpah this early on.

"You have been assigned rooms," Miss Colton announced over her right shoulder. "Three new girls, two senior girls, per room. That's how it's done here."

"We can't request roommates?" Shuli burst out, horrified.

Miss Colton stopped in her tracks and wheeled around.

"I said: That's how it's done here," she said, deliberately enunciating each word to make sure Shuli understood. Shuli went red and bit her lip. Rosie felt like a boat cut adrift from its mooring. This girl, Shuli, was her anchor — the girl who knew all about boarding schools, and she felt safe with her… Well, as safe as she could feel, anyway. But now, everything was changing. Shuli looked unsure and panic-stricken, and Rosie herself felt as if she was in strange and choppy waters and she had the awful, sinking feeling that there were sharks out there.

Suddenly, desperately, she wanted to go home. However awful things were at home, at least it was a familiar awfulness, which she knew how to handle. Here, she was completely alone and unsupported. Rosie had never felt so scared in her life.

CHAPTER TWO

Miss Colton was busy delegating the room assigning to some older girls. Two sixteen-year-olds with a list approached Rosie and Shuli, and to their relief, they were rooming together after all. Along with them, the small, curly-haired girl made up the three freshies in the room; the two sixteen-year-olds were the seniors.

The three freshies stood in the room, awkwardly looking around. It was simply furnished, but the two seniors had obviously stamped their mark on the prime part of the room with posters, cuddly toys, and other personal items. The remaining three beds and the walls around them looked bare, as if someone had recently ripped off her own pictures and personal belongings, which was probably the case.

"First some rules," said one of the seniors, who had introduced herself as Kaylah. "Lights out is at nine. We don't believe lights out applies to us, so we have these flashlights. They're for senior girls only." Kaylah clicked her pocketsize penlight on and off as she continued. "Freshies must keep quiet after nine. You cannot use the showers until we've had ours. Freshies will clean up the bathroom even if they didn't make it dirty. Freshies have to make seniors coffee in the morning…"

"No way!" Curly Hair burst out. "I'm not making anyone coffee! Who do you think you are?"

"We are seniors," Kaylah replied calmly. "You're meant to look up to us. When you're a senior you'll be able to behave like us to the next lot of freshies."

"Hmph. And we're supposed to learn *middos* from *you*?" Curly sneered.

The other senior, a tall girl with bright-red hair in a ponytail looked at Kaylah.

"Looks like we're going to have trouble with this one," she said.

Kaylah nodded in agreement. "There's always *The Cupboard*..." she said darkly. The younger girls looked at each other uncertainly but no more was said on that subject.

"You can have these two closets for your stuff, we have these three over there," the redheaded girl told them.

"Two closets for three girls and three closets for two girls?" protested Curly.

Redhead gave her a distant, sneery look. "We are…"

Curly joined in the chorus. "*Seniors*. Yes, I know."

Rosie couldn't help thinking that the curly-haired girl was really into dicing with danger. Hadn't she heard of getting in people's good books, at least at the beginning?

The two seniors (the redheaded one had told them her name was Rochel) left to go to the senior common room where there was coffee. This left the three younger girls to unpack and get accustomed to their surroundings.

"You're really brave," Shuli told Curly. "What's your name, by the way?"

"Yael. And it's not that I'm brave…I'm impulsive. Sometimes…no, scratch that, *usually*…I do things I regret. But I can't help doing them at the time. Makes life interesting, I feel. Nothing worse than a boring life, don't you think?"

Rosie stared at this diminutive ball of energy and thought she had never met such an unusual girl in her life.

Rochel popped her head round the door a little later, munching on a piece of delicious-looking cake, and said, "Oh, by the way, there are some more rules on that laminated sheet by the window. Read and learn, girls, read and learn." The redhead disappeared again and the door closed behind her.

Rosie had finished unpacking and was testing out her bed. "Oh, you read them to us, Shuli. I can't be bothered to get up now. I'm actually quite comfortable."

Shuli went over to the list.

Yael was throwing stuff from her suitcase into the bottom two drawers of the closet. Rosie watched her in bemusement. "I may not be the tidiest person on the planet," she observed, "but at least I try…at least in the beginning."

Yael looked down at the girl lying on the bed. "But it ends up messy in the end, right?"

"Well, yeah," Rosie acceded.

Yael threw up her hands in triumph. "There ya go! So why bother in the first place? Tidiness is boring."

Rosie closed her eyes and was almost drifting off in a light doze when it occurred to her that Shuli was still standing by the list at the window.

"I thought you were going to read us out the rules," Rosie said.

"Oh, yeah. I was just sidetracked by the stunning view. Look, you can see the ocean from here."

Shuli then proceeded to read out another list of draconian rules that had obviously been drafted by Kaylah and Rochel, not the school staff.

> Seniors get first choice of EVERYTHING. Deal with it.
>
> If seniors have friends or relatives come visit (even from within the school), freshies have to vacate the room to give them space and privacy.
>
> If you see a senior has a nice item of clothing or a pair of shoes, a freshie is NOT allowed to go and buy the same item, even if it is relatively inexpensive, as this will devalue the item for the senior.
>
> Freshies are not allowed to own cell phones. Only seniors are, and freshies may get to use said cell phone occasionally if enough favors have been called in, or tasks done.

These rules went on a bit longer in a similar vein, and Yael and Rosie rolled their eyes.

"Talk about a hierarchy!" Yael said. "Well, I can tell you now, I am not abiding by those rules!"

"No…" Rosie said lazily from the bed, "I would never have guessed…"

Yael sat down at the desk in the corner and started writing. After a while, she got up with her piece of paper and stuck it over the laminated list by the window.

"You can't do that!" Rosie said, with a mixture of horror and awe.

"I just did."

"Read it to us," Shuli said.

Yael read.

I am what I am, not what people try to make me.
I am strong and independent, my power won't forsake me.
I won't be crushed by rules, nor by dictates from above,
For rules they are the sticks, and the carrots; that is love.
What flowers need to bloom, is some gentle rain and sun.
Pounding them with power won't help anyone.
We are young yes, immature, but we are far from fools.
So please treat us kindly, don't crush us with your rules.

Rosie and Shuli stared at Yael.

"Where's that poem from?" Shuli asked.

"I just made it up, it's not from anywhere," Yael replied. "I like writing poetry. It helps me express myself."

"That's genius," Shuli said with a sigh. "I wish I could write like that. In fact, I wish I could *spell* like that."

"Spell?" Yael asked, puzzled. "There aren't any really long words in that poem, what do you mean?"

"Never mind." Shuli seemed for a moment as if she was going to divulge something, but then smiled and said nothing further about spelling.

There was a loud, computerized, buzzing sound, and the roommates heard the pounding of feet towards what they presumed was the dining hall. It was time for dinner. They joined the tide and allowed themselves to be swept along with the crowd.

In the dining hall, for the first time, the girls saw evidence of some obviously Jewish teachers, in the form of a table of *rabbanim* at the front of the hall. These *rabbanim* and their wives between them formed the Kodesh staff.

The head of Kodesh was Rabbi Moslovsky, a kind-looking man in his fifties with twinkly blue eyes and a salt-and-pepper beard. He stood up and spoke, introducing himself and the other members of the Kodesh staff, before telling a short *dvar Torah* from the *sedrah*.

His style and oratory were inspiring and the girls found themselves spellbound but curious.

"What's that accent?" whispered Rosie.

"Oh, it's South African," Shuli whispered back. "We lived in Johannesburg for two years when my parents did outreach work there."

"South Africa?" To a girl who had never left the UK, it sounded like another planet.

"Spent a year there. You wouldn't believe the *kiruv* work my father did there. We had the nicest house too. Our own swimming pool and everything."

"I don't believe you," Rosie said with a stiff turn of her head towards the *rav*. Was she now stuck with an inveterate liar, an impetuous and *chutzpahdik* troublemaker, and two imperious seniors?

CHAPTER THREE

Yael's mother was very young and very alone when she decided that a baby was not what she wanted in her life. The day she decided, she was sitting in a grimy one-room apartment overlooking a railway line. Every fifteen minutes exactly, the fast train to London hurtled by at one hundred and twenty-five miles an hour, and all the buildings in the vicinity shook. Her building, being the closest to the railway, and also the least maintained of all the surrounding buildings, not only shook, but rattled and groaned like an old man trying to get out of a particularly deep chair. It woke her up at night and sometimes it woke the baby up too. She was young, alone, and run ragged with responsibility that she felt she didn't want and couldn't cope with.

She looked at the baby, sleeping for once, in her Moses basket. Bald, but with a few strands of hair round the edges of her head that looked like they might eventually turn into curls. Long, curling lashes lying on her cheeks like delicate spiders. She was so beautiful, and her mother loved her so much, but just wanted someone else to care for her.

With a sigh, her mind made up, she wrote a note asking whoever found this baby to care for her, added that she was Jewish, left it unsigned, and tucked the note down the side of the Moses basket so it wouldn't blow away in the wind.

Then she put on her thin, inadequate jacket and pulled a beanie hat down over her daughter's head. She prepared a bag of diapers and baby clothes, and put in a tin of formula and two bottles. She had thought to nurse the baby herself, but as she was so ambiguous about parenting anyway, she didn't want to bond too closely with a child she would probably not keep.

Another train, another old man creakily shaking his chair as he strove to get up. The building shook. The doors and windows rattled. The young mother went out of the apartment carrying the Moses basket and closed the door behind her.

The baby was found on the steps of the local hospital, and taken in by a nurse, who pronounced her fit and well. The nurses named her "Tuesday," as that was the day of the week when she was found. They cared for her as best they could while Social Services looked for a suitable foster home for her.

This foster home turned out to be a struggling Jewish family called Reed, recently arrived from Israel, who already had five children of their own and desperately needed the income that fostering would bring. They decided to call her "Yael" instead of "Tuesday." As she had no surname of her own, she became "Yael Reed."

"We can only look after her for a couple of years," Mr. Reed told Social Services, "until I get a job and we're more settled. And anyway, we might have more children, and then this baby will be too much for us."

The Reeds were a wonderful, caring family for young Yael. She grew up, cute and curly haired, surrounded by older siblings who adored her. As Mr. Reed never really did get settled with parnasah that well, and more children didn't make their appearance, she remained with the family for far longer than they had first anticipated.

Yael always knew these were not her real parents but it never occurred to her to be upset about it. She wasn't the only child in her class who was living with a family who was not her biological one. She didn't even think, at that time anyway, to wonder about her real mother and why she had given her up.

Fast-forward several years. Yael was now ten, her oldest sibling was away in yeshivah, the next one was in seminary. The family was thinning out somewhat. That year, several things changed, and all of them did not bode well for young Yael Reed.

The first thing that happened was Mr. Reed got a job. A good one that paid him enough not to need the extra income from Social Services for fostering Yael. That in itself wouldn't have been enough for things to radically change things for her, but the next thing that happened was.

Mrs. Reed, after many years of childlessness following her first family of five, gave birth to twins. A boy and a girl. The Reeds were overwhelmed with happiness and gratitude for this wonderful and unexpected miracle. They had never expected to have any more children, and were resigned to having their own five, and Yael to complete the family. Now all of a sudden they had seven of their own, and Yael began to feel like a spare dinner waiting to be discarded. The family was wrapped up in this new event, and, even though she had never known anything else but this family, she felt excluded.

This behavior is common to naturally born siblings on the arrival of a new baby too. But because Yael knew she was fostered, it only served to make things worse. And so she began to react. She didn't even know she was doing it, but she started testing her foster family, to see how much they could stand before they cracked.

She started refusing to go to bed. And to eat the meals that she had previously found so delicious.

"Yael, this is your favorite! Fried chicken and French fries! Eat, just a little, for me!" Mrs. Reed would coax her. Yael was hungry — starving in fact, and the food smelled sooooo good. But she knew eating it would please her foster mother, and she wasn't willing to do that for her. She pushed the plate away.

"I hate your cooking!" she said, and spat into the plate, so no one else would want it either. Then she ran upstairs to the room she shared with her older sister and shut the door. She lay down on her bed, stomach grumbling. Then after a while, and after making very sure no one was coming up, she reached under her bed for her secret stash of cookies and chocolate.

This would sustain her until midnight, when she would creep downstairs and help herself from the fridge. Never quite enough so that her foster mother would notice anything missing; just a little of this, and a little of that.

Her older sister Gila came into the room, her face dark with anger, and Yael stuffed her cookies under her covers.

"Why are you doing this? Mommy made that fried chicken specially 'cause it's your favorite and you've spat in it so it's wasted! She's downstairs crying her eyes out. She doesn't know what she's done wrong."

Yael said nothing, but inwardly she glowed with triumph that her actions had caused her foster mother to cry.

"You should go down and apologize," Gila went on.

"No," Yael replied stubbornly. "I hate it here. Ever since the twins were born it hasn't been the same. No one really wants me here anymore. You've all made it quite obvious."

"Of course we do! You're our sister, just like all the rest!"

"No I'm not. Your mother didn't give birth to me and your father isn't my father. I don't belong here! I want my real mother and father!" It was the first time she had ever expressed an interest in her real parents, and even while she said it, she knew it wasn't really true. She had no memories of them. She knew she had been left on the steps of the hospital. Hardly the behavior of a mother who loved and wanted her.

Gila didn't know what to say to this. Instead of comforting the needy little girl, she got angry and lashed out.

"You're an ungrateful child! My parents took you in, and this is how you treat them?!"

"They took me in for money!*" Yael yelled back. "I was their meal ticket! They didn't love me then and they don't love me now! They used me for parnasah!!" Yael flung herself back on the bed and sobbed with self-pity, aware while she was doing it that several meals' worth of cookies were getting crushed into the sheets and she'd have to clean them up later.*

Gila left the room, defeated and angry, and went downstairs to report this conversation. Yael snuffled her way into silence and then got up to tidy her bed and clean up the crumbs. She sat there, eating the crumbs and crushed cookies, and sniveling. She knew she had made an unforgiveable scene and had crossed an invisible line into unacceptable behavior. She wasn't sure at all that there was any way back.

Later, her foster mother came quietly into her room. Gila stayed tactfully outside, but made sure she was in earshot. Yael pretended to be asleep but Mrs. Reed knew her better. She sat down on the edge of the bed and stroked her hair.

"Yael, Yael, what are we to do with you? I love you. You are one of my children, just like all the rest. Please don't do this to me!"

Yael couldn't bear the tension, and turned to her foster mother. They hugged, kissed, and cried together. Later, she came downstairs for a meal. Mrs. Reed had saved her some unspat-in fried chicken, and she ate it hungrily but in silence. She didn't give her the satisfaction of thanking her for the delicious food, and made sure to leave a quarter of the meal behind, even though she could have easily eaten it and had second helpings. She also decided to leave the dirty dishes on the table instead of her usual practice of tidying up after herself.

Yael knew she was behaving badly but couldn't help herself. She went up to bed, and topped herself up with more sweets from her stash. On balance, thinking about it in bed that night, she reckoned she had just about won that round, but it was a closely fought battle with no clear victors emerging.

After that incident, the Reed family rumbled along fairly well for a while. The twins had quite bad reflux and this made them cry a great deal and throw up a great deal more. Mrs. Reed took them to doctor after doctor and tried medication after medication but nothing seemed to help.

The constant crying was wearing her down and preventing her from sleeping. This made her vulnerable and weepy. But it also made her snappy and irritable, and Yael chose to spring her second round of "testing to see how far she could push them," just when her foster mother was at her lowest ebb. It was extremely bad timing for Mrs. Reed, but triumphantly good timing for Yael.

This time, she rebelled around bedtime.

Her children's bedtime was extremely important to Mrs. Reed, especially as the twins were being so difficult at night. She needed a few hours wind-down time with her husband, and she needed to sit quietly and nurse the twins so that they settled well for the night; it made the difference between Mrs. Reed getting any sleep that night or not. Her older children respected this, and after nine o'clock either went to their rooms to bed, or to read or play quietly. No one bothered the parents at this time.

Yael chose a night when the babies were on a knife-edge between crying all night, and being soothed to sleep by nursing, to throw the mother of all tantrums. She knew, even while she was lying on the floor kicking and screaming like a two-year-old about how all her classmates go to bed at ten o'clock so why should she go to bed at nine, that she was being totally obnoxious. But she didn't care. She wanted to push her foster parents to their limits, and she succeeded.

Mr. Reed pulled her out of the room where his wife was trying to nurse the babies. They were crying now, and twisting their heads away in distress. Mr. Reed was furious. A peaceful night in ruins and all due to this brat of a child who wouldn't go to bed!

"Now look what you've done!" he hissed at her when they were both safely outside the living room.

Yael twisted in his grip and screamed loudly. "I hate you! I hate being here! I want my real parents!"

His expression looked dangerously close to exploding. "Do you not remember that your real mother just left you on the steps of the hospital?" he growled. "Why would you want to find a mother like that? And don't you think that if she'd really wanted to find out where you were, all these years, she could have? Hospitals keep records and so does Social Services. She's made no attempt to trace your whereabouts, so I would imagine she couldn't care less what happened to you. It's about time you grew up and accepted it!"

It was a cruel thing to say and as the words left his mouth Mr. Reed knew he shouldn't have said them. But they were out there and he couldn't take them back. Yael stood still and stared at him in shock. He stared back at her, almost as shocked as she was by what he had just done. He wished with all his heart that he could turn back time and unsay what he had said, but he knew he would, for the rest of his life, berate himself for that look of total defeat in her eyes.

Yael hadn't considered why her mother had never tried to find her. She had just assumed she would, some day. All of a sudden she felt crumpled, like a piece of discarded tissue that someone had blown their nose into and thrown away.

She shook his hand off her arm as he stood there, and then turned and stalked away.

She did not go to bed at all that night, but spent the night huddled in a chair in the den, knees up to her chin, a blanket around her, thinking about her life and how awful it was. She never once had even a moment of hakaras hatov for her loving foster parents and how they had opened their home to her for the past ten years. All she thought of was that she was unloved and unwanted, and alone in the world.

Her foster mother came to her once or twice during the night, to try and persuade her to go back to bed, and said that her foster father was sorry he had said those things, but she was blank, not listening, uncaring. The deed was done; the knife had found its mark. There was nothing they could say or do to repair the damage now.

The next day, Yael refused to go to school. She refused to eat, she refused to get dressed in her uniform. She remained in that chair, knees to her chin, blanket around her, saying and doing nothing, just staring into space. Her foster parents sent one sibling after another in to her to try and talk her round, but it was fruitless. At last, afraid she had gone into some kind of catatonic trance, they called a doctor. The doctor examined her briefly, and called Social Services.

Her social worker, a kindly if somewhat misguided woman by the name of Miss Jones, sat and spoke with her gently and asked her what had happened, and what she would like to do.

At last Yael spoke.

"I would like to leave," she said.

"Are you sure?" Miss Jones said worriedly, thinking of the absence of alternative foster placements in the Jewish community.

"I would like to leave," Yael repeated. "I would like to leave today. Now."

Miss Jones reported this exchange to her foster parents outside the den. Mrs. Reed started to cry, as did several of the children. There was quite a commotion going on, because Mrs. Reed was blaming Mr. Reed for having messed everything up with his cruel and thoughtless remarks. There was a great deal of crying and some shouting, and recriminations galore.

Miss Jones came back into the den.

"The problem is," she said, "that at this present time, we don't have anywhere else for you to go except into care."

"Then I'll go into care," Yael said stubbornly. "Anywhere has got to be better than this place."

"You don't know what you're saying," Miss Jones warned, but Yael was apparently oblivious. In fact she wasn't oblivious at all, but terrified out of her wits at the thought of going into care. At that moment if her foster parents had come into the room and begged her to change her mind, and said they were sorry just one more time, she would have capitulated. She was waiting for that to happen, so that this nightmare could be over. She had seen that her foster parents did love and care for her, and that her siblings loved her too. She had all the proof she needed.

Unfortunately, it was just too late. Her foster father had been yelled at by a screaming banshee that used to be his wife, calling him every name under the sun, and he had had enough. He burst into the den, face like thunder, terrifying the life out of Miss Jones and Yael, and shouted:

"You know what? If you want to leave after everything we've done for you, all the love and care and nurturing you've experienced in our home, go!!! We don't want you here anymore! You have no *hakaras hatov*, no gratitude, no appreciation for the fact that we took you in, an abandoned baby, and brought you up for ten years like one of our own. Get out of my house!! I don't want to see your face anymore!!"

Yael yelled back, "You did it for the *money*!!" and ran out of the room, leaving Mr. Reed stunned into silence and shocked because it was at least partly the truth.

She went upstairs and started packing her things. As she didn't own a suitcase of her own, and didn't want to take anything with her that wasn't hers, she stuffed her belongings into large shopping bags.

Miss Jones waited downstairs, trying to calm the hysterical family down.

"I think she'll calm down and want to come back again," Miss Jones said in a conciliatory tone.

"I don't want her back," Mr. Reed growled. "That girl has broken my family apart. Why should she get to come back whenever she chooses? When she calms down?? What about when we calm down??"

"This is all your fault!" sobbed Mrs. Reed. "You and your big mouth! You've spoiled everything! I don't know if I can ever forgive you!"

Yael appeared at the doorway surrounded by shopping bags. "Don't worry, Mr. Reed," she said coldly. "I shan't be coming back. Ever."

She walked out of the door to Miss Jones' car, leaving the family shell-shocked. Besides the finality of her words, it was the first time in her entire life she had called him anything but Daddy.

Miss Jones sat in her car, a sullen Yael in the back, and made a few phone calls. She was desperately trying to find an alternative placement rather than to put Yael into the children's home. She had never been happy about the children's home, and dreaded what it would do to an already traumatized Yael. But there was no choice.

"Yael," she said, trying one last time, "you really don't want to go to the children's home, believe me."

"You heard Mr. Reed," Yael said, emphasizing her foster father's title deliberately. "They don't want me. I don't want to go back there. Ever."

With a sigh, Miss Jones started the car.

The Yudit Cohen Memorial Children's Home was a bleak place indeed. The entrance hall was cheery, to fool visitors that all was well behind the scenes. But step a little further in, and the rooms and regime were grim, cold, and loveless. She was given a bed in a room of seven other girls, some of whom had learning difficulties and screamed a lot at night. She had a small closet to put all her things in. The curtains at the window were hanging off their rails. The paint was peeling and the atmosphere was one of despair.

The house mother, or eim habayis as she was hopefully called, was an old Germanic woman called Gerda Lipschitz. Gerda was a Holocaust refugee, one of the last of her generation. She had been a small child during the war and was now elderly and should have been stopped working decades ago. She was slightly senile and should no longer have been left in charge of children. She tried her best but was forgetful and doddery and needed looking after herself rather than expecting her to shoulder a caring role.

There were old ladies less doddery than Gerda in care homes being led around by Filipino caregivers and helped to eat. It was a disastrous placement. The girls were unkempt, uncared for, and left to their own devices most of the time. The only advantage was they certainly learned self-reliance, as parenting in any form was totally absent in their lives.

Yael was shocked by this downturn in her life but didn't say a word, as she had insisted she wanted to leave the Reeds. She looked around the home for a like-minded girl she could be friendly with, but the nearest thing was Katya Aarons.

Katya was one of the few girls of approximately her age who did not have learning difficulties. She was eleven, sharp as needles, and as acidic as nitrate. She hinted to everyone who was willing to listen that the reason she was in this care home was that she had done some terrible deed to her real parents, and left the listeners to connect the dots.

The truth was that she had been the human version of a feral cat in her own home, spitting and snarling at any attempts at discipline, scratching and biting whenever love was shown to her, until her parents threw their hands up and admitted defeat. Therapy and family counseling had all been tried and abandoned. The psychiatrist on her case said "to put it in medical terminology, Katya Aarons has a screw loose." Despite her behavioral anarchy, she was still extremely bright and performed at the top of her class in school.

Girls in the home all attended the local Jewish school; the ones with learning difficulties in a special unit within the school. There were only three or four girls who were in the mainstream classes, and Yael and Katya were two of them. The stigma of everyone knowing they were from Yudit Cohen hung around them like a bad smell, along with the fact that their clothes were often dirty and worn, and in need of repair or replacing.

In this respect Katya was brilliant. She could sew like a dream, and offered her coresidents an alteration and repair service. At a price. The administration of Yudit Cohen found it more cost-effective to pay Katya to mend all the girls' clothes rather than buy them new ones. Often people donated their castoff children's clothing to the home, and Katya would alter them to fit.

"I intend to earn enough money to get myself out of the gutter," she told Yael one day as she counted up the day's takings. "And then I shall reach for the stars. Nothing will stop me getting to the top. Glass ceiling? What glass ceiling? Ha!"

"What top? What do you want to do?" Yael asked her in fascination, watching the old, donated sewing machine whizzing through the fabric with Katya's small hands just missing being pierced by the needle.

"Why, I intend to be a top fashion designer, of course!" Katya declared. "Paris, Rome, Milan, New York, London — all the top fashion centers will be my oyster. No one shall get in my way!"

Her green, slightly slanted eyes had a feline look about them, and there was a wild look in them that Yael found quite disturbing. She had no doubt that if anyone did get in Katya's way, they would be trodden underfoot.

Katya was not a good influence on Yael's emerging character. She taught her that achievement was king, at all cost, and nothing — not kindness, not consideration for others, nothing — was more important than getting what she wanted. She also taught her that risks were part of this, and nothing worth having was without risk.

Yael grew closer to Katya as the ensuing years passed. She was, to all intents and purposes, her only friend, and she lived her life vicariously through her. Katya was going to reach for the stars and she, Yael, was going to be up there with her, holding on to her ankles.

They often talked about how Yael would be Katya's sidekick and help her get ahead. They would share an apartment and Yael would do the housework and cleaning, cooking, and shopping, while Katya did the important stuff like designing and sewing the latest fashions for runway models.

Then came the day when Katya was fourteen and Yael was thirteen, and Katya decided her moment had come. She had saved up over two thousand pounds and she was going to Paris to join Dior or Versace or one of the big fashion houses.

In the dead of night, Katya, who did not share a room with Yael, packed her things, took her money and her old, tatty passport, and left the Yudit Cohen Care Home forever. She didn't take Yael with her. She didn't even wake her to say good-bye or even leave her a note explaining her actions. She just left. Ambition at all costs, no matter who was hurt in the process.

Yael was devastated. Doubly so as she felt she had been abandoned by her mother all over again. Her only friend had left her alone, and had gone back on all her promises. Yael was inconsolable. After the tears were all cried and she had no more tears left to cry, she became hardened, angry, and bitter. If this was how people in her life were going to treat her, why should she care about how she treated herself?

A couple of weeks down the line she read in a Jewish newspaper that a girl called Katya Aarons had been run over and killed by a truck while attempting to sneak on board a cross-Channel ferry, Yael could barely muster up a drop of sympathy. The girl hadn't even gotten to France, let alone started a glittering career in fashion design. Served her right. Life was for the moment, and for the moment only. Tomorrow could take care of itself because planning for tomorrow only brought heartache in its wake.

After that, Yael's behavior took a serious downturn in the care home, to the point where she was disrupting the other girls and leading them astray. Gerda Lipschitz had been taken to hospital having suffered a stroke, and the doctors doubted she would ever function normally again. The administration was talking about closing the care home down as no suitable replacement was found. The learning disabled girls were placed in special schools around the country, and one or two regular girls were placed with foster parents.

When Yael heard that the Reeds had taken in two twelve-year-old girls, she went into major meltdown. Miss Jones was summoned.

"I don't know what to do with this girl," she confessed to the administration. "I know she's gone through a lot, but still…" She shrugged helplessly.

It was a horrendous few weeks for Yael. The entire care home had emptied out and she was the only one left. It was like being the last one being chosen for a team game, only far worse, because there were no comforting mothers' arms to run home to at the end of the school day.

Yael spent her days totally alone aside from going to school, where she was regarded as somewhat of a pariah. "You know she's the only one left…" she often heard whispered when the girls didn't think she could hear. She went back to the empty house after school, ate a lonely meal *prepared for her by kindly local women, and slept alone.*

Then her savior came along in the shape of a local entrepreneur and wealthy businessman, Mr. Reuven Salamon. He had heard about the care home problems and had come along to offer what help he could. Everyone was taken care of, he was told. There was only one problem left to solve.

"Ner Miriam would suit," Mr. Salamon told the administration. "It's a Jewish girls' boarding school on the south coast. She'd be nice and far away from everyone here in London. A chance to make a new start. I'll pay her tuition of course."

Yael heard where she was going and shrugged. The coast sounded nice. Far away sounded even nicer.

CHAPTER FOUR

Supper was astonishingly delicious. Rosie had expected it to be dire, but was pleasantly surprised. There were plenty of healthy choices such as salads, stir-fries, and whole wheat pasta with low-fat sauces. Those dishes were followed by vast vats of apple and plum compote made, so the girls heard, from fruit from the school's own orchards. Apparently a certain celebrity chef, who had made it his mission in life to make school food healthier, had visited the school, pronounced the diet of pre-shaped turkey twizzlers and fries followed by steamed puddings as unsuitable for growing high school girls, and had undertaken an entire revamp of the menus.

After supper there was a study period, but as the new girls had nothing to study yet, they were told to go to their rooms. As Rosie, Shuli, and Yael walked slowly towards their room, wondering what punishment lay in wait once the seniors saw Yael's poem, Rabbi Moslovsky appeared and beckoned to Rosie.

All three girls stood still, confused. Rabbi Moslovsky said, "I need to speak to you in private. You girls go on ahead. Rosie will join you shortly."

Rosie felt like she was a branch being torn off the main tree. Even though she was still highly mistrusting of her new friends, and even more so of her new environment, they were all she had. The girls gave her reassuring "You'll be okay, see you soon" glances and went off, leaving her feeling exposed and rather nervous.

"Step into my office please, Miss Bernstein," Rabbi Moslovsky said. *Uh-oh*, Rosie thought. In previous schools no one had ever called her by her last name unless she was in big trouble. What could she possibly have done wrong this early in the game? She hadn't even written that wretched poem, if that was what this was all about!

Rabbi Moslovsky's office was a stark contrast to the glass and steel of the main building, and seemed to have been decorated with a view to recapturing home comforts. His office chair was large, black leather, and exceptionally squishy, and squeaked protestingly when he tilted it backwards. His desk had a similarly battered appearance, as if it had been dragged through the streets to get it here, which might indeed have been the case. It was decorated with large gouges and lines, like an old man's wrinkled face. The walls were book lined, and every inch of wall space was filled with bookcases. The *sefarim* were stuffed in three deep, and some lay on their sides untidily. Rabbi Moslovsky directed Rosie to sit in a comfortably upholstered office chair on the opposite side of the desk.

Rosie stared at him in mute terror waiting for the axe to fall. He seemed at a loss to know how to begin and this scared her even more. Maybe something terrible had happened at home? The atmosphere at home had been terrible enough; now she envisioned scenarios where it was even worse.

Rosie's mind spun like a top. At last, and totally out of character, she burst out, "Are my parents okay? Is everything all right at home? Or have I done something terrible already, on my first day? If I have, I'm really sorry, but…"

Rabbi Moslovsky smiled instantly, and the sun came out for Rosie. She shut her mouth.

"Oh you poor, poor child, here am I trying to formulate my words and meanwhile you're concocting all kinds of scenarios in your head. I'm so sorry; I should have at least prefaced my remarks by saying you've done nothing wrong and everything is okay at home." He paused and at that moment Rosie knew he knew her home circumstances. "Well, as okay as usual. Nothing has majorly changed."

"Phew," Rosie said with a little smile, and held her trembling hands together tightly to stop them from shaking quite so badly. Even though the status quo at home would be awful to most people, it was acceptable to her as long as it didn't get horribly worse.

"No, this isn't about you," Rabbi Moslovsky began. "This is about another new girl, who is coming later on tonight, and she has even more unusual circumstances than you. I've looked through a lot of freshies' profiles, looking for the ideal girl to take this new girl on, and you fit the bill best. You're mature, sensible, and responsible. I suppose being in the situation you're in at home has forced you to grow up beyond your years. I know it's perceived that girls from broken homes are the most common students in a boarding school, but ours has qualities that even the parents of girls from so-called regular environments want."

"I thought seniors were supposed to look after the new girls," Rosie asked, puzzled. She didn't like being singled out as the girl with the unusual home circumstances all the time, but she didn't know what she could do about it so she let it go.

Rabbi Moslovsky waved a dismissive hand and laughed. "Oh, they like to think they're here to lord it over the freshies," he said, "but they're here to just keep an eye on any mischief done in the room. We wouldn't expect a room full of new girls to behave themselves without at least one older girl as a calming influence. As it's unfair to expect one senior to room with a bunch of juniors, we made the rule of two seniors, three juniors per room."

"I see..." Rosie said, not really seeing at all.

"This situation will require a great deal of maturity on your part. You'll need to keep whatever confidences she tells you completely to yourself. This is imperative. To be honest, I was in severe doubt whether to accept this girl into the school at all, with the circumstances she brings with her. But her parents begged and pleaded and said it was *mesiras nefesh* that we take her."

"*Mesiras nefesh*?" Rosie commented, thinking that sounded rather dramatic. "What, is she sick and needs the sea air or something?"

"Nothing like that. But before I tell you, I will need your word that whatever is said here tonight, stays in these four walls." Rabbi Moslovsky got up and walked to the door. He opened it and peered outside. Satisfied that no eavesdroppers stood there with their ears to the door, he came back in and closed the door firmly.

"I've even had this room swept for bugs," he announced, not without a little pride.

Rosie shuddered and looked anxiously around at the floor. She hated bugs. "Ew," she said.

Rabbi Moslovsky laughed. "Not the creepy-crawly type of bugs, but listening devices. Spy cameras. Spy microphones."

Rosie's mouth fell open. "How did you know what to look for?" she asked.

"Oh, I didn't. But *they* did..."

CHAPTER FIVE

"But who are *they*?" Rosie asked.

"Before I tell you who *they* are," the *rav* said in his stage whisper, "I need to know from you that you are trustworthy. Confidentiality is the key in this matter. It could literally make the difference between life and death for this girl. Do I have your word that whatever I tell you and whatever she may tell you, remains a secret?"

Rosie secretly thought the *rav* was being overdramatic but she was far too polite to say so. "You have my word," she said, highly curious now.

To her surprise, the *rav* made yet another trip to the door of the room, another peep behind it for loiterers and eavesdroppers, before returning to his desk, door firmly closed. He leaned over the desk and spoke quietly to Rosie so that any itinerant eavesdropper who had decided it was worth staying with her ear to the door wouldn't be able to hear anyway. Rosie almost rolled her eyes; this was just comical. But his next words sent her into shock.

"Have you ever heard of the term 'Witness Protection Program'?"

"Um…sort of, but I haven't really any idea what it is." Rosie was getting more and more confused and uncomfortable.

"This girl, Nena Sheinfeld, has witnessed a crime. A terrible, ghastly, horrible crime that has affected her whole life. Before she witnessed this crime she was like any other girl her age. Happy, relaxed, doing well at school, confident, and fearless. Now she fears for her life and jumps at every shadow. Her school grades have plummeted and she's started getting into trouble as well. Skipping classes, not doing her homework when she did attend school; she was hiding away at home when we came looking for her. She was obviously terrified out of her wits by what she had experienced."

"Poor girl," Rosie said with genuine feeling. Even with her home life upside down and her school life an unknown, she couldn't imagine being scared to go out.

"Maybe she just needs some therapy," Rosie suggested after a few minutes digesting the story. The *rav* shook his head sadly.

"If only that were enough," he said. "No, unfortunately Nena has a real reason to be afraid. She's due to testify as an eyewitness to this crime, and she's been threatened by the perpetrator that if she does testify, he'll come after her."

Rosie's hand flew to her mouth. "Oh my…"

"So that's where the Witness Protection Program comes in," the *rav* continued. "It's given her a new identity and has paid for her to attend this school, which is very far from where she lives and far from where the crime happened."

"So her real name's not Nena?"

"No, and it's best you don't know it in case you start calling her by it. Even by mistake. One mistake could be enough." He paused to let the gravity sink in. "So now you know why confidentiality is of the essence. You will be the only person in this school besides me — yes, even the other teachers — the only person besides me who knows why she is here. I don't know her real name and neither do you. That's best."

Rosie pondered this for a few moments, then asked, "But why tell me at all? Why not keep the whole thing a secret from everyone? Even you, if it comes to that?"

"The child is only fourteen and is very traumatized by what she witnessed. Besides the whole stress of being threatened by the criminal, she's probably suffering from post-traumatic stress disorder and it might make her behave irrationally at times. This is fine, if at least a couple of people know why this is happening and can offer the appropriate support at the appropriate time. If she was here totally undercover, she would probably flounder and sink. If she has a friend, a real friend, who understands, and can stick up for her if other girls are unpleasant — and I, as head of Kodesh, will make sure the staff don't give her a hard time — she should get through."

"Once she's testified and, hopefully, he's put away in prison, she'll be safe. No?" Rosie asked.

Rabbi Moslovsky sighed. "If only it worked like that."

"Doesn't it?"

"Firstly," the *rav* said, "this criminal has friends. Powerful friends he can call upon to wreak revenge upon whoever had put him away."

"Ohh," Rosie said, the picture becoming clearer and uglier by the minute.

"And even if he doesn't, she'll never be safe. If the justice system I'm familiar with is anything to go by, he won't be incarcerated for life. If he knows where she is, he'll come and find her. No matter how long it takes."

The future for Nena looked bleak. "Maybe she should be abroad," Rosie said. "Maybe this school isn't far enough away."

"Miss Bernstein," the *rav* said, "for Nena, this school is as far away as it needs to be. And no country on this planet would be really safe."

"So which country did the crime happen in?" Rosie wanted to know.

He smiled apologetically. "Sorry."

"But the criminal has been arrested, hasn't he?"

"Yes, and the trial is in a couple of months, maybe less, I'm not sure. But in the meantime she needs to be kept safe. So we are her safe house — this is the Witness Protection Program in action. There will be certain operatives from the program monitoring the school; she won't be alone and unprotected here. Some operatives are already in place, posing as teachers. Secular ones, I might add," he said wryly.

"Oooh, can I know who?"

"Sorry. It might jeopardize their undercover positions, and then the safety of Nena."

Rosie wondered for one mischievous moment whether it might be fun trying to pick out the false teachers from the genuine ones by their lack of skills.

"The fake teachers are actually very skilled in whatever subject they are teaching," Rabbi Moslovsky said, both reading her mind and nipping that idea in the bud with one coup de grace. "You wouldn't be able to spot them."

"Shame," Rosie said with a cheeky smile.

"Undercover operatives have to be just that; undercover and non-discoverable…well not that easily anyhow…not easily enough for a fourteen-year-old schoolgirl to notice, otherwise the whole operation could be in jeopardy."

Rosie thought the whole thing sounded quite exciting and certainly different from how she had anticipated spending her first school semester.

Again the *rav* seemed to be able to read her mind.

"I must admit nothing remotely like this has ever happened in this school, and while it lends a certain air of excitement to the normal, everyday running of the place, it's also a massive, a huge responsibility that we don't do or say anything that could put Nena at risk. I must impress this upon you again. I can't say I would want to be part of a Witness Protection Program on a daily basis; it would be far too much for my blood pressure, which already isn't what it should be…" For a second Rabbi Moslovsky looked a little worried, and reached into his desk for a bottle of pills. "Forgot to take them this morning. Good thing you reminded me."

Rosie wasn't aware she had reminded him of anything, but was glad to accept the praise anyhow.

"So when do I meet this Nena?"

CHAPTER SIX

Nena Sheinfeld wasn't her real name. But that is of little importance for the purpose of telling her story. The whole reasoning behind her name change was to keep her safe, so we will respect that and stick to calling her Nena Sheinfeld. If that's okay with you.

Nena was one of those girls who never stood out in a crowd, never excelled at anything in particular except academics. She wasn't particularly pretty, but she wasn't ugly either. She was just plain, and unremarkable. She had mousy, brown hair that wouldn't stay curled for long if she bothered to curl it, and it became greasy quite soon after she washed it, so it never had that glossy, just-washed look either.

Her eyes were gray, but you wouldn't notice them. They weren't large or fringed with wonderful dark lashes like one of the girls in her class whose teachers had often accused of wearing mascara when she didn't. Nena's were gray, her lashes were fine, and the whole effect was hidden to a large extent, behind strong glasses, as her eyesight was quite poor.

In a world where being thin was king, at least here Nena scored. She was thin to the point of gauntness but it didn't even suit her. She had no idea how to dress to take advantage of her clothes hanger appearance, so she just ended up looking like one. A clothes hanger with a lank mop of hair on top.

In fact, one girl who had been particularly nasty had dressed up as Nena for Purim, and had hidden behind a floor mop on a long stick, with thick-lensed glasses stuck onto the fronds of the mop. She had been disciplined by the teachers for extreme cruelty, and Nena had hidden herself away in a closet and cried for hours. But secretly, somewhere deep down, she was quite flattered by this ghastly caricature, as it meant someone had actually noticed her.

Nena, in general, was to all intents and purposes invisible. If you'd been in her class, then some thirty years down the line when you thought back about your class and who was in it, you'd have almost certainly forgotten about Nena Sheinfeld.

Despite her lack of notable looks, she was bright and academic, particularly excelling in the sciences. She loved nothing better than to study and do well in her tests and end-of-term exams. Unfortunately this didn't increase her likeability with her peers. Indeed it earned her the reputation of being a nerd or teacher's pet.

She had thought about pretending to be dumb and fail tests just to make herself more acceptable, but reconsidered; she didn't think she had any qualities besides her brains that would make up for her classroom peer group skills.

She wasn't talented in any quirky thing like being able to bend her top joint of her finger forwards without moving the second, like one girl in her class could do, or stand on her head and do other amazing gymnastic feats like another could. With her poor eyesight she wasn't a huge asset on the netball field either.

So she managed to drift through elementary school, and part of high school too, like a ghost. A ghost who came at the top of the class at sciences, but at the bottom in popularity. Someone who was there, but only on the periphery.

She did have one or two friends. Other unpopular girls gravitated to her. But if girls had bothered to try to get to know her, and not just judged her by external features and talents, they'd have been rewarded by a warm and affectionate personality, loyalty that knew no bounds, and a deep and abiding frumkeit that a lot of girls in her class could have done well to emulate. Nena didn't just play being frum; she lived it.

"Nena's always saying Tehillim," a popular girl in her class called Rivky once remarked, not in an admiring way, as Nena sat quietly in a corner between classes swaying gently, her lips moving silently.

"Maybe she's saying Tehillim for her hair to stop looking so greasy," said Sheindy, another mean but unfortunately popular member of the class.

"Or her glasses to become flattering!" said someone else.

A small crowd laughed, enjoying the joke at someone else's expense, although many felt uncomfortable doing it. They were like a pack of dogs — and like a pack of singularly cowardly dogs, felt safety in numbers to join in the attack.

Nena was not strong enough or assertive enough to answer anyone back or come up with a biting response. She turned to Hashem, cranked up the Tehillim, and prayed that He would somehow make her life more tolerable than it now was. Maybe something exciting could happen and she'd be at the center of it, and gain some degree of popularity that way?

Be careful what you wish for, Nena Sheinfeld, you might just get it.

Nena's home life was quite normal. She had loving parents, a couple of younger siblings who were both attractive, popular, grounded, and well adjusted. Her parents were proud of their firstborn's academic achievements and brushed aside her fears about lack of popularity.

"You'll prove yourself one day," her mother said. "These girls don't know quality when they see it. They'll wish they were you one day."

Nena thought it must have been a hundred years since her mother was a schoolgirl if she thought that popularity due to good looks and a sparkling personality wasn't more significant than academic skills.

The trouble was, the other unpopular girls in the class weren't very smart at lessons like she was; they were just unpopular due to…well… being blah and unpopular. No looks, no skills, no personality. Nena was the only unpopular girl who was also quite brilliant.

The other A-student in the class happened to be both brilliant and beautiful, and gathered girls around her like the Pied Piper of Hamelin. So the girls who wanted to hang out with Nena were not the sort of girls she would have chosen for her friends. Inevitably, Nena spent a great deal of her free time on her own through choice as well as circumstance.

It was lunch break on a fine, sunny day. Some of the girls chose to sit under shaded trees in the school grounds to eat their sandwiches, and this was a wonderful social opportunity for friendly chatter. There was no place in this group for Nena. She could see the one or two unpopular girls in the class gravitating towards her, wanting to share the lunch break with her as she was actually good company. She was well-read and knew a lot about everything, even if she wasn't willing to spend time chattering about clothes and jewelry and other such empty things.

Nena couldn't face spending her lunchtime with those unpopular girls even though the alternative was to spend it alone. She had her books, and she decided to leave the school grounds and sit in the park to eat her lunch on her own and study a little, whilst listening to music.

The park was just down the street and girls over the age of fourteen were allowed to go there at lunchtime. But because the school had such pleasant gardens of its own, few wanted to take up the opportunity, so Nena had the place to herself. She saw the unpopular girls looking around for her, and she felt horribly guilty as she slid unnoticed out of the school gates and, keeping as much out of sight as she could, made her way to the park. There she found a secluded bench that had a lovely, shady tree over it, and some bushes to hide her from view. She felt safe there. Even if the unpopular girls came looking for her, they were unlikely to notice her there.

Shedding a quiet tear for her solitary state, she sighed, made the relevant berachos, and started eating her lunch. She felt isolated and yet safe and cocooned from the world. She opened her science textbook and started studying for the next test.

In front of her, a robin and its mate distracted her for a while. The brightly colored male bird and the plain, brown female did a dance together catching insects in the warm summer air. She smiled as she watched them; they seemed so tame and unfazed by her being there so close. She felt an affinity towards the dull, brown female, so like herself in some ways — in comparison with the brightly colored male — and hoped one day she, like the robin, would find a suitable life partner.

She felt relaxed, even loved, by nature, if not by man. These little birds didn't see her faults, her lank hair and thick-lensed glasses, her spotty complexion and unfashionable clothes. They just saw a warm, friendly human being who was no threat to their safety, so they played and flew around her without fear. Smiling again, she put down her science book and watched the birds. Science could wait. Indeed, what was science but the beauty of Hashem's wonderful world?

Raised voices made her lift her head. The birds flew away, and Nena felt saddened that they no longer felt safe. She looked to see the source of this distraction, and saw two men arguing loudly as they walked along the path ahead of her little hideaway. She moved along the bench a little until the bushes completely concealed her.

Surprisingly, they stopped to argue only a few feet from where she sat, and seemed completely unaware of her presence. A quick glance around showed the park to be empty except for her, these two men, and the birds. She looked at her watch, and it was time to get back to school, or she would miss afternoon lessons. She started to gather her possessions but something stopped her, and she kept very still indeed.

The men were shouting now, and it didn't seem like an argument that was going to be resolved that easily. Their faces were dark with anger, their arms were waving around, and their voices, speaking in an Eastern European language of some kind, were getting louder. She couldn't understand a word of what they were saying, but she did understand two things. One, they were definitely not friends and two, she had better keep very quiet and still so they wouldn't notice her.

Why had they stopped just there, in front of her? She realized after a moment's wondering, the reason was the little path that led off the park right next to where they were standing. It was obvious. This was the place they parted company; one was going to take that path and the other would go in another direction. But first they had to finish their argument.

She glanced at her watch and wished they would get on with it and finish fighting because she was going to be sooo late and get into sooo much trouble it just wasn't funny!

Be careful what you wish for, Nena Sheinfeld, you might just get it.

One of the men started to walk off up the little path, waving his hands in a dismissive gesture that said, I'm done with this, do what you like. *The remaining man was shouting after him as if to say,* Don't you dare walk away from me!!

The first man went on walking, his back to the other.

Oh good, *Nena thought,* maybe I can get back to school.

The second man pulled out a gun and shot him in the back.

It was all Nena could do to stop herself from screaming. She was so shocked. She stuffed both her hands in her mouth and whimpered. The walking man went down like a crumpled doll and just lay there on the path. The shooter went over to him and bent over him, as if to examine to see his condition. Looking around, he saw no one, so he concealed the dead man towards some bushes.

Nena took her chance. The man was so busy he wouldn't notice her. She grabbed her stuff and ran, trying to make herself as invisible as she possibly could.

She was almost at another exit of the park before she dared look around to see if he had seen her.

He was standing there, looking, it seemed, directly at her. But she was so far away by then that he could not possibly have recognized her face.

She ran for her life.

Sobbing uncontrollably, she arrived at school. She was terrified the man was following her, but nobody seemed to be. Her deputy head, a woman she liked and trusted, was in the corridor, and, in an uncharacteristic display of fear and need, Nena flung herself into the woman's arms, sobbing her heart out.

The deputy head took her into her office, sat her down, gave her tissues, stroked her hair, and waited.

Once the story was out, the woman was in a state of shock. She had imagined a dog had scared Nena on her way back from the park. Never, in her wildest dreams, had she imagined a story like this would emerge.

"Did he see you?" the head asked.

"No, I don't…well…he saw a girl running…I saw him looking at me, but by then I was so far away he couldn't have seen my face."

"We must call the police at once." The deputy head picked up her internal phone to speak to the headmistress, and within a couple of minutes, it seemed, the room was full of people, all crowding around her. She told her story over and over, hiccuping and crying, being comforted in the knowledge that here were adults all around her, looking after her needs.

Little did she know that they were as lost for what to do as she was. They were just waiting for the police.

Meanwhile the story swept around the school like wildfire and Nena Sheinfeld was, for the first time in her life, the center of attention, *although not exactly how she would have wanted it. Everyone wanted to know her, everyone wanted to hear about it, and be a small part of the girl who had witnessed a murder and lived to tell the tale.*

But she was an unwilling celebrity. Even whilst she was surrounded and adored, she recognized that this new pedestal she was put on was made of ice, and would soon melt away in the sun. Nena had always wanted to be liked for herself, not because exciting things were attached to her and made her more interesting. So her instincts were to remain polite but distant to anyone who made what she considered to be false overtures now that she was "famous," and stick to the unpopular girls who had remained loyal to her.

She didn't want to miss lessons but she had to. The police were there, and wanted to know everything she had seen and heard. She told them everything, over and over again until she thought she could recite it in her sleep.

Had she seen the man? Yes, both men had been within only a few feet of where she was concealed. Could she identify him again if she saw him? Yes, probably.

She started to cry when she heard that the second man had indeed died. She had been hoping against hope that maybe, just maybe, he was only injured and would recover. But now it was a murder charge.

Could you get any sense at all of what they were arguing about? No, they were arguing in a foreign language, could be Russian or Polish or Rumanian, she couldn't tell, but it sounded Eastern European. Was the shooting in the heat of the moment or cold-blooded? Here Nena started crying again. He was walking away and the man shot him in the back. How much more cold-blooded can it get?

They let her go after that. They could see she was traumatized. They promised to send a victim support person along for counseling. But she wasn't a victim. She was a witness. Surely this would all go away now that she had given her statement?

The police went away. Nena was told to go home, even though she thought that plunging straight back into lessons would be more therapeutic. She wasn't allowed to do that. No, she had to rest, and recover, in the arms of her family. It was doctor's orders.

At home her shocked and distressed family took charge. But Nena was withdrawn, quiet, and shut herself away in her room. "I just want to go back to school," she kept saying. "I have a science test and I've studied for it!" But whenever she looked at her science book, the one she had been studying from the moment the shooting happened, she only saw the scene in front of her, not the words in the book. Nothing was working any more.

The victim support people organized trauma counseling and she went along with it, but no one seemed to quite get the way she was feeling.

"I just want this all to go away," she kept saying to the counselor. "I want the man arrested and put in jail, and then I'll feel safe."

Be careful what you wish for, Nena Sheinfeld, you might just get it.

Even though Nena had never exactly been Miss Popularity in school or with her peers outside of school, she had been relatively confident and happy. However, after witnessing this murder, it all changed. Nena became silent, withdrawn, and nervous. She saw the incident replayed in her head over and over again as if someone cruel had forced a film inside her head and there was no escape from it. Every time she looked at someone, she saw an overlay of what had happened.

Being able to talk about this in therapy sessions did help somewhat, but it didn't stop the movie in her head.

And then came the day that the police called her parents and told her a suspect had been arrested, and she would be needed to identify him in a lineup.

Her first reaction was to throw a monumental tantrum. Literally, like a two-year-old, she flung herself on the floor, kicked her legs, and screamed that there was no way she could do it. Her parents stood there, totally nonplussed and at a loss. They loved Nena very much but they had absolutely no idea how to deal with this.

Her therapist came to the rescue.

Despite the fact that the therapy sessions hadn't been entirely successful in ridding Nena of her post-traumatic stress, she had become very close to Riva Cohen, the therapist. She was warm, empathetic, and, above all, vulnerable, and that vulnerability struck a chord in Nena. Riva Cohen had been known to cry if Nena frustrated or upset her. Nena had sometimes been thrown into the reverse role and had to comfort Riva rather than the other way around. Little did she know that this was probably part of Riva's strategy, to help with the bonding and to make Nena feel in charge of her life again. It worked, and that was all that mattered.

Nena's mother had called Riva when Nena threw the tantrum, and Riva had come straight over. It was good that she only lived a couple of minutes' drive away, and she had made that drive in defiance of local speeding laws, whether that was advisable or not.

Riva sat on the floor with Nena, who, embarrassed at being found kicking and screaming, now lay quietly sobbing, with both arms covering her face. Childlike, it made her feel like she couldn't be seen.

"She has to identify the man she saw," Nena's mother explained. "That's what's brought this on."

Riva nodded and signaled to her to leave the two of them alone. She stroked Nena's hair.

"You know you have to do this, Nena," she said. "Once you do it, it will all be over. He will be in jail and you will feel safe. It'll only take a minute, and I'll be right there with you. I'll hold your hand if you like."

Snuffles from the floor.

"He won't be able to see you," Riva continued to reassure the girl. "It'll be one-way glass. You can see in, he can't see out."

Nena hadn't considered this, and raised her head to look at Riva. "Yeah?" she asked doubtfully. It had obviously been worrying her a lot.

Sensing a breakthrough, Riva smiled. "Yeah, definitely. He definitely won't be able to see you. There will be five or six men looking quite similar though, so you'll have to pick him out of the lineup. Each will be holding a card with a number. You identify him by the number. Then you walk away and that's it."

"But who are the others?" Riva sniveled, sitting up and mopping her red and swollen face.

"Oh, anyone. Sometimes they just pick people up in the street. Sometimes they're police officers who happen to look a little similar. It has to be fair for the suspect though. They can't get five totally different looking people like old men, children, women, or whatever, and then this guy. They must all be of similar height and build and age too."

Nena nodded. "What if I can't tell the difference? What if I don't recognize him?"

"Then say so. Don't guess. Only pick him out if you are sure."

"So if I can't recognize him, he could walk free?"

Riva could sense she was losing control of the situation again.

"You said you could identify him. In these situations, it's amazing how your brain retains information. You'll be fine. I'll be right there with you."

She hoped she wasn't giving the girl false confidence, but it seemed to work. Nena's whole body relaxed and she hugged Riva. "Okay, I'll do it, thank you! Let's get it over with as soon as possible."

Her parents couldn't have been more grateful to Riva if she'd saved Nena's life. They had felt so helpless in recent days and weeks anyway, and this tantrum was the cherry on the cake of it all.

They were slightly upset that Nena wanted only Riva there when she did the identification. But they decided their wounded pride was worth their daughter's peace of mind, and stayed away.

In the identification room at the police headquarters, Nena stood holding Riva's hand incredibly tightly. The police officer explained the procedure.

"Five men will come in to that room behind the glass but they won't be able to see you, don't worry. They will stand there as long as you need them to. If you need them to speak, they will speak. We've chosen men with Eastern European origins so they will all sound similar in the language they speak, but you and only you can recognize the man you saw by his face and the sound of his voice."

Nena nodded. The police officer signaled to someone, and the men started to file in behind the glass. Nena felt physically sick as she watched them come in. They were all wearing casual clothing, sweatshirts, cotton pants, and running shoes. They were all of similar age and height. How on earth would she be able to tell between them?

"Face the front, please," the police officer spoke into a little microphone that was obviously relayed behind the window. They all faced Nena. They held large cards in front of them, numbered one through five.

Nena, still holding Riva's hand as if her life depended on it, walked slowly along the window looking at the men. Even though she knew they couldn't see her, it seemed to her that each of them was looking straight into her eyes. She thought she was going to faint.

The man holding card number three…

"Could they shout something in Russian or Polish or something?" Nena asked the policeman.

Nena had no idea what they were shouting but number three was the one. She had known it at once, but when he shouted, and his face grew dark and angry, there was no doubt in her mind.

"Number three," she said firmly.

"You sure?" the policeman said, his expression giving nothing away.

"Yes. It's number three. I remember him, and his voice."

"Thank you." He gave no sign as to whether she was right or wrong. His expression was an impassive as a stone statue.

The five men filed out again. Nena looked around her wildly.

"Did I identify the right man?" she asked, panic-stricken.

His stone face softened. "Yes. Yes, you did."

Nena fainted straight into Riva's arms.

When she came round, she was lying on a bed of sorts, still at the police station. She was given a sip of water, and her face was being wiped by Riva, with a cool, damp cloth. A female detective was with her, smiling.

"You did well," she told Nena. "We've been after Ivan Rodchenko for quite some time now. He is the head of the Russian mafia in London and a ruthless gangster. The man he killed was supposedly his friend, but with someone like Rodchenko, no one is his friend. He has killed before. You did well to identify him. Now maybe we can put him away for life."

Nena smiled.

"Of course you will have to testify at his trial," the detective went on casually. Nena froze.

"I have to testify? You mean this isn't over?"

"I'm afraid that's how the law works. Innocent until proven guilty. You identified him; that's gone a long way. But he's entitled to a fair trial and your testimony will put him away for life. As you are under age and have been through a trauma, you can testify via video link so you don't have to be in the same courtroom as him."

"But I'll have to identify him again, I suppose... He'll be on the video."

"Yes. But you won't physically be in the same room."

"Oh. Okay."

There was a long pause and Nena was offered some more water. Then the detective spoke. "There's something else. He knows you've identified him. You said he saw you, from a distance. He's a very dangerous man."

"He didn't see my face! He couldn't have! It was too far away by then!" Nena had a sinking feeling where this was going.

"I know, but he saw your school uniform; it's quite distinctive. He has a lot of friends on the outside, so he'll do his best to track you down and prevent you from testifying. I think the best thing for your own safety is if you go into our Witness Protection Program."

"What's that?"

"We move you to a different area, give you a different name and identity. Maybe even change your looks a little, although I don't think that is going to be necessary."

"Away from home? Away from my school?" Nena was hyperventilating.

"I'm afraid so. It's for your own safety. He'll be sending out people to find you, so the further away you are, the safer you will be."

And that is how Nena Sheinfeld, which is not her real name, left her home, school, and all that was familiar to her, and went to Ner Miriam.

Her parents were of course devastated. They couldn't believe that their firstborn daughter was leaving home and basically disappearing off the face of the earth.

"Is there no other way?" sobbed her mother.

"If you want to keep her safe, no, I'm afraid there isn't," the woman detective told her kindly. She knew it was a big task, asking these kindly Jewish parents to part from their oldest child. She had never put such a young person into Witness Protection before.

"But I can phone her from time to time?" her mother asked eagerly through her tears, clutching at straws. "Or maybe visit?"

"No, I'm afraid you can't. You won't know where she is, and she will be forbidden from contacting you. If contact is made, the villains can trace her."

"Is this forever?" her father asked, his face pale. "Shall we never see Nena again?"

"No such thing as never," smiled the detective, but secretly she wondered if she should be giving the parents false hope.

Her parents both broke down at that point. "How shall we tell the other children?" Her mother sobbed.

"Mum, Dad, I'll be okay." Nena hugged them both, "One day I'm sure I'll be allowed to make contact again."

It hadn't all been bad. Yes, she missed home and all that she knew. But she had made the most wonderful new friends in Ner Miriam, better friends than she had ever had in her previous life — even a girl called Yael Reed who was willing to risk her life for Nena. In Ner Miriam no one made fun of her or mocked her appearance. She felt loved by her new friends, and supported by them. She had even felt safe, for a while…

CHAPTER SEVEN

Rabbi Moslovsky swallowed his blood pressure pills with a sip of water and looked at his watch. "She should be here any moment now. She's being brought to the school by another undercover operative in the guise of a taxi driver. The program didn't want to take any risks whatsoever with regular taxi drivers possibly not turning out to be who they say they are…"

"Wow," said Rosie, the enormity of the situation slowly sinking in. Then she realized something else. Her friends would be very curious as to what had transpired in the *rav*'s office. They would be none too pleased when she was evasive. She had been mistrusting of them until now, had wondered what their real stories were — Yael's predilection to danger and risk, Shuli's stories of *kiruv* in the Congo (what was *that* all about?), and Rosie had noticed Shuli taking a long time to read the rules on the wall… What other secrets did her new friends hold?

And now she was going to be keeping the biggest secret of her entire life — one that could mean life or death for Nena, whoever Nena was really. She couldn't ever reveal what Rabbi Moslovsky had told her, even if it meant losing her new and fragile friendships in the process. How attractive a prospect would that turn out to be?

The *rav* stood up. A phone had rung briefly on his desk. An internal call.

"She's here," he said. "Come and meet Nena."

Rosie followed the *rav* out of his office. She looked around nervously for her friends, but they had obviously concluded she must have fallen into the Bermuda Triangle or some other Black Hole, never to return, and they had gone to their room without her. She was relieved; it saved her from having to explain…yet.

In the huge, glass-and-steel entrance hall, with its marble floors, where her footsteps echoed like a thousand voices and the desire to tap dance never quite left her, Rosie saw a girl standing next to a woman. The woman held car keys in her hand, and Rosie determined from this clue that she must be the taxi driver operative.

Rosie looked at her briefly, trying to sum up in that glance what an undercover operative actually looked like (exactly like everyone else, but this was surely the point…there was little advantage to having a sign across her forehead saying, "Undercover Agent"). The driver wore a black jacket and skirt, wasn't Jewish by her appearance, but had a pleasant face. As if she carried no secrets whatsoever. Impressive, Rosie thought.

She then turned her attention to the girl at her side.

Nena Sheinfeld (as in the absence of any other name that was the name Rosie had to assign to her) didn't look at all as if she was the center of something as dramatic as Rabbi Moslovky's story. She was a thin, plain-looking girl, with a rather unfortunate outcrop of spots on her chin and forehead, and she wore unstylish glasses. Ditto shoes. Ditto her school uniform. Even though the uniform itself hardly lent itself to haute couture, there were ways of making the plain, navy skirt, striped blouse, and navy sweater a bit more chic than Nena had managed to achieve. Even Rosie, who wasn't known for her fashionista tendencies, had belted the sweater over the skirt, and the skirt itself was a flattering A-line rather than a bulky all-round pleat such as Nena wore.

Rosie looked at Nena and Nena blinked at her from behind her thick-lensed glasses. Rosie's first impression was "boring." She sighed inwardly. She was going to have this dull, boring, plain girl trail around after her, have to deal with all her neediness and post-traumatic stress? Oh, pu-leeze! Why on earth did she get chosen for his task? Rosie felt panic rising again. Her strongest inclination was to ask to speak to Rabbi Moslovsky in private again and ask, no, beg him to find someone else to trust with this. She just had too much of her own stuff to deal with.

Rabbi Moslovsky was busy greeting the girl warmly, and paying the taxi driver. The driver nodded and turned to leave. At the entrance to the school the driver turned again and gave Nena a look that Rosie tried her hardest to interpret, but couldn't. Her best try was "stay safe," but she couldn't be sure.

"Which room is Nena going to be in?" Rosie asked the *rav*.

"Right next door to yours," the *rav* replied.

Oh great, Rosie thought. *I suppose it's better than in my room.*

"Well," Rosie said, trying to be upbeat and cheerful while her heart was sinking ever further into her Mary Janes. "Come on, I'll show you your room and introduce you to the girls."

Nena said nothing, but followed Rosie. The one advantage of Nena looking like she did was that she melted completely into the wallpaper, if there had been any wallpaper. She was, to all intents and purposes, invisible, which did make it easier for Rosie not to feel too uneasy being with her. She didn't stand out because of her good looks, that was for sure, and by the same token, she wasn't outstandingly unattractive either. She was just…blah.

Suddenly Nena spoke for the first time. "Let's see the grounds."

Rosie hadn't seen the grounds herself. She glanced at her watch; there was time for a fast reconnoiter. They made their way to an exit and went out.

The land up to the boundary was well kept and tended obviously by school gardeners. But then there were wire fences, high and secure, presumably to keep the girls safely inside and prevent them from having what could be a very nasty accident.

On her way into the school, Rosie had barely registered how close to the cliff edge it was. But here they stood at the wire fence, on a blustery September evening, still daylight, and staring straight into the English Channel. The sky matched the sea, turbulent and gray; the clouds scudded across it frantically, like boats without oarsmen.

"Well," Rosie said, more for something to say than anything else. "*This* will keep us in."

Nena turned to look at her, and for the first time, Rosie saw beyond the plain face with the spots and glasses, to a girl who might be pretty despite all this.

"I'm not so worried about keeping us in," she said. "I'm worried about keeping *him* out."

CHAPTER EIGHT

The two girls walked the perimeter fence for a while, watching the waves crashing onto the rocks below. "Shame there's no beach here," Rosie said. "It might've been fun, having a beach."

"I like those rocks," Nena replied. "They make me feel safer. I don't think anyone coming in by boat could navigate those rocks."

Rosie looked at her, awed at someone who saw everything in terms of her own security.

"You really are scared of this guy, aren't you?" Rosie said.

Nena didn't answer at once. They walked a little further, to where the fence turned inland and away from the cliff's edge. Then she turned to Rosie and the two girls faced each other.

"If you'd seen him... If you'd heard what he said..." She appeared to want to say more, then closed her mouth.

"Tell me," Rosie said gently. "Maybe it'll help."

"I don't know. I don't want to scare you, to bring you into my nightmare. Why should you share my worst fears with me? You're better off not knowing."

"But that's what Rabbi Moslovsky wants me to do, help you," Rosie replied. "It surely can't be good for you to keep it all bottled up."

"Maybe soon. I have to learn to trust you first. Make sure you don't tell anyone. We only met five minutes ago and I'm going to spill everything to you? I don't think so."

Rosie nodded. "That's fair," she said. "I suppose I wouldn't tell you anything just because you'd been chosen to be my confidant either. But just so I understand, why is it so vital that no one knows anything?"

Nena looked at her as if Rosie was completely dumb.

"The more people know, the more likely it is to get out where I am. He's out there, or his associates are, looking for clues as to where I am and what my new identity is."

Rosie blushed and nodded. "I get you. Sorry to be so thick. I've never had much to do with this sort of thing, as you can imagine."

Nena smiled, just a little. "Good. Then we understand each other."

They resumed walking. Rosie glanced at her watch. "I think we'd best be going in now, or they'll start sending out search parties."

The school building had many exits and they found another one and went inside. Looking around, Rosie realized she was completely lost and had no idea where their bedrooms were from here.

"You're almost as new as I am," Nena realized, surprised. "Somehow I thought..."

"I just got here this afternoon," Rosie confessed. "All the new girls did. You couldn't have been assigned anyone more settled unless it had been an older girl. I guess Rabbi M. wanted you to be with someone your own age."

Eventually they found a senior and were directed back to their own part of the building. Yael and Shuli were in their room, distractedly unpacking their things, while obviously waiting for Rosie to return. Kaylah and Rochel were in the common room having a late evening cup of coffee and chat with their friends. This was fine with the freshies, who just wanted to talk amongst themselves.

"This is Nena Sheinfield," Rosie introduced. "She just arrived."

The girls smiled and said hello in a friendly manner, but kept shooting Rosie looks that said, *Nu? What's this all about?*

"What did Rabbi Moslovsky want?" Yael asked curiously.

Rosie thought on her feet. "He wanted to introduce Nena to me and ask me to get all of you guys to make friends, as she's new and doesn't know anyone."

Even to her own ears it sounded unconvincing. After all, none of them had known anyone when they arrived, so why would Nena be a special case? But the girls seemed satisfied with the answer and didn't pursue it any further. Rosie presumed that, as most pupils at a boarding school had a good reason for wanting to board rather than attend a day school, her new friends had concluded Nena too came with her own baggage and it would be inappropriate to question her. Speaking of baggage…

"You didn't bring much," Shuli commented, looking at Nena's small wheelie case. It was the kind plane travelers use for cabin baggage, and hardly looked big enough to carry an entire term's worth of clothing.

"I don't have much. Most of my clothes can be rolled up tight and fit in a small case. My mother said she'd send me some more stuff once the weather gets really cold."

If anything, Rosie felt her friends found this more curious than

Rabbi Moslovsky entrusting Nena into Rosie's care. Most of the girls there, including this trio of freshies, had large suitcases stuffed to the brim and had found difficulty getting enough closet space for it all. Rosie, on the other hand, understood that Nena's lack of clothing was all part of her persona; she needed as little as possible to weigh her down or hold her back. If she had to flee, a small suitcase could easily be packed in an instant.

Nena had a cover story down pat. The trouble was, it didn't reflect well on her. Well, Rosie surmised, telling the truth was obviously impossible, and yet the girl had come to school under such a sense of unusual drama, that any believable cover story had to involve something equally dramatic.

So Nena's story was one of being horribly bullied in school, over the course of a couple of years, by one particular nasty girl. Finally Nena had snapped and attacked her tormentor. The punch in the face put the bully in the hospital with a broken nose, and Nena on the receiving end of a threatened lawsuit by the girl's parents. The story seemed both plausible and even slightly glamorous, yet so far from the real truth as to completely divert the listener and prevent her from probing too much.

She sat there on Rosie's bed, telling her fabricated story with such aplomb and complete lack of guile that Rosie wondered if she herself was the only one of them who had a truthful story behind her. Shuli and Yael listened openmouthed to the horror story of extreme bullying and what it had taken to make Nena finally snap.

"I think," Yael said finally, just before the seniors came in to turn off the lights and force the new trio to separate for the night, "that tomorrow we should have a session of Truth or Dare. We can ask each other something about ourselves, and we have to be honest in our answers. If someone doesn't want to admit the truth, for any reason, the others can give her a dare to do. The limit of the dare will depend on how important the secret is to keep."

"Why would you want to do that?" Shuli said, looking quite worried at the prospect.

"Because," Yael said, smiling enigmatically, "I like living on the edge. It makes life exciting, don't you think? And I think everyone here has a secret to keep."

"I've told you mine already," Nena said, looking straight at Yael with wide eyes that seemed to hide nothing.

Rosie tried to look worried, just for effect, although in truth she was more worried for Nena than for herself.

CHAPTER NINE

Rosie barely slept that night, so worried was she about Nena and the Truth or Dare session that Yael had planned. Despite her misgivings, apparently Nena didn't share them and slept like the proverbial log.

When Rosie crept out of her room in the dead of night to see if Nena was also tossing and turning in the room next door, she opened the door a crack, to see her sleeping the sleep of the totally untroubled. *Lucky, old her*, Rosie thought enviously, and went back to bed grumbling to herself. However, the knowledge itself was enough to calm her; she managed to grab a few hours' precious sleep before the seniors' alarm clock woke everyone up for davening, breakfast, and morning classes.

She awaited the Truth or Dare session with dread and fear, but it was as if Yael's suggestion the previous night had been a dream; she didn't mention it that day, or the next, or indeed anytime. Rosie finally came to the conclusion that maybe she just wanted to see everyone's reaction and had been satisfied, so she didn't actually need to carry out the threat. However, she couldn't help feeling that Yael kept it safely hidden somewhere like a secret deadly weapon, to be brought out if she ever felt doubtful about the trustworthiness of her friends.

Nena fitted into school and social life masterfully. In a way, Rosie felt almost jealous of the ease in which she made friends and managed her cover story with such smooth aplomb. Rosie almost began believing it herself, and it was certainly easier and felt safer, just to slip into the fabricated world Nena had created for herself, than to think about the dark horrors of the genuine one. In fact there were no moments when Nena would take Rosie aside and discuss what was really out there. None. Rosie started feeling redundant. Hadn't Rabbi Moslovsky told her that her role would be one of support and counsel for the fearful times when Nena suffered from the trauma of what had happened? That was an important role and Rosie reveled in the idea of fulfilling it.

But as the weeks went by it seemed that she was out of a job. Nena made no mention of her real life, nor displayed any sign of being distressed by it. If anything, Rosie began to feel that she, not Nena, needed the counseling and support. She found herself tossing and turning at night, jumping at every shadow and starting at every unusual creak of the furniture.

Hashem has His ways of giving people what they need to cope. If Rosie hadn't been so aware, so "on her toes" and nervous, she might have totally missed what happened a few weeks into the first term…

Kaylah and Rochel were indeed high-handed and authoritarian, but hadn't turned out quite as bad as the freshies had feared. It seemed that once they had firmly crushed all attempts at free expression and revolution even before they had manifested themselves in the new girls, and as long as they were quite aware of their places in the hierarchy of the room and its inhabitants, they were quite happy to let them get on with their lives as thoroughly inferior beings.

Uncharacteristically, once Yael had established that the two seniors weren't as awful as anticipated, she had taken down the risky poem she had pasted over the room rules, and it was never spoken of again. Rosie and Shuli had been relieved to avoid confrontation, and had decided it would be prudent not to bring the topic of its disappearance up, in case Yael thought it reflected badly on her daring and reinstated it.

Indeed, Yael, who was unique among the quartet of freshies as being extremely intuitive and insightful, seemed to be most watchful of Nena — who, out of all of them, seemed to be the one with the least inscrutability and mystery. This made Rosie even more nervous and she wondered when Yael, as the prowling leopard on the branch, would finally pounce.

On Tuesdays, the girls had a free afternoon. As the school was so isolated, there wasn't much choice as to where they could go. The town of Bournemouth was a fifteen-minute bus ride away so that was the destination of choice. Bournemouth had interesting things like big stores for retail therapy; a pier with amusements; a kosher shop where they could stock up on nosh; and a shul where they could pop in, meet the rabbi, and get a taste of the real Jewish world they had left behind. Most of the girls piled into the buses that stopped on the road not far from the school and disappeared to Bournemouth for a taste of, if not big-city life, then small, seaside town life at least.

Rosie and her three pals were no exception, but on this particular Tuesday, shortly after the *yamim tovim* ended and the real winter term began, Rosie had a stomach bug and felt a little under the weather. The thought of being jolted around the country roads on a bus did not appeal, so she opted to stay behind and take the afternoon quietly. She thought she might go for a walk around the cliff top and hope that the ozone and cooling sea breezes would clear her head and improve her sense of well-being.

The school was very sparsely populated on free afternoons, as it was too restrictive on other days for the girls not to take advantage of any free time. A couple of teachers no doubt hung out somewhere but Rosie didn't see them; most of them too took their free time seriously.

The sharpness of the breeze whipped around Rosie as she walked, and she wrapped her coat around her more tightly. It hadn't been a warm September, and now it seemed to be descending into winter. She increased her pace to keep warm. She reached the edge of the bluff and looked over at the thrashing ocean below.

Then, at the periphery of her vision, she saw a dark shape moving. She turned her head around to look at it, but as quickly as she looked, the shape disappeared. She wondered if it had been some kind of large dog or even a deer, but somehow she knew that this was a human being, and a tall one at that, and it was moving very fast in the direction of the school building.

A shiver that was not from the cold, swept over Rosie. Something told her that whatever this dark shape was, it had not come here to ask after anyone's good health or well-being. Cautiously, she walked back towards the school, keeping her footsteps light and silent, and her gaze ever watchful.

She hardly dared go inside, but it was cold and getting late and she couldn't stay outside forever. Breathing as quietly as she could, she tiptoed into the corridor and made her way towards her room. Before she could reach it, she heard a loud, piercing scream. It was coming not from Nena's room, but from her own room next door.

"Oh, no!" the female voice cried out. As far as Rosie could tell, it was not Nena. "Help me! Please help me!!"

CHAPTER TEN

Rosie had sometimes thought of herself as quite heroic. After all, she was stoic in the face of unimaginable stress at home, and had been the strong one of the siblings — the one they had turned to when they were all crying in distress at their parents' parting of ways. So she had fondly imagined she would be heroic in the face of this new and terrifying situation.

But to her extreme surprise she found herself absolutely petrified of what she might find if she went into her room. She approached cautiously, but then found that she just couldn't take another step towards it, so hid in an empty bedroom nearby, shivering and shaking and cowering like a kitten in the rain. By the time she plucked up courage to take further steps towards the room, her door was open and Rabbi Moslovsky was standing there, looking very grave indeed.

"Did you hear the screaming?" were his first words. Rosie nodded, unable to speak.

"I'm afraid we've had an intruder in the school. He has kidnapped…"

"Not Nena?!" Rosie burst out, finding her voice at last. She entered the room, looking around fearfully. But aside from her and the *rav*, it was empty, and there were no signs of a scuffle.

"No, not Nena. Miss Colton. Our deputy head. She was doing some rounds of the rooms, as she does when the girls are out for the afternoon, and…he grabbed her."

Rosie sank back onto her bed, so shocked her mind was almost blank. She couldn't think of a single useful thing to say. Rabbi Moslovsky said, "We can't be certain that this is connected to Nena, but I'm presuming so, and that this man wants some kind of leverage to get to Nena through this kidnapping."

Rosie was dimly aware that her whole body was trembling. The one thought going through her mind now, over and over was finally voiced. "You can't let him get to Nena because of this!"

"I know we can't," the *rav* said, sinking back into a chair. He was trembling too, she noticed. "But I can't just sit back and let my deputy head come to harm either."

Other staff members now entered the room. There was a tumult of talking and discussion, all of which excluded Rosie. It was probably because she was one of the only, if not the only, girl remaining in the building, that they didn't notice her presence. She decided it would be best to keep quiet and observe, rather than speak up and risk being sent out "while the grown-ups talk."

She had learned, over the last difficult divisive months at home, how to make herself so invisible that her parents could argue and fight and assume they were alone, when she was really sitting like a mouse in a corner, blending into the furniture like a chameleon. As then, now she shrank down and the adults milled around, so shocked and horrified by the turn of events that for the moment, at least, no one thought to ask her to leave.

"Where was Barbara when she was taken?" one teacher asked. Rosie presumed that Barbara was Miss Colton's first name.

"It must have been in this room or the next one," Rabbi Moslovsky replied. "She must've been on her room rounds, checking things while the girls were in town."

"Why Barbara though?" someone else asked.

"Wrong place, wrong time?" someone else suggested. "There weren't a whole lot of us about, and I think no girls at all."

Rosie, shrinking back to form part of the paint of the walls, marveled at how this teacher didn't take in the fact that she was there.

"But what can the kidnapper possibly want?" asked the art teacher, an eccentric single woman in her forties with wild, paint-spattered hair and multiple bead necklaces. Rosie's glance darted at the *rav* to see how he would handle this. He merely shrugged.

"We can only hope it's financial. A ransom we can cope with; we can raise the money to free her. *Pidyon shvuim* is a huge mitzvah anyway. But if he doesn't want money…well, the alternative hardly bears consideration."

Rosie couldn't imagine what the alternative might be.

"What do we do?" the English teacher, a Miss Colton lookalike, asked. Then Rosie realized why she was a lookalike. "I'm so worried for my cousin. Barbara may look very capable and in control, but in fact she falls to pieces in a crisis. She can't cope with too much stress."

"For now, we've informed the police," the *rav* said.

"Is that a good idea? Don't these kidnappers usually threaten goodness-knows-what to their victim if the police are involved?" asked the art teacher, pulling at her beads distractedly.

"That's what they use to scare people into not calling the cops," Miss Colton's cousin said. "I've read about it. But the cops always tell you to call them and they'll be discreet. You can't do this on your own."

"They're on their way, anyways," the *rav* said, pacing the room. "I don't know what they can do…maybe search for evidence that the kidnapper left behind or something."

"The girls will all be back within the hour," the art teacher said suddenly. "What chaos there's going to be then."

"You're right," said the *rav*. "I doubt the police will be able to do much with hundreds of girls milling around the place. We have to keep them away, at least until they've done an initial search."

"How on earth are we going to do that?" another teacher wondered. And indeed, it would not be an easy assignment. The girls came back from Bournemouth in dribs and drabs, by small busloads, and it would be almost impossible to head them all off.

"We'll get Mr. Wilkins on the job. He's always fancied himself as more than just the school janitor. Let him get busy on this." The *rav* was looking pleased with himself for the idea.

And so it was, that as each group of girls arrived back at the school, Mr. Wilkins was standing there like a Roman centurion, on guard, telling them there'd been an "incident," and no one was allowed back in the school until further notice. They were all herded into a large outbuilding. That Miss Colton might also have been brought here and thus the place be full of trace evidence, had obviously not occurred to anyone in authority, but it seemed deserted and bore no signs of having been used recently.

The girls were annoyed, cold, tired, hungry, and needing the bathrooms. Luckily there were some outside facilities, but no chairs or refreshments, so they just had to sit on the concrete floors and wait for readmission into the school.

Rosie decided she didn't want to be the only girl in the building when the police came, so she managed to slip out and join her classmates. She sat down on the cold stone floor next to Shuli, Yael, and Nena.

"Where were you?" Yael said at once. "I didn't see you in Bournemouth."

Rosie turned her head away so her friends wouldn't see her blushing. "I, er…went for a walk instead. Needed the fresh air. Had a bit of a stomachache." It wasn't a lie and it wasn't the whole truth either, but it would do for now.

The noise of the police cars arriving made everyone look curiously out of the windows.

"It's the cops!" one girl called. "There's about five cop cars out there! And a crime scene van too! What on earth has been going on here this afternoon?"

CHAPTER ELEVEN

The girls were still huddling in the outbuilding, looking at the police vans and the officers spilling out of them like toys someone had tipped out of a toy box. They were discussing what could possibly be the cause of all this excitement.

"A murder! Maybe one of the teachers has been done away with!" suggested one dramatic girl.

"No such luck," said the school renegade drily, and everyone laughed. "No, it's probably some boring old burglary…someone's stolen Miss Colton's hairpins…the ones she uses to keep that rock solid bun in place." More laughter ensued. But it was a nervous tittering rather than a relaxed, enjoyable kind of laughter, and soon the girls calmed down and stopped making jokes.

"Looks serious; they've got rolls of that 'Crime Scene — Do Not Cross' tape with them. I wonder how much of our school is going to be a crime scene…"

Rosie became aware of her three friends looking at her very curiously. "What?"

"You weren't in Bournemouth with us this afternoon. You were here, weren't you? You know what's happened, don't you?"

Rosie shot a glance at Nena, who was looking at her even more sharply than the other two. One look between the two girls and Nena was instantly made aware that whatever had gone on that afternoon was connected to her. She went white and turned her head away, hugging her arms around herself.

Luckily for Rosie she didn't have to answer then and here. The English teacher, whose name was Miss Freedman, came into the outhouse looking pale but officious.

"All right girls, you can come inside the school building now, but you will see part of it has been cordoned off. I want everyone to use the bathrooms if they need to, and then gather in the assembly hall, where Rabbi Moslovsky will address you. If your room or your nearest bathroom is behind the police cordon, please don't attempt to cross it to gain access to your room. Use a different bathroom for now and we will explain what is happening during the assembly. Now move quietly and quickly towards the second entrance."

The girls were all so relieved not to have to sit on the cold, hard concrete floor any longer that they wouldn't have cared where they went, as long as it was inside the building. They made their way in a surprisingly orderly fashion. The girls all sat expectantly down in the assembly hall, waiting to be informed as to what on earth was going on. There was the minimum of murmurings; they were all silenced by anxiety and a sense of foreboding. When the *rav* entered the large hall he too had a solemn expression.

"Someone's definitely died…just look at his face!" the school renegade whispered, and in the way of broken telephone, it passed along the rows of girls that someone had definitely died and there had been a gruesome murder.

"There has been a shocking crime perpetrated here this afternoon. Something that hasn't happened in the entire history of our school," the *rav* began without preamble. "Our deputy head, Miss Colton, has been kidnapped by person or persons unknown, and we don't know the motive for it either. "

At the name being revealed there was a collective intake of shocked breath amongst the girls. Miss Colton, of the iron-gray bun and the apparently iron-gray personality, was human and vulnerable enough to be a victim of such a terrible crime! Heads turned to each other, whisperings and murmurings spread throughout the hall, until they were silenced by a sudden rap on the podium by Rabbi Moslovsky. The *rav* continued.

"The police are, even as I speak, doing a fingertip search of the area in which we believe this staff member was abducted, which is why we cannot allow you access to this area until their search is completed. The Scene of Crimes Officers, known as SOCOs, are collecting forensic evidence that could lead to the apprehension of the kidnappers. We have no ransom note or any indication of why this crime has happened. But one thing is perfectly clear."

Rabbi Moslovsky cleared his throat and swallowed before continuing. "Just by calling in the police we were taking a huge risk. Kidnappers like to keep the police out of their negotiations and put fear in our hearts by threatening to harm their victim if we call them. So we have to do damage limitation here, and the buck stops with you, girls.

"Thankfully our school is extremely isolated. However, we live in the twenty-first century and there are phones, and mobile phones, and other means of communication with the outside world. I do not want any one of you talking about this to anyone outside of this school. It is vital that the news of this kidnapping does not spread. To that end, and because I know how hard it is to keep quiet about such things, until this matter is sorted out, I am cancelling all free afternoons in town, I am confiscating all students' cellular phones, and I am disconnecting all the phones and Internet lines out of the school. Only the staff will be able to communicate with the outside world until it is safe again for us to allow you to do so."

While he had been talking — no doubt to preempt the obvious desire of some girls to get a last-minute text to friends and family in — Miss Freedman and other staff members had been moving along the rows of girls, collecting their cell phones and dropping them into a big bag. The girls were outraged and horrified.

"If your parents or anyone needs to contact you, they can do so via the school office," the *rav* assured everyone. "You will not be totally un-contactable. But we cannot allow you to speak directly to your family and friends until it is safe to do so. I'm sure you understand the necessity for such stringent measures."

"Basically, they don't trust us," Renegade said sourly.

"Do you blame them?" someone else said acidly. "I'm the first to admit I'd be on the phone like a shot blabbing. This is the most exciting thing that's happened in this school and we aren't allowed to talk about it! I mean, come on!"

There was a murmuring and nodding of heads in agreement to this.

"I'm really sorry to have to do this to you girls," the *rav* finished his talk, "but we took a risk calling in the police. We took a bigger risk telling you all about it, but we thought that if we didn't, speculation would be rife, and the gossip-mongering would be worse than the actuality. So if you know the truth, you can understand why secrecy is of the essence, and we have to, absolutely *have* to, keep this under wraps. This incident stays within the walls of this school building. Do I make myself clear?"

"Yes, Rabbi Moslovsky," the girls murmured in unison. Somehow the seriousness of the situation lent it a certain amount of importance that the girls shouldered with excitement. They were in charge of an important secret and they held Miss Colton's life in their hands.

They filed gravely out of the hall and slowly moved around the building to see which rooms were available to them and which were out of bounds. Rosie already knew her room was the Ground Zero of the investigation, but she waited for her friends to find it out for themselves.

"You know what, girls," Yael said as she was turned away from their bedroom and had to go into another room for the moment. "This isn't just a school anymore. It's a prison."

CHAPTER TWELVE

"A prison?" Shuli asked, shocked. It sounded so overdramatic.

"A prison," Yael insisted. "What part of a prison wouldn't you call this place? We aren't allowed to leave the building. We aren't allowed to communicate with the outside world. Heck, it's worse than a prison. In a prison there are phones and the inmates can use them."

"You're right," Shuli said. "It's the worst kind of prison. Like in some nightmare."

All four girls were sitting on the bed of a willing friend who knew their rooms were out of bounds.

Yael turned to Rosie and Nena. "You're very quiet," she commented, looking hard at the two girls.

"We're shocked, that's all," Nena said.

"You know more than you're letting on," Yael accused Rosie. "You were here when all of us were in Bournemouth. Come on, spill the beans."

"I didn't see anything," Rosie said, relieved that she could be truthful. "I was too terrified to go into my room after I heard the screams and…"

"You heard screams?" Yael pounced on this tantalizing tidbit of information.

"I was outside, taking a walk, as I said," Rosie said slowly, "and I heard screams coming from inside. I was too terrified to investigate. I hid in a spare bedroom. I'm ashamed to say I was a real wuss."

"Don't be ashamed," Shuli said kindly. "You weren't a wuss… you were just being normal. I doubt many of us would have had the guts to be all gung-ho and go in there when there was a kidnapper about."

"I would've," Yael declared, and the other three had no problem believing her.

"Yes and you might've got yourself killed," Shuli said sharply. "Being brave and being reckless aren't the same thing. You have to know how far to go when you take risks, and I honestly don't think you do."

"I do," Yael protested unconvincingly, and no one looked as if they believed her.

"You take risks for the sake of it," Shuli went on. "And I'm still trying to figure you out on that one. Do you have a death wish or something?"

Yael turned her head away. "You don't wanna know."

There was a short silence. Then Nena said, "I wonder why they wanted Miss Colton…"

She shot Rosie a glance that said, *Play along with me, please…*

"Maybe she's really a rich princess or duchess or something,"

Rosie said obligingly. "I mean, how much do we really know about her? Or about any of the teachers, for that matter?"

The girls seemed to like the idea of Miss Colton really being a secret Royal. They talked about it for a while and it defused the situation, letting Rosie and what she knew off the hook.

Suppertime came and went and still the girls weren't allowed back in their bedrooms. The police were everywhere, it seemed, and the SOCOs, with their white paper suits, hats, and overshoes, plus their latex gloves, looked like science fiction characters.

"We're going to have to sleep in your bedroom," Shuli told the obliging girl who had allowed them access to her room. The girl didn't look too pleased at this. But then, at ten o'clock that night, the police finally packed up their stuff and left the building, and the girls were allowed back in their own rooms.

"I never thought I'd be so pleased to see this bedroom again," Yael said, flinging herself gratefully down on her bed. Kaylah and Rochel who had of course also been displaced, were already taking showers and preparing for bed. Rosie had a good look around to see what the police had done, but besides a few items not being where she had left them, they had left the place pretty tidy. She noticed some traces of white powder, and presumed it was fingerprint powder. As if reading her mind, Miss Freedman came into the room.

"All of you girls will have to be fingerprinted tomorrow," she announced. "The police said they really should have done it tonight, to avoid having to come back, but as it was so late and they knew you needed to get to bed, they've agreed to postpone it till tomorrow. They will be doing next door's, as well as the cleaners and anyone else who had access to this room."

"Why us?" Kaylah asked, mortified. "We didn't kidnap Miss Colton!"

"To rule you out," Yael said before Miss Freedman could confirm this was indeed so. "Our fingerprints will be everywhere, so they need to know all of ours, so they can look for other prints that aren't ours. It's called 'elimination.'"

"Hmph," Kaylah said, annoyed that she had been put in her place by a freshie.

"Goodnight, girls," Miss Freedman said, and went out, closing the door.

"I'm leaving a night-light on," Rochel said suddenly. "I don't feel safe."

"I don't think anyone of us does," Kaylah agreed, and everyone nodded. A small night-light glowed reassuringly in a corner, lighting up five sets of frightened eyes.

"I shan't sleep a wink tonight!" Rochel declared dramatically. But despite the tension and worry in the atmosphere, four girls in that room were asleep within the hour. Only Rosie lay awake, deeply aware of the knowledge she carried that no one else did. That Miss Colton had probably been abducted as some kind of leverage to get to Nena. The question was, who did the school value more? Were they willing to give up Nena to save Miss Colton? Did the school regret taking on a "liability" like Nena, a girl on a deeply flawed Witness Protection Program who had obviously already been traced, and now they were going to give her up? Rosie could hardly believe that would happen, but who knew?

After a while of tossing and turning, Rosie got up and went out into the corridor. The school was silent; everyone was asleep. It was after one in the morning. But a shadowy figure suddenly emerged from the darkness and Rosie almost cried out in shock.

It was Nena, also sleepless, looking for a friend.

Rosie and Nena sat on a bench in the corridor in the darkness, shoulders just touching, saying nothing. There was nothing to be said. After half an hour or so of this companionable silence, they both went back to their beds, and slept until morning. It had been nothing much, but it had helped.

Fingerprinting the next day was exciting if a little messy. About two dozen girls and some of the staff had to press each of their fingers into the pads the SOCOs had laid out for them, after which the fingerprints were carefully labeled and indexed, and fed into a computer to be uploaded to an online database. They had their own laptops with Internet access, so didn't need to use the school's, which was restricted by the new rules.

Some of the senior girls complained that the fingerprint powder didn't come off and was ruining their perfectly good manicures, but on the whole everyone found it a welcome diversion from classes. Then the police were gone, and there was nothing more to do but wait.

"We have no doubt the kidnappers will get in touch with you very shortly," the chief investigating officer of the case told Rabbi Moslovsky. "No one kidnaps without a reason. You just have to sit it out till that reason comes to light. Money is the most common reason, but there are others of course. Someone around this school must know why Miss Colton was taken and what leverage her abduction has." The officer looked very closely at Rabbi Moslovksy. The *rav* took the officer into his office and closed the door.

"Can I talk to you in confidence? Somewhere we are guaranteed not to be overheard?" asked the *rav*.

"Outside, on the cliffs?" suggested the officer.

The sea pounded the shore and almost drowned out their voices as the two men walked and talked.

CHAPTER THIRTEEN

The chief investigating officer, whose name was James Nesbit, nodded sagely as Rabbi Moslovsky filled him in with the details of Nena's arrival at the school.

"I feel pretty sure the two events are linked," the *rav* surmised, and Nesbit agreed.

"Certainly seems to be too much of a coincidence to be anything else. Makes it much more complicated, though."

"Why?"

"Well, there's nothing like a straightforward kidnapping for ransom. We can and do handle those all the time, usually by handing over the money but watching the drop, as it's called, and following whoever picks it up until we can make an arrest. Always making sure, of course, that the victim is handed over as soon as the drop is made so that nothing can go wrong once we pounce. Sometimes the victim's family is too scared to call the police and ends up just paying the ransom themselves anyway. We don't recommend this, as it just encourages kidnappers to repeat their crimes. If we're extremely discreet, we can usually fool the abductors into thinking that the police haven't been contacted."

"Usually, but not always, I presume," Rabbi Moslovsky pointed out. "And then the victim is put at grave risk."

The officer shrugged. "We can't guarantee anything, but we have highly trained teams of officers who handle ransom demands with the utmost secrecy and discretion."

"But I don't think money is going to be involved here," the *rav* mused.

"I think you're right. This appears to be a kidnapping for leverage, at least from what you say about the girl. Makes it much more difficult to decide how to handle it."

"Nena was entrusted into our care. I can't hand her over just to save another person. Who says one life is more important than another? It's a very difficult conundrum, discussed in many of our holy books, as it happens," the *rav* said.

Nesbit seemed intrigued. "Your Torah seems to encompass everything," he observed with a serious expression. "But in the meantime, no demands have been made for the return of your teacher so we don't know how to react to anything."

"So we just wait?"

"Nothing else we can do. But of course we picked up some trace evidence at the crime scene, which we are processing in the hope that it'll give us some clues as to who took her."

"Processing? How long does everything take?" Rabbi Moslovsky asked in frustration.

"We have to send it to our forensic laboratory, and they'll work on it as fast as they can but it isn't instantaneous. Those crime movies give people the idea that right after you find evidence you can process it and learn its secrets. Unfortunately, real life grinds along more slowly."

"And in the meantime Miss Colton is…" Rabbi Moslovsky shuddered.

"We're doing all we can," the officer said in a tone of voice meant to comfort but achieving absolutely nothing.

The two men walked slowly back to the school building again, where the SOCOs had finished fingerprinting everyone relevant and were once more packing up to leave.

"Classes as usual now girls, the fun's over," called Miss Freedman to the communal groan of the students. Being fingerprinted had been fun and a diversion. It was only a couple of days since the new, draconian rules had been put in place but already the cracks were beginning to show. The girls were getting restless and irritable. Their weekly trips to town, and phoning home for news of family and friends, had been a lifeline that was now denied them.

"I've got cabin fever," whined Yael between classes, as she looked out of the window at what was turning out to be a lovely autumnal day — sunny, breezy, and still quite warm for October. She danced around the classroom like a kickboxer, and pretended to kick out at the filing cabinets. "I need to *do* something!"

There were murmurs of agreement.

"The school grounds are quite large you know, girls," Miss Freedman said consolingly. "And you have the freedom of the entire campus to walk around. It's not as if we're keeping you indoors. Why don't you go out to the sports field and have a good game of netball or baseball or something energetic to work off all that excess energy?"

The seniors were grumbling that they were denied their weekly trip to restock their cosmetics and get their hair and nails done, particularly after the damaging effects of the fingerprinting.

Rabbi Moslovsky sat in his office after classes, head in his hands. Not being able to do anything to expedite matters had to be the most frustrating experience of his life. And he knew the girls were getting restless and antsy and needed something interesting to divert them. Having the school in such an isolated location had its definite drawbacks.

The art teacher, Miss Murkel, she of the ropes of beads and wild hairstyle, knocked and came into his office.

"Yes, what is it?" sighed the *rav*.

"I was thinking, Rabbi," she said. "Girls in their teens need their dose of retail therapy. The older they get, the more they need it. I mean shopping, in case you don't know the terminology."

"I do know the terminology, Miss Murkel," Moslovsky sighed. "I've been married for thirty years and also have daughters."

"Well then," she went on, warming to her theme, "if the girls aren't allowed to go to the stores in Bournemouth, bring the stores to the school!" She said this with a flourish of her ropes of beads that threatened to put the *rav*'s eye out. He backed off nervously.

"And how exactly do you intend to do that?"

"I have a cousin who lives in Bournemouth and owns a small kiosk. She sells all kinds of things. Makeup, cosmetics, knockoff handbags and sunglasses, sweaters and skirts. I'm sure she could be persuaded to bring her wares to the school say once a week or even more often, while all this is going on, and open it up in the school grounds. She might even know others in the same business who'd be willing to do the same thing. Bring a market to the school. The girls would love it! And," she added coyly, "so would I and most of the female staff members! None of us can leave the school premises either."

Rabbi Moslovsky grinned. This arty, over-the-top woman had quite cheered him up and given him something positive to plan for. "It sounds like a splendid idea, thank you. Get onto it at once."

Miss Murkel skipped out of the room full of excitement.

The phone rang on Rabbi Moslovsky's desk. It was James Nesbit asking if there had been any communication from the kidnappers.

"No, nothing yet, but my art teacher came up with a rather good idea for a diversion…" he explained to the officer, who made a strange noise over the phone.

"Everyone who enters and leaves your school premises has to be vetted," he said. "How do we know that the kiosk owner isn't the kidnapper? Unlikely I know, but we have to be sure. Get your art teacher to give us the name of everyone she plans to bring onto the campus so we can check them out. And do it *before* she asks them to come."

"Oh, "Rabbi Moslovsky said. "I hadn't thought about that."

He hung up and was just about to call Miss Murkel's cell phone (the teachers' cells had not been confiscated), when the phone on his desk rang again. He picked it up. A coarse voice said, "We have your old bag of a teacher. If you want her back alive, do exactly what I say…"

CHAPTER FOURTEEN

Rabbi Moslovsky was so shocked that for a moment he could not assimilate what he had heard on the phone.

"What?" he asked stupidly. He felt like he was swimming and water filled his ears.

"You got hearing problems?" the coarse voice reiterated. "I said we've got your old-bag teacher and if you want her to stay alive you have to do exactly what I say. Geddit?"

The *rav*'s heart was pounding so loudly he was sure the man at the other end of the phone could hear it. He was slowly rallying back to his senses.

"How do I know she's alive now?" he asked. "I need proof."

"You've been watching them crime programs," the voice said with a grating laugh that made the *rav* shudder. "Okay, you want proof, here's proof." There was a pause. "Bring her here."

There was a scuffling noise and a muffled protest. "Say something, to prove you're alive."

"Is that Rabbi Moslovsky?" Miss Colton burst out. "Please help me, they're…mmmffmfff…"

"Proof enough for you? We can't take much more of her yakking. She's been driving me mad. Talk, talk, talk. She never shuts up. "

The *rav* was shaking so badly he thought he'd drop the phone. "What do you want from us?" he said at last, trying to control his voice from trembling.

"Whatja think? The girl of course. The witness. We can't have her walking around free, about to give evidence in court. My mate's in custody, on remand, they wouldn't even let him out on bail… He tells me to come and get her. Without her, there's no case. You bring her, you can have your old lady back. With pleasure."

"What girl? What witness?" The *rav* was stalling for time because James Nesbit had fitted a tracing and recording device to the phone and had told him that if anyone called, to keep them talking. Officers were monitoring the call and needed as long as possible.

The voice grew dark and angry. "Don't play games with me," he said. "I know the girl's at the school. You play games, we'll send back your teacher all right, but you won't like the condition of the package you get."

"What do I do?" the *rav* croaked.

"We'll call again with instructions. Be ready." The caller hung up. Instantly the phone rang again, and Moslovsky picked it up thinking it was the kidnapper again. It was Nesbit.

"Well done," he said. "We got that and we're working on it. One thing we're sure of. There's more than one kidnapper."

Rabbi Moslovsky had been so traumatized he hadn't picked up on that. "How do you know?"

"The man who called you asked someone else to bring Miss Colton to the phone. So there were at least two of them."

"Oh, of course." The *rav* blushed at his own ineptitude.

"Miss Colton sounded in fighting spirit though," Nesbit went on, "which is good. Her voice sounded as normal to you?"

"Oh, yes, perfectly as normal, just distressed."

"The bad news is that it is as you feared; they want Nena in exchange for Miss Colton," Nesbit went on, "which is a lose-lose situation all round. We'll have to call in our kidnapping experts; they've no doubt met this before and might have some input."

"Not forgetting Jewish law," reminded the *rav*.

"I'll bear that in mind." Nesbit hung up. The *rav* sat there shaking. He had given up smoking ten years earlier, but now there was nothing he wanted more than a cigarette, to calm his nerves. Resisting the craving, as he had been a very heavy smoker and the doctors had warned him of heart attack risks, he sat there, wondering what to do, who to speak to. Who could he speak to when the whole situation was so secret?

He pressed a buzzer on his desk and his secretary answered. "Yes, Rabbi?"

"Please ask Rosie Bernstein to come in here."

Rosie had been in her room, chatting to her friends, when the summons came. They all looked at her curiously, especially Nena, who had joined them as she usually did; they were very much a quartet now.

Rosie had never seen Rabbi Moslovsky look so gray and old. It was as if he had aged twenty years in the past twenty-four hours. His normally twinkly eyes full of light and humor now had the look of the eyes of a fish on a slab; dead and without hope. Without preamble he told her of the phone call from the kidnappers and what they wanted. Rosie went pale.

"You can't give up Nena for Miss Colton! It's… It's so wrong!! You can't! Please, Rabbi Moslovsky!"

The *rav* nodded. "I know we can't, and don't worry, I have no intentions of doing so. Anyway there are halachos that clearly say there is no obligation for one person to give himself up for the life of another."

Rosie caught the meaning behind the words.

"No *obligation*, you say. But he can volunteer if he so chooses?"

The *rav* put his head in his hands. "Yes, he can. I mean she can. But I would never ask it of her. She has been through too much and has come here as her last refuge. I wouldn't even suggest it."

"What do the police suggest?"

"They're bringing in their experts. It's an unusual case; most kidnappings are for ransom, not leverage."

"Nena must not be told," Rosie said firmly. "She'd want to hand herself over; she'd be devastated to think another person was being sacrificed for her sake."

"I agree," Moslovsky said. They both sat in silence.

Then Rosie spoke the unspeakable.

"Maybe if the police were willing to protect a decoy…"

"A decoy? You mean a stand-in for Nena?"

"Yes. That's exactly what I mean."

"But who would do such a risky thing? Would you?"

Rosie sat rooted to the spot considering the matter. "I'd want to do it in theory," she said at last, "but after the way I reacted when I heard the screams, I honestly think I'd go to pieces in a crisis. I'm afraid I'm not cut out for heroism, much as I'd like to be."

"It's good you're honest, with me as well as with yourself," the *rav* said kindly. "It would be no good at all if you played a false heroine and then cracked under pressure and put both Nena and Miss Colton at even more risk. It would just infuriate the kidnappers, and make them act precipitously."

Rosie's mind was whirring. "I think," she said, "that you should consider taking one more girl into your confidence about this whole matter. A girl who I feel would be prepared to do this."

The *rav* nodded. "Go on, who do you have in mind?"

CHAPTER FIFTEEN

Rosie went back to her room, her mind whirling with what she was about to do. She had received very guarded and cautious permission to allow one other person into this closed circle around Nena and her Witness Protection Program and she just hoped against hope she was doing the right thing.

The girls were still there chatting just as she'd left them. Three pairs of curious eyes turned to her, none more curious than those of Nena Sheinfeld. *What was that all about?* her gaze said quite clearly. Rosie smiled at her as guilelessly as she could. There was absolutely no way she was going to fill Nena in on anything that had transpired in the *rav*'s office.

"Oh, he wanted to talk to me about something that's happening at home. Nothing to do with anything here," she said, thinking on her feet as Nena's look became more pointed. She obviously wasn't going to let Rosie off the hook with a simple "Oh, nothing much." Not this time, not after everything that was going on.

Rosie's home life, unsettled and unhappy though it was, did prove useful as a decoy sometimes. It could always be called upon as a reliable diversion in time of need. Nena's eyes cleared and she visibly relaxed.

"So," Rosie said brightly, sitting on the bed and trying to look as if she didn't have a huge elephant of a task sitting on her shoulder, "what's everyone been chatting about? What have I missed?"

It had been decided with the *rav* that Rosie was not to do anything at all in front of the other girls, but to wait and bide her time for the right opportunity to speak to the girl they had in mind.

She felt like such a fraud. Here she was sitting on a bed in a student bedroom pretending to be just like everyone else. And she had always wanted to be just like everyone else — a regular girl, with a regular, settled home life and family. Hashem, it seemed, had other plans for her.

The *rav* paced his office. He was so scared that the second phone call from the kidnappers would come before the new plan was set into motion. Nesbit had been cautiously optimistic about the plan, even congratulating Rosie on the idea, having run it past his kidnapping expert.

"We can't one hundred percent guarantee anyone's safety in any given situation," Nesbit had concluded after much discussion, "but if the person you have in mind does what's expected of her and doesn't deviate from the plan of action, I'd say we can pretty much ninety percent guarantee it will be okay."

"What I don't understand," the *rav* said, "is what's the point of a decoy? We're still putting someone's life at risk and it isn't even the right someone."

"The point is — and *only* if your student Rosie is right about this girl," Nesbit explained, "that the real Nena is likely to be traumatized by her experiences in the past, and extremely stressed, and it'll show in how she behaves. If the decoy has none of this baggage in her past, and is brave and somewhat fearless, she'll remain calm and in control of her actions. I want to have her psychologically assessed before we agree to this plan though. To make sure she's what she says she is."

"Of course I can't move an inch before I have the girl's parents' okay to put her in this situation," the *rav* stressed. "And in order to gain that, I need as firm an assurance from you that you will be with her every step of the way, protecting her against possible harm."

"I'll personally speak to the girl's parents once we have her evaluated as suitable for the mission," Nesbit assured him. "And I'll give them as much assurance as I can. Unfortunately this all takes time, of course."

"Then we'd better move fast," the *rav* said nervously. "I just don't want that second phone call coming till everything is set."

"It probably *will* come before everything is set, but don't worry," Nesbit said airily with the relaxed confidence of someone for whom danger was an everyday occurrence. "You can always play for time. Say Nena is sick or something and can't be moved for a day or so."

"It's all very well for you," Moslovsky said. "I've never done this before and that phone call frankly gave me the heebie-jeebies. That gritty, coarse voice!" he shuddered. "I'm not so sure I won't just capitulate and fall to pieces if I hear that voice in my ear again."

Nesbit decided the time to play softball had passed.

"Listen to me, Rabbi," he said with a hard edge to his voice. "We're dealing with teenagers here, young teenagers at that, only fourteen years old, and they're holding up better than you are, from where I'm sitting. The lives of at least two people are at stake and if you act like a scared, little baby you won't be doing yourself, or the school, or indeed your religion, much credit. Grow a backbone for Heaven's sake!"

No one had ever spoken so harshly to Rabbi Moslovsky before and he was shocked. Even though he couldn't think what on earth his religion had to do with anything, he decided to accept the rebuke meekly.

"I apologize," he said, trying to sound like the action hero of his schoolboy dreams. "I won't let Nena, or anyone else, down."

"Yes, the sooner Rosie recruits that girl the better for the overall plan," Nesbit said in a softer voice. "But she can't rush in all gung-ho and risk the security of the operation if others are about. She has to choose her moment carefully. Even if it means a slight delay."

Now, hearing those words in his head again, Rabbi Moslovsky paced his office and fretted. He almost thought of disconnecting his phone so the kidnappers couldn't get through at all, but then he remembered, *Grow a backbone for Heaven's sake!* However as he paced, he kept eyeing the phone sitting menacingly in the middle of his desk, glowering with its own new inner power to scare the living daylights out of him.

Rosie, meanwhile, watched and waited for the right moment. It came at last when the girls decided to go out for a walk in the school grounds. This was proving a popular pastime in the absence of any further expeditions. Miss Murkel's idea of a kiosk was still being assessed, but in the wake of the kidnapper's phone call it had all been put on hold.

It was a beautiful autumn evening. The sun was still warm on their backs, the breeze was light, and the sea reflected the azure-blue sky. Even the crashing waves were rocking relatively quietly below the cliffs. The girls turned their faces to the sun and tried to imagine that this was true freedom, instead of life in a caged enclosure from which there was, for the moment at least, no escape.

As they walked, the girls naturally fell into smaller and smaller groups as they gratefully spread out and enjoyed the extra space of the outdoors. There was a neat path around the school buildings, but most girls chose to walk on the soft grass, just to feel something natural, as opposed to man-made, under their feet. Shuli was skipping; she was so pleased to be outdoors in the sunshine.

Rosie maneuvered herself next to her target and started to gently edge her away from the rest of the group, the way a lion might carefully separate the weakest calf from a herd before attacking.

"Yael," she said, "I need to speak to you. Alone. And you must promise me you'll keep what I'm going to say entirely, and absolutely, to yourself. Do I have your word?"

CHAPTER SIXTEEN

Barbara Colton was a fifty-year-old spinster from South Devon. As a young girl she had cared for her sick parents instead of having a social life. By the time her parents died, she was in her late thirties, and life, it seemed, had passed her by. Not being Jewish meant she didn't have access to the *shidduch* system that might have been able to match her up with someone in a similar position.

So she decided to devote her life to teaching. Despite having no siblings, Barbara had quite a few cousins, and those cousins soon saw a promising and cheap source of extra study sessions for their lagging children. Barbara used these sessions as much as the cousins used her, to gain experience and attitude, and then applied for a job at Ner Miriam on the south coast — as far away from her family as she could manage to be employed. The fact that her cousin Mildred, the English teacher, had followed her to the school was a constant source of irritation to her. But she bore it stoically and worked on moving up the ladder until she was deputy head and had left her disliked cousin far behind in her vapor trail.

But now, sitting alone in a locked room, in an unnamed place, with captors who kept their faces covered by ski masks, she would have given anything to have Mildred, yes even Mildred, there with her. Once her captors had ascertained that she was an unlikely escapee, as she lacked the agility to climb out of locked windows and the ingenuity to work out other escape routes, they stopped tying her to a chair and allowed her the freedom of the small room and its adjacent bathroom.

But she was lonely, frightened, and miserable, so whenever her captors came into the room she talked to them incessantly just to have someone human to interact with. She knew it drove them nuts, but she needed human contact, even if it was evil.

She listened intently when the two captors talked to each other, to see if she could pick up any clues as to their identity or the whereabouts of her incarceration. One was a man; he of the gritty, gruff voice, and he had an accent. The other didn't speak in her presence, but from her slight shape and the odd piece of long, blonde hair escaping from the ski mask, she had deduced the other was a woman.

The woman came into the room now, ski mask in place, bringing Miss Colton lunch. A store-bought sandwich and a cup of tea.

"Oh, that looks nice, what's in it?" Miss Colton asked, hoping to elicit a spoken response.

The figure put down the tray and gestured to her to eat, and another gesture to stop talking. Then the man came in pulling on a ski mask, and Miss Colton was rewarded with a glimpse of bearded chin.

"You'd better hope your rabbi gives up the girl," the man said gruffly, "or else." Even though she couldn't see his face, Miss Colton knew he was smiling grimly.

"Could I possibly have a little walk outside?" she asked. "I've been stuck in this room so long I'm getting claustrophobic."

The man threw back his head and laughed as if this was the funniest thing he had heard all year.

And it was then that she saw the tattoo.

A small dragon tattoo at the base of his neck, just where it joined his collarbone. And there was something entwined into the dragon, letters… What were they? One looked like an M and the other…

He stopped laughing and the tattoo disappeared. He looked at his co-captor.

"Tie her to you by the wrist and take her for a walk around the garden or something. You can take her to the bathroom first."

The woman nodded and fetched some twine. She carefully tied a knot around Miss Colton's wrist and held the other end firmly, rather than tying it to herself as he had suggested. Quietly, Miss Colton followed her out of the room.

The woman allowed her to use the bathroom without being tied to her. Gratefully, Miss Colton took her time cleaning herself up. She looked around to see if there were any negotiable windows she could climb out of but the only window was both high and small, and she was neither agile nor slender. Sighing, she gave up the idea of escaping through it and emerged to find the woman waiting for her. Her captor picked up the end of the rope and jerked her head to signify that they were going outside.

The house she was being held in was a small semidetached with an equally small back garden, fenced on all sides. They walked round and round, while Miss Colton tried to get a bearing of where she might be, but this could be any house, in any street, anywhere. The only thing she knew was that they hadn't travelled for more than half an hour after leaving the school, so they must still be somewhere on the south coast of England.

Miss Colton sniffed surreptitiously. And there it was. Ozone. The smell of the sea.

They were somewhere on the coast, and by the distance and the built-up area the house was in, she guessed Bournemouth. Not that it helped much, but it was something.

She turned to the woman. "I've got some money stashed away," she said to her in a whisper. "You can have it, all of it, if you somehow let me escape." With the words "let me" she made quotation marks in the air with her two hands, even though one hand was tied to the captor.

The woman shook her head.

"You don't really believe in what he's doing, do you?" Miss Colton went on intensely. "Using me as leverage to get a young girl to give herself up for a fate I can't even begin to imagine? I'm sure you're a good person, really… Just help me escape and you'll be able to live with yourself. You can't really want to do what he says…"

The woman turned to her and Miss Colton could see her whole body language was one of hopeless surrender. Then, for the first time, she spoke. Her voice was definitely female, as Miss Colton had suspected. But the accent…that was what threw her. It was pure Eastern European. Russian? Polish?

"You don't understand," the woman said in a low voice. "I have no choices. If I don't do what he says, he will kill me… I would help you if I could…but I can't. I'm sorry…"

"Just let go the rope… Say I wriggled free. He won't do anything to you if it wasn't your fault. Then, here's my phone number…" Miss Colton plucked a pen from the woman's top pocket and scribbled it on the captor's forearm. "And I promise I'll give you the money."

"I would let you go, if it was that simple," the woman said sadly. "I would never come to you for the money, because I would be dead…whether it was my fault or not. He would kill me."

CHAPTER SEVENTEEN

"Surely he wouldn't kill you or hurt you in any way if you were totally blameless?" Miss Colton whispered urgently as they continued walking around and around. She was beginning to get dizzy, but the fact that her captor had spoken was a huge step forward and she wasn't willing to let it go in such a hurry.

The word "blameless" seemed to be a little beyond the woman's vocabulary, and she turned a querying masked face to Miss Colton. It was weird how, despite the captor being masked, Miss Colton could tell by body language alone what she was thinking.

"I mean, if it isn't your fault," she supplied. There was a gesture of recognition.

"He wants the girl," the woman said. "If he no gets her, he will be very angry. You are his ticket to get her. If you not here, he will be very angry. And believe me when I say you do not want to see Alexander when he is angry." A hand flew up to cover her mouth as she realized her slipup. Miss Colton pretended not to notice, but inside herself, she was exultant. She had clues. A dragon tattoo at the base of his neck and now a name. Alexander. It wasn't much but it was something.

As they continued to walk, Miss Colton's mind was whirling. This was probably why Alexander had instructed the woman not to speak. He knew she was likely to give something away, so she was better off staying silent. She could only hope that the woman wouldn't admit to him that she had spoken, so that he wouldn't punish her.

Miss Colton took a deep breath and smiled at the woman.

"Mmm," she said. "I do so love the smell of the sea, don't you? And it seems so close too!"

She was hoping for some more slipups as to their location, but the woman was on her guard now.

"I not tell him I spoke with you, or he will beat me," she said. "And if you want more walks like this, you not tell him either, okay?"

Miss Colton patted the woman's arm in a comradely fashion. "Your secret's safe with me, my dear," she said with a smile. She thought maybe if she created a bond with her female captor, she might have a better chance of more clues. But fear was uppermost in the woman's mind.

"You seem very scared of him," she commented artlessly.

The woman turned to her. "You have no idea," she said. "He is vicious. No mercy."

"How on earth did you get involved with him?"

"I was part of a human cargo from Russia. All women, all young. We were told, come to the UK, you will find work, and big apartments, and make lots of money to send home. In Moscow I lived with my family in a very small apartment. They told us all lies to get us to come here. They said I could be a fashion model." The woman snorted. "Look at me...I am much too short to be a fashion model. But I wanted to believe, so I believed. So did my friends. The UK was our utopia. Alexander took money from us, from all of us, for the fares to UK. I gave him all the money I had, just to get here.

"Once we were here, instead of big, fancy apartments and jobs, we found ourselves in a big house, all together, locked in. Alexander was the boss of the whole thing. He found work for some of the girls, but not legitimate work. Some were sent out to steal, and they had to give all their stuff to him. And me, he picked me for some reason, to work with him. Maybe I'm the prettiest. I don't know why he chose me."

"Oh, I'm sure you are very pretty," Miss Colton assured her.

"Some of the other girls are already dead," the woman said. "Some of the others are in jail. They never pointed a finger, so he was never exposed. They were all terrified for their lives."

Miss Colton was so shocked she didn't know what to say. This was so far removed from her genteel upbringing that for once they had no common language.

"Do you want to bring him down?" she asked at last.

"Of course I do," the woman said. "I want to be free of him. But he is very powerful."

"Maybe if we worked together..." Miss Colton suggested.

The woman looked at her and laughed. "You, old, fat woman? What can you do? I am young and strong, I have purple belt in martial arts, and I can't do nothing. What can you do?"

Miss Colton swallowed the insult. "I could...sit on him!" she suggested. "While you tie him up or something... Then me being fat is actually a good thing."

The woman looked her critically. "You not fat enough. He could throw you off."

A compliment at last and also a shred of hope.

"Worth a try, don't you think?" Miss Colton tried her hardest to keep the pleading note out of her voice. "He won't kill me, he needs me too much. As you say, I'm his ticket."

The woman glanced towards the house. "We better go back in, he will start becoming suspicious." Miss Colton felt disappointed that there had been no firm answer, but on the other hand, the woman hadn't said no. Give her time to mull it over and who knows? She allowed herself to be led back to the house but there was a new spring to her step.

The man was waiting. Even with his mask in place Miss Colton could see his aggressive stance as he looked at the female captor.

"You were a long time," he said accusingly.

The woman shrugged and gestured to Miss Colton as if to say, *She needed the fresh air; give her a break.*

The man shrugged in turn. "It's time to contact the school again with instructions." He turned to Miss Colton. "Now we'll see how much that precious school of yours values your life."

"Against the life of a defenseless child?" Miss Colton blurted out. "I've lived my life. She has it all in front of her. I'd hope they'd put her first."

"You've lived your life?" scorned the man. "Never married, no children. A dried-up, old spinster... How is that living your life?"

Miss Colton flushed. "I am fulfilled. I looked after my parents, and now I have the girls to care for."

"Ha!" he mocked, throwing back his head and revealing the dragon tattoo again. "Useless, old woman."

The female captor looked at him sharply at this clue giveaway, but he seemed unconcerned. "Go and make some coffee," he told her, and pushed her away like an annoying cat that had jumped on to his lap. "I am sure our honored guest would like a cup of coffee, yes?" He looked at Miss Colton.

"Tea would be nice," she said.

"You English and your tea! Okay, two coffees, one tea, Svetlana, and make it snappy. I have a phone call to make."

The woman left the room and he gestured that Miss Colton be seated at the table. She sat down meekly but inside she was exultant.

He had let her name slip. Svetlana. Alexander. Miss Colton had two names, a dragon tattoo, an almost-location, and what's more, Svetlana seemed predisposed to help her. Things were looking up.

CHAPTER EIGHTEEN

Rosie had segregated Yael and they were now walking in some little-explored part of the school grounds. Slowly, hesitatingly, she started telling her about Nena, and what she was really doing here. The girl's eyes grew round as saucers as she listened.

"It's like a movie!" she said, hardly able to contain her excitement. It was all she could do not to jump up and down. In fact, she did cave in and do some jumping. She was like a boxed spring that had just escaped.

"It's not a movie, it's real life and there are real live people involved," Rosie reminded her.

"I know, but…"

"And your parents will have to give their permission for you to be involved in what could be a very dangerous mission," Rosie continued, as briefed by Nesbit and Moslovsky. At this, Yael stopped jumping and looked hard at her.

"My parents?"

Rosie was rather taken aback by Yael's confrontational attitude to this. She had thought it was a no-brainer that a fourteen-year-old girl would have to have parental consent before being sent on such a quest.

"Well, yes, of course. It wouldn't be right otherwise…"

Yael's body language had changed from jack-in-the-box to skulking feline afraid of its own shadow.

"My parents care diddly-squat about me. Never have, never will. Why do you think I'm like this? Risk taking to the point of recklessness — everyone says it about me. I've come to agree that it's true. If they don't care about me and what happens to me, why should I?" Her face had taken on an unpleasantly dark color. Rosie was alarmed.

"That can't be true," she protested. "I mean, look, they sent you to this school, which costs a pretty packet from what I understand. They must care something about you. They haven't turfed you out into the street, have they?" Rosie finished triumphant that her point would strike home. Yael snorted.

"They might as well have," she growled. "You think *they* are paying for my education?"

There were a couple of flattish rocks at the point they had now reached, and the two girls took advantage of them and sat down side by side. Rosie, horrified, could hardly assimilate what she was being told.

"My parents abandoned me as a baby. They left me wrapped in a blanket, on the steps of our local hospital and did a runner. I haven't heard from them since. No one has." Yael sighed. "They were very young. That's the only excuse I can come up with."

"That's awful!" Rosie exclaimed, her voice full of pity for her friend.

Yael glared at her. "I don't want pity. Never have. I'm okay. I was fostered out to a nice family who brought me up, but it was never going to be a permanent arrangement. They kept me far longer than they had originally intended, but by the time I was ten and exhibiting all this kind of behavior, they couldn't cope with me any longer. I was sent into care. Four years in a children's home is enough to make anyone crazy. I managed to stay sane. Just. Then a wealthy entrepreneur in the community decided the best place for me would be this one. Away from everyone, everyone could just forget about me here. He became my legal guardian, but it's not as if he really cares about me. He's 'doing a mitzvah,'" Yael made quotation marks in the air as she said this, "by paying for me to be out of the way. That's all."

Rosie didn't know what to say. She was appalled.

After a short pause Yael smiled wryly. "So you see, Rosie, I'm perfect for this mission. I'm brave, fearless, and reckless because I have nothing to lose. I have absolutely nothing to lose."

"You have your life to lose!" Rosie protested. "That must be worth something!"

Yael shrugged. "My life wasn't worth anything to *them*." She jerked her thumb to indicate those who were meant to care for her. "So why should it mean anything to me?"

"So you can prove to them that you are worth caring about," Rosie said firmly. "And at the very least, you have to care about what happens to you — otherwise you could put the mission at risk. You *have to*."

There was a silence. Both girls sat staring off at the sea. Then Yael spoke.

"Of course I care. I'd be lying if I said I wanted to die, or didn't mind if I did." She paused. "But I was born to do this. To prove that I'm worth something. Which no one else seems to think I am."

Rosie hugged her.

"Not you, and the others," Yael said, accepting the hug and hugging her back. "I know you know I'm worth something. I'm talking about my various parents and guardians. The whole lot of them."

"Rabbi Moslovsky must know about your home situation, though," Rosie said, puzzled. "So why did he say we had to get parental consent?"

"I think my guardian kinda kept that side of it quiet. No one in the *frum* community wants to admit to something like that. So to the wide world out there my guardian is just a kindly *askan* who undertook to pay for my education. Hardly anyone knows I was abandoned at birth."

"I see," Rosie said. She had the distinct feeling that she was being educated in life far beyond what was usual for girls her age.

Yael shrugged again with a false-happy grin. "So you see, my dear friend Rosie, that I don't need parental permission! Come on, let's join the others or they'll start worrying we've both been kidnapped too!"

The two girls got up from their stone seats and walked back to where the rest of the class was congregated, sitting on benches and on the grass overlooking the sea. The strong wire fences were a secure barrier to anyone falling. Or to anyone climbing up the cliff face. Not that it had helped poor Miss Colton in her hour of need, Rosie thought.

"Where have you been?" Shuli asked curiously as the two girls sat down with her and a very sharp-eyed Nena who was looking for a signal from Rosie. She felt unable to give one but just sent her a *we'll talk later* message with her eyes.

"Oh, just exploring," Yael said cheerily and tossed her unruly curls artlessly.

The look in Shuli's eyes made Rosie think, *Oh, dear. Shuli's the only one not in this loop now. She must feel so excluded. What can I do to fix this?* She couldn't think of a way at present but resolved to try and make her not feel so left out when the opportunity presented itself.

Rosie related the information she had gleaned from Yael to Rabbi Moslovsky. He was very still as she talked and his expression was one of great sadness. When she had finished he sighed and spoke.

"I had my suspicions that something was amiss with Yael's home life but I had no idea it was as bad as this." He was quiet a while longer and then said, "I think Nesbit wants her to have a psychological assessment next, to see if she really is as suitable for this as she says. She'll have to be trained and prepared. It's all going to take time, and time is a luxury, I'm very afraid, that our Miss Colton may not have."

CHAPTER NINETEEN

Alexander had either made or received a phone call, which he had taken in another room. For some reason he'd left the door open, enabling Miss Colton to at least try and monitor what was going on. From his agitated state upon hanging up, she guessed it was the prisoner on the other end — the man Nena had witnessed.

He now seemed jumpier, but he also seemed less confident about his course of action. Miss Colton had strained to eavesdrop on the phone call, but as it was in Russian, no matter how much she heard, it wouldn't have helped her decipher it. However, she prided herself on being astute at picking up on tone and voice expression, and Alexander's tone of voice grew more and more agitated the longer the phone call went on. She guessed he was being told off, or threatened, by the prisoner. Something like, "Get on with it and make sure you don't mess this one up! Everything depends on it, including your life!" Of course they could have been discussing the laundry for all she understood of Russian. So she sought out Svetlana.

Svetlana was in the kitchen preparing dinner. She wasn't wearing her ski mask since the cooking was making her face too hot, Miss Colton figured. She looked horrified to be caught and looked around for the mask and somewhere to hide herself.

"You mustn't tell him you saw my face!" she pleaded. As Miss Colton promised her she wouldn't, she studied the pretty, young face in front of her and stored it in her memory.

"Where is Alexander?" Svetlana said desperately, pulling on her ski mask.

"I don't know where he is now," Miss Colton said, "but he was on the phone before, talking in Russian. I wonder if you overheard any of it."

Svetlana stirred whatever was in the pot furiously and for a while Miss Colton thought she hadn't heard. Then she spoke.

"He is angry. Very angry. He says we are too slow. That we should have the girl by now."

So I was right, Miss Colton thought.

"Who is angry? The man in prison?"

A quick nod. "It is all taking too long. The longer we take, the more we risk getting caught."

"So what's the delay?"

Then they heard Alexander's heavy footsteps coming into the kitchen. He was wearing his ski mask — he was obviously not as lax as his female counterpart. He spoke to Svetlana in Russian. Miss Colton presumed he was asking her what they had been talking about. Svetlana replied but what was said Miss Colton had no idea.

"She is good cook, yes?" he said to Miss Colton in proud tones.

"You are sensible English woman learning good Russian recipes. English cooking is the worst in the world. You can learn from us."

So Svetlana had told him they had been discussing the contents of the stew pot. And Alexander wasn't even pretending to be anything but Russian. It was all unraveling, like a ball of wool played with constantly by a cat. And that cat was Barbara Colton.

At first, when she had been captured, she had presumed she would shortly be rescued, so had waited passively for her knight in shining armor to ride up on a white stallion. When after a couple of days this was apparently not happening — although of course she had no idea of what was going on behind the scenes at the school — she decided to be more proactive. She was a resourceful woman. She could find a way out of this!

Her captors had relaxed their vigil somewhat. When she had first been taken to that house, she was tied to a chair in a locked room by day, and tied by her wrist to a bed at night. That was horrible. Then as she had health problems that necessitated frequent restroom trips, they couldn't be bothered to keep tying and untying her to the chair or bed, so she was given the freedom of the room and its adjacent bathroom.

Now, since the walk around the garden, she more or less had the free run of the house. The front door was heavily locked, and they had worked out that a woman of her age and size was unlikely to make a bolt through the windows, even though they were also locked. So they allowed her the freedom of wandering around the small house, although she was never left alone in it. If one of the captors went out, the other always stayed behind to watch her.

Miss Colton wanted to lull them. To make them think she was a fat, non-athletic old woman who was not a flight risk because she couldn't move with ease. To this end, she developed a limp, a lopsided way of walking that spoke of a hip problem, and every now and then she would complain about pain.

"I need medication," she would whine. "I take painkilling medication every four hours back at the school, and I've been without it. I'm really beginning to suffer."

The first time, Alexander had looked at her closely. "You seemed to be walking around the garden just fine," he commented. She didn't know what to say to this, but then, to her surprise and delight, Svetlana had come to her rescue.

"Oh no, she was limping. I noticed it. I had to walk really slowly with her. She is in pain."

During quiet moments alone, Miss Colton tried to work out why Svetlana would do that. Then she realized. This was her way of helping her. She couldn't do anything active or she'd risk her life. But she could passively play along with her ploys, even though she had no idea where they would lead or what Miss Colton was planning to do.

"So what? You want I should get pain medication?" Alexander growled at her. "What you think this is? A clinic? You are a captive!"

Miss Colton had shrugged and continued to hobble around looking agonized. She never got her meds, but then again, she didn't really need any. She was overweight, but fit, and there was nothing wrong with her hip. But it served its purpose. Alexander had a picture of her in his mind as a sick, helpless old woman who would be no real escape risk. And so the security around her gradually became more and more lax.

The next afternoon they left her unsupervised when both of them were taking a nap. This had never happened before. Miss Colton was free to explore the house and look for escape routes. The trouble was, there weren't any. The front door was dead bolted and had more locks on it than a prison. The windows were open-able with a key, but she couldn't find one, and they were too small. It was hopeless. Her ploy of pretending to be sick was useless — there was no way out of this house.

Then she discovered the coal cellar.

In the olden days when the house was heated by a coal fire, the fuel was delivered directly into a small cellar beneath the house where it was stored. That cellar had an opening into the street so the deliveries could be done without the owners needing to be at home. Now empty of coal, it was down a very narrow flight of steps off the kitchen. Miss Colton had found it during one of her nightly walks around the house, and thought she might just be able to squeeze down it. She presumed her captors didn't yet know of its presence. And this was how she wanted to keep things, until she made her escape.

CHAPTER TWENTY

"Where's Yael going?" Nena asked Rosie. Yael had just been taken from the school in what Chief Inspector Nesbit hoped looked like an innocuous, normal car, but was in fact an unmarked police car driven by a plainclothes policeman. She was going to her psychological assessment, but of course no one was to know this.

Rabbi Moslovsky had briefed Rosie on what to say under such circumstances. The whole project had to work like oiled machinery if it was to succeed.

"Oh, she heard that her grandmother isn't well. She's been given compassionate leave to go and visit her for a few days," Rosie replied. She hoped against hope that Yael hadn't filled Nena in on her home life, which would have made a sick grandmother about as realistic a story as a fairy tale. But Nena nodded, accepting the excuse.

The two girls were walking outside to get some fresh air, as the school was still on major lockdown. They had watched Yael getting into a plain, dark car and being driven away.

Miss Colton was still missing and it had been five days now. School was continuing more or less as usual, with other teachers filling in for her classes. Her disappearance was no longer referred to. If the girls asked one of the teachers what was happening with the deputy head, most of them shrugged with genuine blank stares and said they didn't have a clue. And they were being truthful.

The only one who looked uncomfortable when this question was put to him, was Rabbi Moslovsky. He was genetically programmed to be honest and truthful, and it was clearly killing him to be this secretive and even to tell white lies.

The two girls stared at the dark car disappearing down the hill. Nena turned to Rosie.

"Okay Rosie, spill. What *is* going on?"

"Nothing's going on," Rosie said quickly, probably too quickly.

"Look. Miss Colton has disappeared, apparently been kidnapped. As far as I know there's been no ransom demand. The police were swarming all over the school looking for clues, took all our fingerprints, and now, nothing. It's all gone quiet and so has everyone. The school's on lockdown but nobody's talking. And you're telling me nothing's going on? What kind of an idiot do you take me for?"

Rosie started walking away from the entrance, round the side of the building to where it was quieter, Nena at her side.

"What do you *think's* going on, Nena?" she said at last.

"I'm pretty sure this is something to do with me."

"Not everything has to be to do with you," Rosie said in the hope that it would divert Nena away from being the center of her own universe.

"Of course not, but it's too much of a coincidence to be anything else." Rosie's diversion tactic wasn't working, and Nena was too astute for it to work, anyway.

"And why do you think I know any more than anyone else?" Rosie said desperately. She felt like a chess player trying to work several moves ahead of her opponent and she could already see that she was going to have to tell Nena something, even if not the whole truth, just to keep her from probing too much.

"Because you're the only one around here who doesn't look totally lost and puzzled. You have a look that says you know more than you let on. And I think I have the right to know what that is. After all, it's my life we're talking about."

Rosie thought Nena was right but was still unsure how to handle things. She stalled for time. "Come, let's find somewhere private. There are too many girls here."

They found an outhouse where gardening tools were kept. On the way there Rosie's mind was churning, but the more she scrabbled for a foothold in her thoughts, the more the ground slipped away from her. Nena was eager for disclosure, so she went ahead, opened the outhouse door and stood expectantly inside to prove it was empty and isolated.

She motioned to Rosie with both hands.

They sat down on a rather grubby workbench after wiping it perfunctorily with a cloth they found lying around. Rosie turned to Nena and took both her hands in her own.

"Look, Nena, you know how confidential all of this is. I've been drawn into it and to be honest, I wish I hadn't been. I like a quiet life. All this drama may seem exciting, but it's not, it's just plain scary. I have enough problems of my own at home and had chosen to come here to get away from all of that."

"I'm sorry," Nena said, looking genuinely distressed for her friend. "You've been great — a fantastic choice for whatever the *rav* chose you, but if you'd rather drop out now…" she let the rest of the sentence hang in the air.

Rosie shrugged. "Even if I did want to, I couldn't. I'm in too deep now. Let's just hope Hashem will in some way protect me as well as you and make this all work out for both of us."

"Amen to that," Nena said with feeling.

"I'm really not sure if I'm supposed to tell you anything at all, but you've obviously figured out that Miss Colton's abduction is connected to you somehow…and you're right about that."

Despite Nena apparently having figured it out, the admission of it made her go pale with shock.

"How is it connected?"

Rosie looked away. This was the difficult part.

"Look, if I tell you, I know you're going to try and play the heroine but you mustn't. Do you hear me? You absolutely mustn't. It wouldn't help anyone, least of all yourself, and anyway, there are other plans in the works."

Nena nodded slowly, realization dawning. "They have Miss Colton because they want to exchange her for me."

Rosie said nothing. Maybe she could say later that she hadn't in fact told Nena this, that Nena had taken her silence for confirmation.

Nena processed this idea, swallowed hard, and said, "And you thought I'd want to sacrifice myself for Miss Colton?"

Again, Rosie thought it was prudent to say nothing. Nena swallowed again. "I'm afraid I'm less of a heroine than you give me credit for. I'm far too scared and have been far too traumatized, to offer myself up to get Miss Colton back. I know maybe I should, but…"

"No, you shouldn't! Rabbi Moslovsky was telling me — you have absolutely no *chiyuv* to save her by sacrificing yourself."

"So what's the plan then?" Nena asked.

Now it was Rosie's turn to swallow hard. "It's Yael. That's where she was being taken. Not to her grandmother. I don't even think she has a grandmother. She's being psychologically assessed…"

"For what?" Nena's voice was rising in panic.

"She says she was born to do this. She's being assessed to see if she really is suitable, or will just be a liability. She wants to be your decoy. We'll know by tomorrow if the plan is good to go."

CHAPTER TWENTY-ONE

Rabbi Moslovsky was pacing. In fact, he had spent so much time in recent days pacing up and down his office that, when he was able to see any humorous side in this horrible situation — which wasn't often — he told himself this was the most exercise he had had in years.

The school continued to function as normal but it was no thanks to him; he was unable to lead it in his usual way. His mind was totally immersed in this kidnapping; it had consumed him, swallowed him whole, and he could think of absolutely nothing else. Luckily his deputy head of Kodesh, Rabbi Simons, was willing and able to take over the task of running the Kodesh side of the school.

Rabbi Moslovsky was terrified that the phone call he dreaded would come before Yael had been assessed and deemed suitable to be the decoy for Nena. He was equally if not more terrified of what would happen if she was not deemed suitable.

The phone on his desk rang. He looked at it in abject terror, as if the phone itself would jump out of its cradle and attack him. In fact, this ordeal was affecting his health badly and he was genuinely frightened that he might not survive it. He reached into his pocket for one of his heart pills, and then picked up the phone, steeling himself for the gruff Russian tones of the kidnapper.

"Is that you, Rabbi?" said Nesbit.

The relief Moslovsky felt almost made him faint on the spot. Groping for the arm of his chair, he sat down, and felt his whole body shaking. He was definitely not cut out to be an action hero, he decided.

He said yes in such a croak that Nesbit sounded doubtful that it was indeed him.

"Rabbi?"

"Sorry," he said, trying to make his voice sound normal. "I just thought it might be the kidnappers. It got me nervous."

Nesbit sounded worried. "Rabbi, you aren't a well man. Maybe this is too much for you to handle. Can you find someone else to deputize for you on this matter and maybe you go back to running the school?"

For a moment Moslovsky considered this idea and it sounded like heaven. Not to have to worry about Nena and Miss Colton. To hand the whole thing, lock, stock, and barrel, to someone else and just go back to being plain, old Rabbi Moslovsky, head of Kodesh again. But then he wondered who would deputize, and how much telling yet someone else about everything would jeopardize the whole mission, and he realized that like it or not, he was in for the long haul.

"I'll be fine," he said finally. Nesbit didn't press the matter or insist he step down, and by this Moslovsky knew that it was indeed important to keep the inner circle of those in the know, as small as possible.

"I called to tell you about Yael," Nesbit went on.

"Oh, yes? How did she do?"

"Fantastic. She's a natural. She'll make an amazing spy one day. In fact I have contacts in MI5 — that's the British Secret Service — and have asked them to take an interest in her. See how she develops as she grows up."

"A spy? Maybe not a career for a religious Jewish girl," the *rav* said doubtfully.

"You never know. She might need to earn her own living…and she has all the qualities."

"Well, I suppose it beats working as a secretary in an office," the *rav* said, thinking the whole thing was a pipe dream anyway.

"We've been briefing her, training her, and assessing her and she picks up the nub of what she needs to do in an instant. No messing about. Most impressive. I think we're good to go, when you get that phone call. She knows exactly what to do, and I'm pretty confident that she won't mess up."

"So what happens now?" the *rav* asked, still shaking slightly. He was relieved from the phone call not being the kidnapper. He was remembering his wife's birthing classes and the breathing they learned there, and practiced some deep calming breaths. To his surprise, his pulse slowed and he felt better.

"I've just put Yael in a car; she's on her way back to the school. Oh, and I've given her a wire to wear when she actually acts as decoy."

"That's a bit risky, isn't it?" Moslovsky asked worriedly, his pulse rising again. "They're bound to check her for listening devices, aren't they?"

Nesbit laughed. "Get with the program, Rabbi," he said. "The latest bugs are virtually undetectable unless you scan for them. She'll wear it deep inside her ear and no one will notice it. Unless they're very clued in to the latest technology, which I doubt. It's a two-way device — we can talk to her, she can speak normally or quietly and we'll be able to pick it up. And on our end, it records everything that's said."

"Wow," said the *rav*. He had barely gotten the hang of his cell phone. "Well, let's hope she doesn't lose the bug… She's only a young girl after all."

"That is a risk, I agree," Nesbit said. "But Yael, despite her apparent devil-may-care attitude, is in fact incredibly with-it and focused on what she needs to do. I doubt very much she'll be careless with the bug. Anyway, if she loses one of them I gave her a spare."

"So now…?"

"Now, my rabbinical friend, we watch and wait. For the phone call, for the instructions."

"Is there nothing you can do in the meantime to try and find Miss Colton?" Moslovsky asked. "Maybe she's absolutely desperate, or being tortured, or maybe she isn't alive anymore. And all due to the fact that we haven't made any attempt to find her." His pulse was throbbing dangerously. He took some more calming breaths but this time they didn't work so well. He felt rising panic.

"If we had the least clue as to her whereabouts, maybe we could search for her. But she disappeared off the face of the earth and could be anywhere. Anywhere at all. It would take far too much manpower and a ridiculous amount of wasted time to even begin to work out where she might be. She could be on the moon for all we know."

If Nesbit had known that at the moment he uttered those words,

Miss Colton was a mere three miles away from the school, in a small coastal house, contemplating an escape route, he might have thought otherwise about a rescue attempt.

CHAPTER TWENTY-TWO

Miss Colton was having a "bad day" with her hip. The fact that her injury was manufactured and artificial passed Alexander by completely, and even Svetlana wasn't sure if this was a recent development in her health or a ploy. Miss Colton had been a consummate actress in her youth; she had even acquired a theatrical agent, which meant she had some level of credence in show business. She'd performed in various minor stage productions and once had a supporting role in a movie — even if it had never been released in the cinema. But she could act, and right now she was calling up all her hidden acting talents and asking them to work for her.

She had spent the morning hobbling around in an agonized fashion, making a lot of low moans and sucking in air through her teeth to signify pain. She sat down, then stood up as if sitting was even more painful. All in all it was a picture of a woman who didn't know what to do with herself.

"I have pain medication at the school," she kept saying. "I have to take it four times a day. You keeping me here means I'm sixteen doses behind and I'm really suffering. I need my medication!"

Alexander was clearly losing patience with the complaining and moaning. He said in Russian to Svetlana, "If that old woman doesn't stop her groaning, so help me I'm going to put her out of her misery…permanently!"

"And how will that help us exactly?" Svetlana hissed back at him in the same tongue. "We'll lose our only leverage to get the girl!"

"Pah!" Alexander said and bashed the wall in frustration.

"When are we doing the exchange?" Svetlana asked him.

"I'm making the phone call in the morning. Everything has to be set up just right so we don't get caught."

Miss Colton moaned again and yelped a little to signify her hip had sent a sharp bolt of pain through her.

Alexander cracked. "Okay, okay!" he shouted. "I will go to pharmacy and get you some painkilling medication. Just tell me which one!"

"You can't get it over the counter," Miss Colton said artlessly. "You need a prescription."

Alexander came up to her far too close for her comfort and pushed his face even closer. "Now see here you fat old woman," he growled. For a moment she was sure he was going to strangle her, but she stood her ground. "I cannot get a prescription. I am not going to walk into the school and say, 'Hey, everyone, I am the kidnapper. I need Miss Colton's medication. Do you know where it is kept by any chance?' So, as we cannot get you to a doctor and I cannot get your medication from the school, what exactly do you suggest I do?"

She stared straight back at him even though she was quaking like Jell-O inside.

"Why can't you take me to a doctor?" she said.

"Because —" he snapped back and then paused. He looked at Svetlana and Svetlana looked back at him and shrugged as if to say, *I don't know, don't ask me!*

Alexander whipped his head back and forth between the two women. "If I get you to a doctor and get you your medication, will you stop moaning after that?"

"I shall be as quiet as a lamb," Miss Colton said.

He looked at Svetlana again, who said something in Russian that seemed to reassure him.

"Okay. We go down to the local clinic now and get your stupid prescription. But so help me, if you carry on moaning after this…" he added threateningly.

"Quiet as a lamb," Miss Colton assured him with a smile.

She had no idea what she was going to do at the doctor's. She had never had painkilling medication and didn't even know the name of a strong one likely to be prescription only. But it was a chance to interact with the outside world and if it prevented her having to squeeze herself into that coal cellar, it was worth a shot.

"I just need to use the bathroom before we go," she said.

"You and your bathroom! You live in that place!" he grumbled. "Go! Be quick!"

In the bathroom Miss Colton tore off a few sheets of toilet paper. Her captors had been very careful to make sure she had no writing implements with her. But she found a sharp-edged piece of tile and quickly pricked her finger with it. She wrote a message on the paper with her own blood and stuffed it into the waistband of her skirt. She then pressed the tiny wound hard with another piece of paper until the bleeding stopped, then flushed and emerged.

"Okay, let's go," Alexander said. "I want to get this over with."

"Oh, so do I," Miss Colton assured him. "I really need those meds."

For the first time in four days, Miss Colton stepped out beyond the garden gate into the street. She took the opportunity to have a good look around her to see if there were any landmarks she might recognize for later, but it was a bland suburban street and there were no signs where she was standing. Alexander told Svetlana something in Russian as they got into the car, and Svetlana covered Miss Colton's eyes with a scarf, presumably so she couldn't make out where she was.

The car drove for about half a mile and then stopped, and she was helped out of the car still blindfolded. The two captors formed a huddle around her as they walked her into a building and it wasn't until she was inside that the blindfold was removed.

It was a walk-in doctor's clinic. They sat in the waiting room for a while, and Miss Colton looked desperately at the notices on the wall to see if there was a clue to its location. Without her glasses she couldn't see so far, and her two captors made sure she was sitting a good distance from the notice board. She peered and peered until Alexander whispered in her ear that if she didn't stop trying to read the notices he would put the blindfold on again and tell the other waiting patients that she had a bad reaction to light. She had managed to read a few of the notices in larger print, but all they talked about was getting inoculations and staying safe. No addresses.

When it was her turn they walked her into the doctor's office. He looked curiously at the threesome, perhaps wondering why someone needed two chaperones, but said nothing. The doctor was middle-aged and impatient. He listened to Miss Colton's symptoms but did no examination.

"I need some stronger painkillers than you can get over the counter," she said.

"What have you been prescribed till now?" he asked predictably, and her heart sank.

She struggled for a moment, then said with a little laugh, "Senior moment, you know… I can't remember the name of the thing!"

"Well, for arthritic pain we usually prescribe…" and he named a product she had never heard of.

"That's it," she exclaimed gratefully. "As strong a dose as you're allowed to give; it's really bad!"

The doctor seemed pleased to have the appointment over and done with so fast, scribbled something on a prescription pad, tore it off, and handed it to Miss Colton. Alexander grabbed it from her hand and said "Let's go." The two Russians turned to leave and as they did, Miss Colton took her chance and slipped her note onto the doctor's desk. Then she walked out.

Before the next patient came in, the doctor noticed a blood-stained piece of bathroom tissue on his desk.

"Ew," he said. "Some people have no manners." He crumpled Miss Colton's note without looking at it more closely, and threw it into his wastebasket. Then he buzzed for his next patient to come in.

CHAPTER TWENTY-THREE

After two days' absence, Yael slipped into the school early in the morning. She was almost unnoticed by everyone, except Rosie and now Nena, who had been briefed to the nth degree and was extremely curious. The car had been one of those large, black, silent ones that cost a fortune; its sheer costliness had manifested in its ability to glide up to the school gates like a wisp of smoke, disgorge its passenger, and glide back down the hill without any noticeable engine noise to attract attention to itself.

Rosie and Nena, who were waiting for her, grabbed her as she tried to sneak back into the school, and pulled her towards one of the outhouses for a full-on student debrief.

Yael's curly hair looked a little disheveled and her normally chirpy disposition was somewhat lacking. She sat down on an old box and looked at Nena questioningly, then at Rosie for confirmation. The other girls pulled up boxes to sit next to her.

"I filled her in," Rosie admitted. "I had to. It was only fair." There was a slight pause. "I didn't tell her anything that you told me… about…you know. Just thought she ought to know about the decoy thing. If you were laying yourself on the line for her, that is."

Yael nodded her acceptance of this truth.

"So, c'mon, c'mon, give!" Rosie burst out.

Yael was silent for a while, staring at the ground between her feet, and Nena looked a bit panicked.

"You've changed your mind; you're not going to do it," Nena said with a sigh.

"No, no I haven't changed my mind. Don't worry, I'm going to do it. It's just… Well, you know I'm the reckless, take chances, and never-mind-the-consequences type?"

The two girls nodded.

"Well, the past two days have been a real dose of cold water on my head. I've had a reality check such as I've never had in my life. I've learned that even though I am, as I thought, born to do something like this…and…did you know they thought I'd make an ideal spy one day?"

"No!" the two girls chorused.

"Yeah, well, I had someone from the Secret Service visit me while I was down there and check me out. He's going to get in touch when I'm about twenty or so. See if I'd be interested in signing up."

The two girls were more than impressed; they were speechless.

"Anyway, back to the point…even though they assured me that I was suitable for the mission, the reality of it, the knowledge of what responsibility it carried, and the risk that I might not even survive it, was *hugely* sobering. They drummed it into me that I can't be reckless and do stupid things, and go off on tangents of my own just because it seemed a good idea at the time. If I'm to have a good chance of carrying this off I have to stick with the program one hundred percent and not deviate from it one iota.

"We did lots of practice runs, and role-play and worse case scenarios. It was absolutely awful. And it didn't do my hair any good either," she tried to joke in a lame effort to inject humor into a horrific scenario. The two girls were gaping at her, awestruck at what she'd gone through.

"I can't let you do this for me," Nena said firmly. "It's too much to ask. You could get harmed! I'll give myself up."

"Don't be silly," Yael scolded her. "If you go, you'll for sure get hurt. If I go as your decoy, there's a good chance, with the plan the police have up their sleeves, that we'll all come through this okay."

Rosie nodded and touched Nena's arm. "I know how you feel, but you're going to have to step back and let Yael do this."

Nena was quiet and then nodded. "So when?"

"We don't know. When the kidnapper phones Rabbi Moslovsky with instructions, I guess."

"Let's go back to school," Nena said, getting up. "Besides anything else, all this is cutting Shuli right out of the loop and I feel bad for her. She's the only one of us who doesn't know."

"Do you think she should?" Rosie asked. "It's really your call." They all walked back towards the school building, mulling this over.

"We've been a foursome since the beginning," Rosie said. "And in fact Shuli was the first one to make friends with me. I'm not saying what you should do, but..."

"Yes, I think she should know," Nena said decisively. "Let's go tell her. We have a good half an hour before classes begin."

Shuli did look a little miffed to see the three girls approaching her. "What's going on, guys?" she asked. Nena linked arms with her and all four walked back to their bedroom together.

After Shuli had been filled in and was in a suitably jaw-dropped mode, Rosie impressed upon her — as she meant for all four of them — the need for utmost secrecy.

"I know it's a huge secret," she said sternly, "and the temptation to share it with just one other girl must be almost irresistible. But the story stops here, with us four. Or the whole operation will be in jeopardy. 'Cause that one girl will tell another 'just one girl' and that's how the whole thing will spread like wildfire. Then Miss Colton might die, and the kidnapper will have nothing to lose in coming to get Nena openly."

They all nodded sagely. Shuli kept mumbling, "Oh my gosh," and "Wow," over and over. Then she spoke. "I think it's time you all knew my secret," she said. "It's really nothing, certainly when compared to this, but since all of you've brought me into this huge secret, I think you should know."

"I didn't even know you had one," Rosie said honestly. "Except all that stuff about your parents doing *kiruv* work in South Africa, and having a house with a swimming pool, which I didn't really believe from day one. Is that your secret? That you made that up?"

"No, that's absolutely true. A lot of people in South Africa have houses with swimming pools, and it was only a rental anyway. No, that wasn't my secret."

"Then what was?" All the girls were curious now. Shuli blushed.

"Remember when I was reading those rules the seniors left by the window and I took such a long time? Well, the reason is that I have a hard time reading stuff. I'm severely dyslexic but I like to hide it and see if I can get by without people knowing. I've been getting extra tutoring and it's really helping."

There was a pause. "And?" Yael said, confused.

"And…that's it," Shuli said, still bright red.

"Aww, that's nothing!" Yael reassured her. "Lots of girls are dyslexic. It's no big deal. Why are you so embarrassed about it?"

They all hugged Shuli and she stopped blushing and felt so loved. And for a short time they all forgot about the momentous task ahead.

CHAPTER TWENTY-FOUR

The doctor at the walk-in clinic was packing up his stuff for the day. The cleaners were already moving in around him, dusting, vacuuming, and generally making a nuisance of themselves. Once the cleaners were around, the doctor wanted to get as far away from the clinic as he could. He wanted nothing more right now than to go home to his wife, put his feet up with a large glass of whiskey, and forget about his day.

The cleaner in his office was emptying the wastebasket into a larger bag. She appeared puzzled as she looked at crumpled-up piece of bloodstained tissue. Painstakingly, she unfolded it until it was legible.

"Look, hurry up, will you?" the doctor said impatiently. "I want to lock up and go home."

"I think you should look at this, Doctor," the cleaner said. She smoothed the piece of toilet paper out on his desk in front of him so he could read the message.

"What the…?" he said, staring at it. Suddenly his dream evening evaporated. For a split second or two he thought of ignoring the message written there, and just putting it down to some nutcase. Then he remembered who had left it on his desk. It had been that woman with the despairing look in her eyes, who had come in, oddly, he had thought at the time, flanked by those two people — a large, gruff-looking man, and a small, blonde woman. They looked foreign even though they hadn't actually said anything, but the patient herself… Why would she need two chaperones like that?

He recalled writing a prescription for her, and he quickly checked his records. Barbara Colton. And the way they had hustled her out of the room… It had all been rather odd, but at the time he had been so stressed and busy he hadn't given it a moment's thought.

Sighing, he sat back down again and picked up his phone. "Police, please."

Miss Colton was back at the house with the unneeded medication Svetlana had picked up on the way home; she'd been blindfolded and left in the car outside the pharmacy with Alexander so she couldn't assess where they were. She was surprised that the cavalry, or at least the local police, hadn't come looking for her. After all the trouble she'd gone to writing that note, she'd been expecting a dramatic rescue soon after, and was very downhearted that it didn't seem to be coming. Her captors had left her alone in her room, and she sat there, mulling over what had happened.

Slowly it dawned upon her. Even if the doctor had taken immediate action on reading her missive, all she had managed to write on it was *I'm being held captive; Barbara Colton*. She couldn't give an address as she didn't know where she was being held. She hadn't had enough time, or blood for that matter, to name her captors either. So aside from the vaguest clue as to the geographical area that she had been in, there wasn't a lot for the cops to go on.

Barbara Colton sat in her chair with a huge, deep sigh and realized that, for all intents and purposes, her efforts in blood had been a waste of time.

The phone on Moslovsky's desk rang threateningly. The *rav* jumped out of his skin with shock. Oh, could this be the call he'd been dreading? With a shaking hand, he picked up the handset, almost knocking it to the floor with his nerves.

"Nesbit here."

Moslovsky sank back with relief. "Oh, it's you."

"We might have a lead. Miss Colton was taken to a doctor by two kidnappers and managed to leave a note on the doctor's desk."

"What?" The *rav* sat up straight in surprise. "Where is she? What did the note say?"

"That's the problem," Nesbit said. "The note didn't say much. Just that she was being held captive, and her name. No address or other names."

"What's the use of that?" the *rav* asked despairingly. "Why didn't she write where she was or some information as to her captors?"

"We can't know," Nesbit said. "She obviously took quite a risk even doing that. The note was written on toilet paper, and in blood. Her captors weren't taking any chances giving her writing implements or anything."

"In blood!" Rabbi Moslovsky said, shocked. "Poor woman. I hope she hasn't been harmed."

"I doubt it. The amount of blood used was very small; it looked more like she had pricked herself deliberately to write the note. We've done some tests on the blood and we need to know her blood type so we can match it up."

"I can let you know that, we have that on record somewhere. But how is this all going to help? She hasn't given away much in that note."

"No, her note didn't give much information. But the toilet paper itself did."

"The toilet paper?" The *rav* was confused.

"It's not a standard brand you'd find in supermarkets," Nesbit explained. "It's a minor brand available in small convenience stores and only in a small geographic area. She had no idea when she wrote the note, but she gave us a much narrower search area by using that toilet paper — providing the kidnappers bought it locally to where she's being held. And it makes sense that if you buy a product in a small convenience store, rather than in a big supermarket, that it's close to where you live. I've already got local cops doing house-to-house inquiries in the area. It's a very small town close to Bournemouth. So not very far away at all."

"I can't see them giving up Miss Colton without a huge fight," the *rav* said worriedly. "She's their ticket to Nena."

"We know that," Nesbit said. "If we do go in, it'll be with our armed response unit. We wouldn't risk our unarmed officers. We don't plan on firing a single shot unless we absolutely have to, but we have to be prepared to. There could be quite a shoot-out. Of course we have no idea if the kidnappers are themselves armed, but we have to assume they are."

"Miss Colton could get hurt in a shoot-out," the *rav* said. His panic levels were rising again.

"Yes it's possible, but our men are highly trained, and will do everything they can to avoid that scenario. I'm sure she'll be just fine. We'll instruct her to get out of harm's way if possible." Nesbit paused, then went on. "She's really done extremely well. How she got her kidnappers to take her to the doctor is anyone's guess, but it was her best chance of leaving a message and she did it. We're most impressed here."

They said their good-byes, and the phone call ended. The *rav* sat back in his chair, smiling to himself. *Good old Miss Colton! Even without realizing it, she had led the police to a searchable area.* He was relaxed and upbeat when his phone rang again. He reached for it without a second thought.

"Hello, Rabbi," said the gruff voice of Alexander. "Have you missed me? I've missed you, Rabbi. Oh, yes. I've missed our little talks quite a lot…"

CHAPTER TWENTY-FIVE

Rabbi Moslovsky's heart was pounding so hard that he thought it would burst. Here it was, the call he had been dreading and fearing for so many days. That gruff foreign accent, those threatening tones… He reached for his medication and then realized he had taken some only a short time ago, so couldn't take any more without risk. He would just have to use other strategies to calm himself down. He did some slow, deep breathing and felt his pulse slowing.

"You there, Rabbi?" came the gruff voice, sounding a little worried.

"Yes, I'm here." Moslovsky sighed in a resigned tone.

"You were very quiet there for a while… I thought maybe you had fainted or had a heart attack or something." The voice laughed. "And we don't want that, do we? At least not before we have done the exchange… After that you have my full permission to have as many heart attacks as you like." He laughed again, and it was not a pleasant sound. The *rav* felt his pulse picking up again and he did some more slow breathing.

"Well, here's the deal. My friend, who is locked up in prison because of the girl you have in your school, he wants justice."

Moslovsky couldn't help giving a contemptuous snort at these words. "Justice? Don't you mean revenge?"

The voice took on a sharp edge. "I say what I mean and I mean what I say, Rabbi, and I thank you not to question me." There was a pause while he obviously expected the *rav* to apologize. When only silence was forthcoming, he went on, "I see you are going to be difficult. You do not want something terrible to happen to Miss Colton, do you?"

The *rav* shuddered. "No, no please don't hurt her. I'll do whatever you say."

"Then apologize for being rude and questioning me." The voice brooked no debate.

"I apologize." Even though it practically strangled him to say the words, Moslovsky saw he had no choice but to totally capitulate, or at least to appear to do so, if there was to be any chance of getting Miss Colton back safe.

"Say: 'I apologize for being rude and questioning you,'" the man insisted. Gritting his teeth and clenching his fists, Moslovsky did so, and the man gave a low, throaty chuckle of satisfaction.

"Good, good, now we make the progress, no?"

"Yes," the *rav* said in a small, defeated-sounding voice. He was aware that there was a bug on the phone and the police were monitoring the entire call, so maybe his stubbornness, if it lengthened the call enough, was a good thing.

"Now. Here's what I want you to do. I want you to bring the girl. You, alone, no one else with you, and a mobile phone. I will be giving you instructions along the way. I am not going to tell you the meeting place yet. I will be watching you, and if I see any evidence of police or anyone but you and the girl, I will immediately drive away with Miss Colton. Is that clear?"

The words ate into his soul like acid and burned him. "I hear you," Rabbi Moslovsky said hoarsely. His heart was pounding again and no amount of deep breathing was easing it.

"Good, good. You learn fast. You good student, yes?" Again that horrible laugh.

"When do you want me to do this?" the *rav* asked through the burning in his throat.

"Tomorrow. You will give me your cell phone number now, and I will call it to verify." Rabbi Moslovsky told him the number. The phone rang and the gruff voice was there. The *rav* looked for the caller ID but the number was listed as "Unavailable."

"You leave the school at nine on the dot, with the girl. Not five minutes to nine, not five minutes past nine. You will check the time on a radio-controlled clock to be sure. You will drive down the hill and make a right at the bottom, as if you were driving towards the coast. Keep on the road for at least two miles and I will call you again. So make sure you have your Bluetooth hands-free working."

The caller hung up both lines. The *rav* was left alone, trembling violently. In a minute or two his phone rang again — his cell this time, and it was Nesbit.

"Good, you did great," Nesbit said.

"That was so awful," the *rav* replied, and to his embarrassment found himself close to tears.

"Yes, it was pretty rough. The good news is, we were able to trace the call."

"Oh, good!! So where —"

"The bad news is, it's a call box in a service station on the M3 motorway."

"Oh well, that narrows it down to only about sixty miles," the *rav* said sourly. "Should be a breeze finding out which one."

"The guy is obviously going out of his way to remain untraceable," Nesbit said. "He didn't use a cell phone; we could've used triangulation to within thirty feet if he had."

"Anyway," sighed Moslovsky, defeated, "you heard the rest, no doubt."

"Yes. I'm coming to the school later on to brief Yael, and we need to set up your car."

"Set up my car? With what?"

"Sensors, bugs, and a two-way thingy that means when you are talking to the kidnapper getting instructions, I can hear him as well as you can. And I'll be able to give you instructions in your earpiece that will remain inaudible to the kidnapper. You need to wear a wire, and so does Yael, and maybe even a bulletproof vest."

"They'll detect a wire in an instant," Rabbi Moslovsky said in a worried tone.

"Not ours; they're virtually indetectable. You wear them deep inside your ear, they're flesh colored and invisible to the casual observer — and even the not-so-casual one."

"I'll be so nervous, I might crash the car. I'd be a liability, and then what good would I be to anyone?" Moslovsky said this and then realized how childish this sounded. Two lives were on the line and he was behaving like a baby! "Don't worry," he assured Nesbit, "I'll be okay. The adrenalin will kick in and I'll step up to the plate and do my duty."

"Yes you will," Nesbit said sternly. "Otherwise, if you dare come back dead, you'll have me to deal with."

The humor in this was totally lost on the *rav*. Nesbit sighed, and said, "I'll be there soon. Get Yael ready for the briefing."

CHAPTER TWENTY-SIX

In the *rav*'s office an hour later, Nesbit carried on their conversation as if it had taken place only minutes before. "You realize, however, that if the kidnapper uses a cell phone tomorrow, we *will* be able to triangulate his location."

Rabbi Moslovsky nodded. "Will you be in the area?"

"Of course. Discreetly so, but we'll be right behind you all the way. We don't want you or the girl to get into any real danger, obviously."

"They may figure that out," the *rav* said.

"I'm using our top men for this assignment. Really, I'm only along for the ride. I'm not heading this up, I'm not the best qualified. I've called in kidnap negotiators and top brass who know exactly how to handle this sort of situation. They know exactly how to follow the drop car — that's your car — without the kidnappers being the least bit aware of the fact."

The *rav* looked somewhat mollified. "I'll take you to Yael. She's ready and waiting."

"Ready and waiting" was hardly the description that fit Yael at that moment. She was in her bedroom with her three friends in a state of nerves — hugging and being hugged, getting up and sitting down, pacing and standing stock-still, staring out of the window at the rolling surf below.

Nena said she felt the most responsible for this mission, and felt terrible. She alternated between desperately wanting the whole thing to stop; her doing the right thing and be Nena, and not expect someone else to take the fall for her; and knowing that she would, in fact, jeopardize the mission far more than Yael would.

Yael had dressed in some of Nena's clothes. This was totally unnecessary, as the kidnappers and presumably the criminal in the background didn't know what clothes Nena owned. But Yael had chosen to do this to "get into character," to become Nena. She had also studied the way Nena walked, her mannerisms and gestures, and Shuli had spent the best part of the early morning trying to blow the curls out of Yael's hair so it would look more like Nena's. The curls were defiant, and as soon as Yael got damp with nerves they would spring back into action, but the attempt had been made anyway.

"Say something, say something!" Yael kept commanding Nena so that she could copy her voice and intonation. Nena was getting a bit irritated by this.

"Look, they don't know what I sound like; I don't think I did anything else but scream for help when I witnessed what I witnessed," she said. "So give it a rest, will you?"

Yael would not be put off. "Show me how you scream for help then!" she insisted. "I might well need that and end up sounding very different from you."

Nena looked unsure. "Oh, go on," Rosie sighed. "Yael's nervous and it's obvious she needs you to do something to calm her down. So go ahead and scream."

"Screaming will calm her down?" Nena laughed, but did it all the same. "Help, help!" she said, not very loudly.

"That's no good," Yael scolded.

Nena sighed. "Okay, okay. HELP, HELP!!" she yelled at the top of her lungs.

Yael immediately copied her. "HELP, HELP!! Is that right?"

"Sounds about right…" Rosie said, impressed, just as Nesbit and Rabbi Moslovsky burst into their room looking extremely anxious.

"What's going on, what was all that screaming, are you okay?" Moslovsky asked. Nesbit looked worriedly round the room but the girls were collapsed on the bed in fits of giggles.

"What, you think this is a joke?" Nesbit said angrily. Rabbi Moslovsky fell onto a chair, looking pale and shaken. The girls sobered.

"I'm sorry, it's my fault," Yael said. "I was getting Nena to scream for help so I could copy her voice, that's all."

When everyone had calmed down and Rabbi Moslovsky's color had returned to normal, Yael realized how irresponsible that particular little activity had been and apologized profusely to the *rav*.

"Look, tomorrow's the day," he said at last. "I need you to be focused and responsible. Silly girlish pranks like this one won't be tolerated. Is that clear, Yael Reed?"

Yael hung her head. "Yes, it's clear."

The other girls were very quiet. It was dawning upon them how very serious this whole thing was and they regretted acting so childishly.

"Okay, okay, lighten up now," Nesbit said with a smile. "I need Yael on her own today to prepare her for tomorrow. So off you go to class, the rest of you."

The girls all hugged Yael again and wished her luck. They reluctantly left her behind and went off to their classes.

Rabbi Moslovsky fanned himself with his hand. "That was... frightening."

"Sorry," Yael said again, feeling ashamed.

"I'm taking this young lady off your hands for a while," Nesbit told him. "I suggest you go back and lie down or something. We don't want you flaking out at a critical moment."

"Don't I need to go through the steps with you myself?" the *rav* asked. He felt shaky just thinking about it.

"No. Not the way you are now. In fact…I'm strongly thinking of replacing you with a decoy too. I think you're a liability, to be honest. With your health in its present state, I don't think you should make the drop tomorrow."

"But…who would you get?" Rabbi Moslovsky couldn't help a feeling of elation at the thought of not having to do the terrifying journey tomorrow. He felt a hundred times better already.

"I have an officer who is originally from South Africa, so he has your accent. He happens to be bearded, but we'll add to that, and make him look as Jewish as possible. He's a good man, a brave man, and a competent man, and he's not on the brink of a heart attack either. I've been thinking of using him instead of you for a while, so I've been briefing him in case. But watching you just now has made me make up my mind. Sorry, Rabbi, you're off the case. Go and lie down and leave it to us."

"I feel so useless," the *rav* said helplessly, but was only too happy to go back to his quarters, make himself a hot drink, and have a short rest. He had never felt so healthy in his life as he did at that moment; he knew it was the adrenalin kicking in from knowing he didn't have to do the exchange. Even though he felt he'd let people down, he knew the risks of letting them down tomorrow were far greater. He shot Yael an apologetic glance and she responded with a smile. He left the room.

"Okay, Yael, we're going to go through all the steps one more time," Nesbit said, leading her towards an empty classroom. "One of my sergeants will role-play the kidnapper, and I will play the officer who is taking the rabbi's place tomorrow. We have to get this right. For everyone's sake."

CHAPTER TWENTY-SEVEN

The two Russians seemed extremely panicky this morning, Barbara Colton thought. Alexander had gone out ostensibly to buy milk and bread, but had returned empty-handed, pale, and shaking. He spoke to Svetlana in urgent, nervous tones, and she responded in kind, shouting and waving her hands around. They both kept going to the window overlooking the street and peering out. Miss Colton retired to her room quietly, not wanting to be conspicuous, but wanting to see what they were looking for too.

There were two windows in her room, side by side. There was nothing of interest to see in the garden, so she turned her attention to the street. It was a quiet side street, and there was nothing unusual going on that she could discern. She had almost decided that Alexander was being paranoid for nothing, when something caught her eye. The flashing, blue light of a police car in the distance — not in their street, but at the top, by the main road. It was parked, and there were more than one of them. It was quite far away and hard to discern but Miss Colton was pretty sure there were two police cars up there.

Of course this didn't mean anything; police cars were everywhere. It didn't mean they were looking for them specifically. So Miss Colton wondered why Alexander was so nervous.

She was still waiting for her opportunity to escape down the coal cellar route, but had yet to take it. Maybe, while the two of them were so distracted…? She started shaking and perspiring heavily. This could be her opportunity. She crept out of her room again and, without attracting attention to herself, observed what her captors were doing. They were both at the window peeking out of the tiniest corner of the net curtains.

Curtain twitching, she thought drily. *A practice long beloved of nosey, old busybody ladies wanting to spy on the neighbors and assuming no one can see them. But of course everyone can see the curtains twitching from the outside.*

She walked as silently as she dared towards the door leading to the coal cellar. But it was hopeless. The house was so silent with the two of them practically holding their breath watching the police car, that as soon as a floorboard creaked they both turned around sharply, startled and anxious.

"I'm just going to the bathroom!" Miss Colton said airily, waving a hand towards it. "Darn nuisance, these old lady debilitations of mine, you know!"

"Debilitations?" Alexander asked, baffled.

Miss Colton had no idea if the word even existed. "Debilitated" meant incapacitated or injured, so she had made a noun out of it without knowing if there was such a noun.

"She mean old ladies need bathroom more," Svetlana said out of the corner of her mouth. Neither of them had moved from their watching places at the window, just swiveled their heads in her direction like puppets.

"I am never going to be old lady," Alexander declared. "Too fat, too stupid, too slow, and too much going to bathroom!" He roared with laughter briefly, and then remembered about the police and stopped suddenly as if someone had flicked a switch off. Svetlana did not laugh with him, presumably because she hoped one day she would be an old lady.

She left the bathroom. Alexander was looking more agitated. A cursory look through the living room window told Miss Colton that the flashing, blue light of the police car was slowly creeping down their road and approaching ever nearer.

He was speaking to Svetlana in Russian and pointing. From the tone and gesticulation, Miss Colton surmised he was saying something like, "They're doing house-to-house searches and they're getting closer!"

Svetlana responded by looking for Miss Colton and then looking away when she realized she had been standing there the whole time. She said something in Russian to Alexander but Miss Colton couldn't even guess what it was.

Then Alexander's cell phone rang. He spoke into it, then hung up and turned to the two women, speaking in English.

"We have to move her. The exchange is on in two hours."

Svetlana gestured at the window. "How we going to leave the house with the police crawling all over the street?"

Alexander looked out of the window again. The police were

definitely getting closer. He muttered an expletive in Russian and threw his hands up to the ceiling in a gesture of hopelessness.

"Are we trapped?" Miss Colton asked with an artless, faux-worried expression on her face.

"You keep quiet, fat old woman. You give me headache enough without talking!" Alexander spat.

The two Russians spoke excitedly in their native tongue for quite a while. Miss Colton could only guess what they were saying, but from the multiple gestures to the window and to herself, she guessed they were getting worried about how they were going to achieve the exchange with the police were bearing down on them at a steady pace.

"Dear me, you *do* have a bit of a problem, don't you?!" she said, unable to help an amused note entering her voice. It was a mistake. Alexander swung round and put his face so close to hers she felt sure he was going to head-butt her. Her heart raced.

"You don't understand. If no exchange happen…you get hurt. Do you get it now?"

She backed off, shocked into silence. She managed a small, frightened nod.

"So how about you try help think of a solution to how we get out of here?" he said, following her backward progress across the room, his face still in hers. "Then maybe you might live to see another year in that stupid school. If it doesn't fall into the ocean first…"

"There's always the coal cellar…" she squeaked.

They both stopped in their tracks and stared at her.

"The what?" Alexander growled. "What you talking about?"

"The coal cellar. Come with me. I'll show you."

It had been her secret escape plan. Something she had hugged to herself for days now. But now she knew she could have never pulled it off anyway, so Plan B had to be to use this secret escape plan to save her own skin.

They followed Miss Colton, bemused, to the little locked door in the hallway. She pulled the key out of the hiding place she had made for it, a little niche in the plaster of the wall, and unlocked it.

"What were you thinking of, woman?" Alexander shook his head.

They went down the dark, narrow stairs together and into the cellar, Miss Colton leading the way. At the bottom, the small, empty chamber once filled with coal. And a hatch leading to the street. She gestured to it.

"Our way out."

"This leads where?" he asked, snorting in disdain. "To the street where the police are looking? How will that help?"

"No," Miss Colton said, "it leads to an alleyway *behind* the street. In the olden days, gentrified people didn't want coal delivered at the front of their houses; that's why the alleyways were built."

Alexander looked at her through narrowed eyes. "For a fat old woman, you not quite as stupid as you look," he said. "Let's go. Now."

CHAPTER TWENTY-EIGHT

The girls crowded round Yael as she made her last-minute preparations for the big decoy mission. She had no idea what she could do to prepare herself, but the girls davened and said *Tehillim* and cried on each other's shoulders and murmured platitudes about how amazing Yael was to undertake this. No one cried more than Nena, the person everything was being sacrificed for.

Rabbi Moslovsky spent quite some time training his stand-in

to act and speak like an Orthodox Jew. A bearded South African police officer, no matter how convincing he looked at a casual glance, did not yet have the mannerisms down and could be easily detected. The stand-in, Jim, had watched documentaries and movies featuring Orthodox Jewry, and that together with Moslovsky's on-the-spot training had brought him up to speed. By the time the mission was ready to roll, even the *rav* had to admit, Jim was almost Jewish!

He followed Moslovsky around, mimicking his mannerisms to the point where the *rav* got quite irritated. "I'm sure I don't wave my hands around quite that much!" he told Jim crossly. "And what about all this fiddling with my beard? Surely you don't mean I do it that much?"

"Oh, but you do," the cop assured him with a grin.

Nesbit stood by looking tense. A team of undercover cops would be following the drop car at a safe and discreet distance. He wouldn't be among them, just in case the villains would recognize him.

"It's time to go," Nesbit said, looking at his watch.

Jim, aka Moslovsky, assumed a suitably worried air. The kidnappers knew Moslovsky was nervous and unwell, so for him to appear calm and in control would be an instant red flag. He had a false nose spray to copy the Rabbi's heart medication, and made sure he held it close at hand so he could use it when he thought he was being observed. He and Yael went out to the waiting car, while the other three girls, Nesbit, and Moslovsky watched through the windows of the building. The rest of the school was blissfully unaware of what was happening, and lessons were continuing as normal.

"The car isn't bugged, is it?" Yael asked Jim worriedly as she settled down in the seat and strapped herself in.

"It's been swept for bugs and is clean," Jim assured her. "Aside from our own bugs of course, which we need. The kidnappers haven't gotten to this car and bugged it, don't worry. We can talk freely unless the kidnappers are on the phone, when you must keep quiet as a mouse."

"What if they want to hear me talking?" she asked anxiously.

"Well, talk. That's not a problem. They don't know what Nena sounds like anyway, and it's not as if you have a different accent or anything."

"That's true."

Jim shot Yael a sideways glance as they drove down the hill towards the main road. "Hey, I thought you were this fearless, brave girl everyone's been talking about," he said with a smile. "What's this worried look I'm seeing on your face?"

"I'm not worried for me… I'm worried for Nena," Yael said. "She's what this mission is all about, and I mustn't mess it up for her."

Jim nodded. "Neither of us can afford to do that."

The car reached the road and, as instructed, Jim turned right and started along the coast road. It was relatively quiet for the time of day; not too many travelers headed for the beach this late in the year. He drove slowly, carefully along the road. Even though he was prepared for the phone to ring, and was trained to deal with the call, the ringing made them both jump. Yael clutched her chest. Jim motioned her to calm down as he pressed the button on the car dashboard that would activate the hands-free phone.

"You there, Rabbi?" came the gruff voice.

"I'm here," Jim replied, making sure to inject the right amount of quavering into his voice so it didn't sound too calm and confident.

"We have slight delay," the voice said. "The police are crawling all over my street. We are trying to get out of our house so we can do the exchange. So far we have managed to leave the house through the coal cellar, but now we are in the alleyway behind the house and we can't go any further. Police are everywhere. You have to tell the policeman to call off his men or the whole thing is off."

Yael shot Jim a panic-stricken look. Jim again signaled for her to be calm.

"How can I tell the policeman?" he said, "You told me I'm not allowed to speak to anyone but you."

There was a short silence on the line. "Now you are trying to be clever with me and I don't like it!" he said. "Obviously you have to speak to policeman. I am telling you to. Call off his men. Now! We are in alleyway and can't move until they go!"

The line was cut. Jim pulled up at the side of the road so he could call Nesbit. "A lack of coordination there, sir," Jim said. "Sending those guys to do house-to-house searches just when the kidnappers are trying to leave to do the exchange."

"I could call them off," Nesbit said slowly, "but if they told you they're in an alleyway behind the house, they shouldn't be too difficult to find either. We could just go and pick them up."

Yael looked disappointed at this idea.

"And risk them hurting Miss Colton? And then coming after the girl?" Jim said.

"There's going to be a stage of this operation — however we do it — when the kidnappers realize we're not handing over anyone in exchange for anyone. Miss Colton's life will be on the line, sooner or later. Does it matter if it's now or then?"

"You could always pretend to call them off," Jim said slowly.

"I think the kidnappers will figure that out pretty quick," Nesbit replied. "Hmm… What shall we do? Go ahead with the fake exchange, or go in and pick them up now? What would be safer?"

CHAPTER TWENTY-NINE

Nesbit paced back and forth while talking to his colleague Mark Gross, the police squad's kidnapping and terrorism expert.

"Call off your men," Gross advised him. "Or at least appear to. Make them disappear, but not entirely, in case Miss Colton is in danger. Are all the men in uniform?"

"Yes," Nesbit said. "House-to-house officers usually are in uniform; that way they don't scare the residents."

"Hmm… It would be better if they could be replaced by plain-clothed officers. A SWAT team. I'm sure you have a Special Weapons And Tactics team on standby don't you?"

"Of course. I'll get them down there at once and recall the uniformed officers."

"Get the SWAT guys to lay very, very low," Gross said. "Maybe get them on road maintenance or something. Digging up gas pipes or electricity cables, that sort of thing. You'll have to okay it with the Bournemouth Town Council of course. Can't just start digging up council property. Make sure they know it's a top secret mission. Get them hard hats and high-visibility jackets so they'll look the part."

Nesbit couldn't help a smile. "Quite ironic, isn't it…high-visibility jackets when we're trying to pretend they're not there at all." The jackets were fluorescent yellow and designed to be as noticeable as possible for the wearer, in case of traffic.

"That's the way it's played." Gross grinned back. "We don't usually notice things that are right under our noses. How often have you taken a look at the guys digging up the road?"

"You're right," Nesbit said. "I'll call Jim so he knows what to say when the kidnappers call back. Then I'll get the SWAT team outfitted and on the scene."

Jim received the call from Nesbit and told Yael the plan. She looked relieved; she'd been fretting about what they would say if the kidnappers rang back. This also meant the exchange was going to happen and she was too excited about it to have it cancelled at this stage.

"Is that you, Rabbi?" the Russian accent came over the phone line again.

"Yes, it's me."

"Well, what have you decided?"

"I spoke to the police and they're calling off the search. You should soon be able to leave the alleyway."

The man spoke in Russian to someone, obviously his accomplice; it sounded like he was giving instructions to see if the street was clear of cops. Jim waited patiently, giving Yael calming looks every now and then.

In the alleyway, tension was mounting high. Alexander and Svetlana could hear the police getting closer. They were now ringing the doorbell right next door to the house they had occupied only a short time ago. They were sure they would be captured imminently, and planned to try and kill Miss Colton if this happened. They had to send a message to the police and to the people at the school that they were not to be messed with.

Miss Colton, meanwhile, was praying more than she ever had in her life. She had seen the look in Alexander's eyes when he had glanced at her, and knew it didn't bode well. She wasn't Jewish, but she was playing it safe and praying nonetheless. After all, she had lived amongst Jews long enough to know it couldn't do any harm to put a good word in for herself.

"Stop that mumbling!" Alexander yelled. He was very tense. Svetlana had just gone to peek round the edge of the alleyway for the third time in fifteen minutes, to see if the coast was clear. The first two times nothing much had changed; the police were still advancing relentlessly. This time, however, Alexander himself heard car doors slam, engines rev up, and cars pull away.

Svetlana came back smiling. She nodded and said something

brief in Russian that Miss Colton presumed was "They've gone."

Alexander growled something back, perhaps "Let me see for myself." He peeked outside and also came back grinning. "There are workmen in yellow jackets out there. You stupid English. Always digging up the road for something or other. Come on, the police have gone."

Alexander picked up his cell phone and dialed. "Okay, I want you to go to the service station called 'Little Cook'; it's on the main road, about five miles from the coast. I will meet you in the parking lot. We will stay in our car, which is a blue Toyota Prius. You will park two spaces away. The girl will get out of your car and the teacher will get out of mine. We will do the exchange. End of story. Got that, Rabbi?"

"I think so," Jim said, sounding as if he was struggling to assimilate the information, which was being relayed straight to Nesbit. "I go to Little Cook on the main road about five miles from the coast and park two spaces from a blue Toyota Prius. What happens if there is more than one Toyota Prius? And what happens if the lot is full and I can't find a space?"

"Stop making difficulties!" growled Alexander. "I chose Little Cook because the food is so bad there that no one goes to it. You won't have a problem."

Jim gulped. "Okay."

"We will be there in fifteen minutes. We are going to go slowly and make many detours, to make sure we are not being followed. If we are being followed, you'll never see Miss Colton again. Get it?"

"Yes," Jim said.

"I don't want you getting there before me. So drive around a little. Pace yourself. Time your arrival for not earlier than in fifteen minutes. I want to be there first, so I can observe your arrival."

"Drive around a bit," Jim repeated in a suitably nervous-sounding voice. "Okay. Got that."

Alexander hung up.

Yael looked at Jim. "What are they going to do if they can't follow the kidnappers?" she asked.

"I don't know, but I guess they have a plan."

"Do you know where Little Cook is?"

"Not a clue," Jim said with a cheerful grin. "But we can always stop and ask someone. I have GPS on my phone but I'm not allowed to use that phone."

Yael looked out at the quiet road. "I don't see anyone around to ask for directions." She was beginning to realize how dangerous their predicament was, and it was not a nice feeling.

The phone rang and they both jumped. Jim pressed a button on the dash and Nesbit's voice came over the loudspeaker.

"Don't stop and ask directions," he said firmly.

"I wasn't going to, don't worry," Jim said. "I knew you'd tell me the way."

Nesbit gave him precise directions to Little Cook.

"What are you going to do about following them if they're looking out for a tail?" Jim asked. "You don't want to risk being spotted and Miss Colton's life being put at risk."

Nesbit's voice came over the speakers of the car. "Don't worry. Our team won't follow them. They're already there, waiting."

CHAPTER THIRTY

Little Cook was a motorway service area that had its heyday in the 1980s — back when a trip on the open road was a reasonably enjoyable occasion. Topping the outing with a meal at Little Cook was the highlight of a working-class family's experience. Alexander was right — attendance at the dilapidated facility was sparse. The future for Little Cook outlets was bleak, but this one now had an important mission to fulfill. Its tumbleweed-looking parking lot was to be the scene of an incident so different from that of families parking to get a greasy, fast meal, that it was hard to imagine it ever being the same again.

"There it is, up ahead," Yael said, pointing to the restaurant's sign. She felt her palms dampening with nerves.

Jim glanced at his watch. Plenty of time had elapsed; if the blue Prius wasn't there by now something was badly wrong. He approached the parking lot slowly and with trepidation.

The phone rang. It was Nesbit. "Our guys are the petrol station attendants," he said. "This is a small enough place that the petrol station is close to the parking lot, so they're on red alert. There's also two of them working the gardens at the edge of the parking lot. Okay?"

"I see them," Jim said.

"Once Miss Colton is in your car and Yael is in theirs, our guys will move in fast, before the kidnappers have a chance to get away. The two gardeners will block the main exit and are armed; they'll attempt to disable the driver without risking anyone else."

Yael didn't like the word "attempt," but kept quiet. She'd be in the car with two dangerous kidnappers and people were going to be shooting at them! Well, this was what she'd signed up for so she had to be fearless, just like she'd boasted she was. Only she didn't feel quite so brave now.

"There's the Prius," Jim said, gesturing with his head. It was easy to spot, as Alexander had said; the lot was almost deserted.

Yael davened from her little siddur. She had been davening the whole way there — a bit like a bride saying *Tehillim* on the way to her chuppah, only there was no element of *simchah* in this. On her head rested the safety of Miss Colton and Nena, plus Jim and several others. It was a frightening sense of responsibility.

Slowly, deliberately, Jim drove into the parking space two spaces from the Prius. He looked inside and saw two figures in ski masks, and a woman in the back — presumably Miss Colton. He waited.

The phone rang in his car.

"You there, Rabbi?" came the gruff voice again.

"Where else would I be?" Jim answered.

This did not please the captor. "Don't be clever with me; not at this stage. Are you ready to let the girl out of the car?"

"Yes, but only when Miss Colton is more than halfway towards us."

"I'm the one making the decisions, Rabbi."

The back door of the Prius opened and a shaky Miss Colton got out. She appeared disheveled and pale. She looked at Jim and her eyes widened. Jim panicked. She had noticed it wasn't Moslovsky and it wasn't Nena either. Yael's eyes met hers and they held each other's gaze. Was she going to give the game away?

But no, her eyes grew calm as she absorbed the implications of the switch. She walked a few steps and stood between the two cars, equidistant.

The phone rang in Jim's car again. "Send out the girl, Rabbi. Now."

Jim looked at Yael. "You ready?" She swallowed hard and nodded. He nodded at the door of the car. She slid over and opened it. She had never felt more terrified in her life.

Standing outside the car, not knowing quite what to do next, Yael saw Miss Colton moving towards her. Some kind of signal passed between them as she moved towards her teacher, looking into her eyes. Miss Colton nodded almost imperceptibly as they passed each other. She was nodding her understanding of the situation; she had taken it in at one glance.

Miss Colton got into the car driven by Jim and the door closed. Yael continued to walk towards the car with the two kidnappers. The car door opened and the smaller of the two kidnappers pulled her inside. The door closed.

Alexander spoke in Russian and switched on the car engine.

Svetlana held on tightly to Yael who was looking around wildly, wondering when rescue would come. Surely by now…?

The car drove quickly towards the exit.

Nesbit was speaking urgently to his men on their phones but something was wrong. They weren't acting fast enough. The car was speeding away from the parking lot and the officers weren't stopping it the way they were meant to. They were so sluggish! What on earth was happening? Jim was on the move too, but trying to circle round to see what had happened to the men on duty — the men who were supposed to stop the kidnappers' car from getting away.

The phone rang in Jim's car. It was the Russian captor.

"I don't know who you are, Rabbi, or if you are the rabbi, but it really doesn't matter if you are or not. While we were waiting for you to arrive, my delightful colleague here went round to all the workers in the parking lot and slipped them a little something by injection. Something to slow them down, make them drowsy and disorientated. They wouldn't have felt much, just a little pinprick. If they were genuine, it would just affect their work for a few hours. If they were police, it would stop them doing whatever was planned for us. Do you really think we are that stupid? We knew if no one was following us, that the police probably had someone waiting for us at Little Cook. Thank your policemen friends for being so predictable. It has helped us a lot. And now we have the girl. Thank you for that too. The exchange went perfectly, no? We shall celebrate with some good Russian vodka later. *Nasdrovia!*"

CHAPTER THIRTY-ONE

The silence that followed the exchange was deafening. It filled the world. Jim tried to follow the Prius, but it sped off at such a pace that there was no way he could keep up. It disappeared down a side road and Jim completely lost the trail. He stopped the car and sat there, banging his fist on the steering wheel in frustration. Miss Colton sat in the back of the car completely frozen in shock, unable to speak a word. Yael had been sacrificed for her, and Yael's fate was now sealed. There was nothing left to say.

Nesbit called Jim after a while. "What the heck went wrong there?" he shouted on speakerphone. "It was all going so smoothly!"

"They were just one step ahead of us, Boss," Jim said. "Sedated the team at the parking lot."

"Sedated the SWAT team? They're our best men! How could they?"

"The woman. She just walked up to them, smiling, and slipped a needle into them. It just slowed them down, didn't knock them out or anything."

"Can they identify her?"

"They said she was blonde and pretty. That was all. Their memory was all fuzzy from the sedatives."

"Is Miss Colton all right?"

"She's fine."

"You sure you've lost the car? No chance of picking up the trail again?"

"I can drive around a bit more but I think it's hopeless. I do have the registration number of the car though."

"They'll probably switch license plates as soon as they can." Nesbit sighed. "But you have the make and model of the car, and unless they ditch the car and get another one, that's something to go on at least."

"They're probably going to switch cars," Jim said hopelessly. "What happened to triangulating the cell phone signal?"

"That only works if it's switched on. And doesn't have blocking software. As soon as they got Yael they switched it off. So much for that idea." Nesbit paused and exhaled. "Get back here. I want to question Miss Colton. Find out what she knows about the kidnappers."

"You're just going to leave Yael with them?" Miss Colton said from the back of the car, horrified. It was the first time she'd spoken since she'd gotten in the car.

"Your evidence can help us trace her," Nesbit said. "And we have CCTV surveillance cameras in the area. Our best people can try and trace the movements of the car using camera evidence at least until the kidnappers switch vehicles. Look, there's nothing more you can do out there for now. Come back to the school."

By the time the car with Jim and Miss Colton had returned to the school, Rabbi Moslovsky, Rosie, and Nena had been informed of the tragic turn of events. They told Shuli at once and the three girls sat on Yael's bed sobbing, hugging, and davening in turn. Moslovsky was in such shock that he was unable to function. He sat in his chair, shaking, pale as a ghost, his heart pounding so loudly that it reminded him to take his medication. Having a heart attack now would not help matters.

Having taken his meds and feeling his heart calm somewhat, the only thing he could rationally think of doing was to call his own *rav* and mentor, a certain *dayan* whom he always turned to in times of need. The *dayan* listened to the *rav* and recognized he was close to tears and closer to despair. His heart bled for him and for the whole situation.

"If there is any good in this situation," the *dayan* said softly, "it's that you yourself didn't undertake this mission. Then not only would you have blamed yourself — and that's a terrible, awful burden to bear — but everyone else would have blamed you too. I know it's scant comfort, but at least a top policeman was involved in this matter, so the fact that the kidnappers were one step ahead and got away with the girl, is horrendous of course, but shows that even our best officers couldn't outsmart them."

Moslovsky hadn't considered the *dayan*'s perspective, and it was indeed a source of comfort, however little.

"I suggest you call a *taanis tzibbur* for the entire school, and a day of davening and saying *Tehillim* for Yael," the *dayan* went on. "And perhaps announce a special task for everyone in the school, like taking upon themselves a *cheshbon hanefesh*, and not to speak *lashon hara*."

Moslovsky nodded even though the *dayan* couldn't see him. "The only thing is, we've kept the incident a secret from the rest of the school. Only Yael's immediate friends know about it, and of course Nena, the girl she was acting as decoy for."

"Sometimes the power of communal prayer, improving *middos*, and a fast, can be more useful than keeping things a secret," the *dayan* said. "You don't have to give all the details, just say that she has been abducted and is in grave danger."

"The Rav is right, thank you," Moslovsky agreed. After a few more exchanges, the connection was severed, and Moslovsky was once again alone with his thoughts. He did feel better; the *dayan* had given him a sense of purpose, something to do. He called in his deputy and other members of the Kodesh staff, to tell them the *dayan*'s suggestions.

Miss Colton, meanwhile, was holed up in a side room at the school, with Nesbit, Jim, and various experts including a sketch artist. She had seen both kidnappers without their ski masks on and was helping the sketch artist draw a likeness of them both.

"The one whose name is Alexander — he had a dragon tattoo at the base of his neck…just here…" and she demonstrated on her own neck where her shirt collar met it. "I could only see it when he threw his head back to laugh or growl," she added. The sketch artist drew and showed her the dragon.

"Like this?"

"No, smaller. Much smaller, and the dragon's tail was sort of curled around its body. It was also colored dark red."

The artist erased what he had drawn and tried again. "How's this one?"

Barbara nodded, impressed. "That's pretty much it!" she exclaimed.

"We can put that sketch in our database back at headquarters to see if it matches with anyone known to us or to Interpol," the artist told her. "You've done well. Any other distinguishing marks or features?"

Barbara thought for a bit.

"Well, Alexander was very tall, over six feet, I'd say. He had thick, black hair, like really thick. Unusual in a man of his age when most of them are going bald."

The artist drew.

"How old would you say he was, approximately?"

"About forty-ish."

"Facial hair? A beard or moustache?"

"Yes, he had a moustache. He didn't have a beard, but he had stubble, like he hadn't shaved in a few days."

"Eyebrows?"

"Yes. He had eyebrows."

The artist sighed. "No, I mean were they bushy or fine? Joined together in the middle or shaped?"

Miss Colton blushed, and then thought back. "Bushy but not joined. Dark, like his hair." The artist drew some more.

Somewhere in the south of England, where Yael was being held, terrified and alone, Alexander grinned to himself in the bathroom mirror. He pulled off his thick, dark wig, revealing a shiny, bald head. He winced a little as he pulled off the bushy eyebrows, revealing pale, almost invisible, blond ones. Then, arching his neck, he peeled off the dragon tattoo, which had, after all, been nothing more than a sticker. Foolish old woman! He deliberately made sure she saw the tattoo often, so she would report it and send the police off on the wrong trail.

CHAPTER THIRTY-TWO

The assembly that Rabbi Moslovsky called was a somber affair. The girls filed in silently, looking as if they were going to be told someone had died. They barely dared to breathe until they heard what the story was. They instinctively knew it wasn't great news.

The *rav* took the podium and looked at the sea of upturned, pale faces in front of him gravely. He felt his heart pounding, so sprayed some medication into his mouth. Someone at the back of the hall started crying, spontaneously, unexpectedly, before she had even heard him say a word.

"Girls," Moslovsky began, "today I am going to ask you all to undertake a very adult task. You are going to be asked to take upon yourselves a *taanis tzibbur*, and I and all the members of staff will fast as well. This will take place tomorrow, from *amud hashachar* until dark. The exact times will be posted on the notice boards around the school. There will also be communal *Tehillim* in the hall at one o'clock tomorrow afternoon. Besides this, I'm asking each of you to do a *cheshbon hanefesh* — to look inside yourselves and see how you might improve your *middos* and behavior. One important thing I think you should take upon yourselves, is to speak no *lashon hara* for at least the duration of the fast tomorrow, and if possible, for longer." He paused.

"The reason for this turn of events…is that one of our girls has been kidnapped and is in grave danger."

There was a huge intake of breath across the hall. Talking broke out as one girl turned to the other, mystified and shocked.

"To save speculation, the girl in question is Yael Reed. I do not intend to fill you in with any more details than that. Suffice it to say that your *tefillos* are extremely necessary for her well-being. You are not to tell anyone about this, as it could mean the difference between life and death for her if it becomes public knowledge. So for now, the ban on the use of your phones and the Internet will remain in place, as will the curfew on leaving the school grounds." Rabbi Moslovsky swallowed.

"Unfortunately Yael has fallen into the hands of some villains who do not wish the best for her. At this stage, all we can do is turn to Hashem, our Creator, and cry and weep to Him, and beg Him to save her. Of course the police are doing whatever they can, but it would be a huge mistake to rely on them and not on Hashem. So fast tomorrow, and daven your hearts out for poor Yael. Thank you."

The *rav* stepped down shaking, a broken man. Rabbi Simons, deputy head of Kodesh, faced the girls. There was a slow bubbling up of noise, questions, and panic. He needed to keep them calm.

"You heard the *rav*," he said. "You need to grow up now, be adults. For the first time in your lives, how you behave can have a real effect on someone else's life. Yael is in danger, and you can help her. Not by panicking, not by speculation, and above all not by blabbing to *anyone*. If an outside worker comes to fix something, or do the gardens, you must not blab to him, however tempting it might seem at the time. He may promise not to pass on the information, but you can bet your bottom dollar that he will, and that's how news spreads. And that could be very bad news for Yael. So, do we have agreement on that?"

Nods all round from the stunned girls. Simons continued.

"Rabbi Moslovsky was unsure whether to fill you in at all, but he asked *daas Torah* and was told that the power of fasting and prayer outweigh the risk. So Yael's life is in *your* hands."

Shocked back into silence, the girls sat immobilized as the blunt Rabbi Simons marched off the podium. The class teachers, also shocked and traumatized by the event, gathered them together and herded them back into their classrooms. The girls went quietly, unable to think of anything to say that would not make the matter worse.

Back in the side room, the sketch artist was getting frustrated with Miss Colton. She, on the other hand, was drooping badly. She had had enough, but the artist was still milking her for any information he could glean from her memory.

"Nose?" This time the artist thought he'd better not overestimate his client's ability to cope with questions. "Big, small, medium? Hooked? Bulbous? Pointy?"

Miss Colton's eyes glazed over and her hands trembled with exhaustion. "I don't remember… It was just a nose…"

The artist could see she was getting tired, and that he wouldn't get more out of her today. He showed her his drawing.

"It's not exactly like him, but something like him," Miss Colton conceded.

"Shall we talk about the woman next time?" he asked.

Miss Colton nodded gratefully. "The woman was less distinctive. Small, slim, blonde hair to here," she said, touching her shoulders, "and pretty. Nothing much else to say about her, really."

She got up from the chair and felt herself almost about to faint. The artist moved to catch her but she waved him away. "I'll be all right. I just need a bath and a lie down at home. We can continue this tomorrow."

As she walked out the door, the artist, sketching away, asked, "Did she wear her hair up or down? In a ponytail or loose?"

Gathering her last remaining reserves of adrenalin, Miss Colton turned on him and snapped, "How would I know if her hair was down to here if she wore it up? Really, some people!"

And somewhere in the south of England, where Yael Reed was being held, terrified and alone, Svetlana stood in front of a bathroom mirror. She carefully removed her shoulder-length, blonde wig, revealing a dark, spiky pixie cut that she fluffed out with her fingers. The only thing poor, deluded Miss Colton had gotten right with her description was Alexander's height, and that Svetlana was a very pretty young woman.

"Stupid, fat old witch," said Alexander, grinning at Svetlana. "And stupid, stupid British police!"

Svetlana did not grin back.

CHAPTER THIRTY-THREE

Nena was totally hysterical, sobbing on her bed. The other two girls sat with her, not knowing how to comfort her.

"It's all my fault!" she sobbed. "I should've done the right thing and given myself up. Now Yael's in mortal danger and I'm here sitting pretty while she could be killed because of me!"

"If anyone can get herself out of this, Yael can," Rosie said in as convincing a tone as she could muster, for she barely believed it herself. "You wouldn't have been able to cope at all, so give her some credit and let's see what happens. Meanwhile you heard the *rabbanim*. We're fasting tomorrow, and saying *Tehillim* and not talking *loshon hara* for as long as we can manage…"

Nena turned a red, swollen, tearstained face to the two girls.

"I don't know if I can do this…the saying *Tehillim* and stuff. I don't know if I can believe in a G-d who would do this to an innocent girl who was only trying to help!" She burst into fresh sobs. "She was so brave!! And I'm such a coward! I don't deserve her help."

"Hey," Shuli said, patting Nena's shoulder awkwardly. "We all have crises of faith when things don't go so well for us… Don't despair. Hashem is there and if you want to have a rant at Him, I'm sure He can take it."

Nena stopped sobbing and looked at Shuli in surprise. "Have a rant at Hashem?"

Shuli blushed a little. "I haven't told anyone this before…but when I found out I was dyslexic and would need special ed all my life, I thought it was just so darned unfair. I'd have to struggle when everyone else just got on and learned to read like it was no big deal. Heck, I had a *six-year-old brother* who could read books much easier than I could!" She threw her hands up in the air.

"I had a rant at Hashem then, told Him I thought I didn't deserve to be 'special needs.' But then, when I listened to myself, and listened to what He was trying to tell me in reply, I realized he was giving me *nisyonos* that only I could overcome. So I was determined to do at least as well as everyone else, if not better, and to hide my dyslexia to see if anyone noticed. And you didn't notice, did you? So my plan worked."

There was silence in the bedroom. Nena sniffled and blew her nose, hard. Then she said, "I might have that little talk with Hashem later."

"Good for you," Rosie said and patted her approvingly.

The school served an extra nice dinner that night to enable the girls to fast better. Times of the *taanis* were posted all over the school. Moslovsky had been warned off fasting by his doctors, but had gained permission to fast until midday, providing he drank small amounts of water if he felt the slightest bit faint or his heart started acting erratically. Even the non-Jewish staff members decided to fast. Some had never fasted in their lives before.

Miss Colton was not allowed to fast even though she wanted to join in. Her constitution, even though she thought of herself as robust for a woman her age, was severely compromised by her experience with the kidnappers. A regime of rest and healthy food was prescribed for her. She had a long, hot soak in her bathtub, and, thinking her descriptions of the kidnappers were useful to the police, she slept like a baby.

Meanwhile, the sketch artist took the drawing and description of Alexander back to headquarters, where officers ran it through the database. They found several contenders for the dragon tattoo but none of them were in the right place, and none looked remotely like Miss Colton's description. The police found this puzzling.

"Thick, black hair; bushy eyebrows; and a moustache?" Nesbit snorted, looking at the sketch and reading the report. "Purleeze. This has got to be a disguise. I'm willing to bet the tattoo is a stick-on one too."

"So that puts us back to square one?" said his underling.

"Not quite," Nesbit said. "We still have recordings of this guy's voice making calls to the rabbi. Unless he's disguised that too, we can try to match that up with something we have on record. I would suggest we play some of the recordings back to Miss Colton in the morning and let her tell us if that sounds like him or not."

Miss Colton awoke refreshed and so glad to be back in her own bed. In captivity, she had been given a bed to sleep in, but it was narrow and hard. She hadn't slept well because, besides being uncomfortable, she was constantly afraid that her captors would decide she was no longer worth anything to them.

She lay there, content that she was back home, and rather pleased with herself for her session with the sketch artist. She felt ready to go in and continue. Stretching, she got out of bed, and prepared to meet the new day. She made herself a hearty breakfast of all the foods she had missed during her captivity. While she was eating it with relish, her phone rang. It was the sketch artist.

"Oh, hello!" Miss Colton said cheerily. "I'm feeling much better this morning and I'm ready, willing, and able to tell you about the woman now — as well as anything else I remember about Alexander!"

The sketch artist, for some reason Miss Colton could not understand, sounded less than thrilled at this. "We have a problem," he said. "Most of the distinguishing features you described...were probably fake. He could look totally different from how you remembered him."

Miss Colton swallowed. "Fake? What? Oh my gosh…"

She thought back. How could she have been so gullible? Such thick, dark hair on a man of forty — but it hadn't occurred to her it might be a wig. And she'd been so proud of herself, noticing the tattoo whenever he threw his head back to laugh… Of *course* he had shown it to her — he *wanted* her to notice it, to describe it to the police! How stupid could she have been?

"So it's even more important that you try and think of things he couldn't fake," the sketch artist continued. "Like the shape of his nose, for example…and his ears. We also need you to listen to voice recordings so you can tell us if he disguised his voice during the phone calls."

"I don't tend to notice ears," Miss Colton said downheartedly. "But I'll try and think. And, oh…"

"What?"

"If he disguised himself, I'm willing to bet Svetlana did too. She might not be blonde at all."

"What color eyebrows did she have?"

"Brown. I did remember thinking it was rather strange…as she had such blonde hair, to have such dark eyebrows…but I thought maybe she just dyed it…so many girls today do that…oh dear, oh dear, oh dear…"

Miss Colton pushed her breakfast away as a deep sense of hopelessness set in. Her delicious meal had totally lost its appeal.

CHAPTER THIRTY-FOUR

Yael opened her eyes and saw only darkness. For a moment or two she panicked, but then she remembered that her kidnappers had blindfolded her. She was alone, tied up to a chair, and couldn't see. She took long, deep breaths to calm herself. An hour or so ago, someone had led her to the bathroom to use the facilities and had waited there until she was done. She was pretty much aware that person was female, just by the feel of her hands — soft and smooth. No one had spoken to her yet.

She was drawing on every reserve she had — of her feeling that she had nothing to lose, so who cared? Of her training that the police had given her. She remembered how they told her what a great spy she might make one day. And last, but by no means least, she drew upon her faith in Hashem. She didn't know many *tefillos* by heart, but what she did, she recited over and over again. What she didn't know, she just made up. She was sure Hashem would accept her *tefillos* whether from the siddur or from her heart.

Someone came into the room. By the heaviness of the tread she presumed it was not the woman who had accompanied her to the bathroom. And then he spoke to her. A deep, gruff, male voice.

"So. You are the girl my friend in prison wants dead. You saw his crime and you are going to testify against him. We can't have that, now, can we?"

Instinctively, Yael wanted to tell him to go take a long walk off a short pier, but she knew she had to be Nena, not herself. She had been trained for this. She got into role smoothly, as if she was drawing it in with her next breath.

"Please!" she said in a tremulous voice that was not like her at all. "I won't tell anyone, I promise!! Please! Don't hurt me!"

He snorted. "Yes, of course. We will just let you go, and you won't tell a soul about what you saw him do." He snorted again to show his total disdain of this plan.

Yael began to cry. It was as genuine as she could make it. She was thinking of what Nena must be going through at this moment, and the tears came naturally.

"Before we kill you," the voice said, "my friend in prison wants to meet you. He wants to see the girl who put him there — and the one who won't be testifying. Because she'll be dead."

Yael thought about this. This was an unexpected development. Had Nena actually been spotted by the villain in prison? Could he actually identify her as the wrong girl if he saw her? In her training, the police had assured her that no one knew what Nena looked like, but how could she be sure that was true?

"My assistant will give you something to eat. We are making plans to take you to the prison without being caught. It takes time to organize."

"I only eat…kosher," Yael-Nena said pathetically.

"You will eat what we give you!" the man growled. "That stupid woman didn't make so much fuss about food! Wassa matter with you?"

"She isn't Jewish," Yael said.

He growled something unintelligible and left the room. A little later, the door opened again, and this time lighter, softer footfalls could be heard. The woman, obviously. She spoke. A soft voice with a Russian accent like the man.

"What you can eat?"

Yael thought. There was no point in starving herself; she could make allowances for things like *chalav stam* in a situation like this. She needed her strength to cope with whatever lay ahead.

"Do you have cereal and milk?"

"Yes. You want?"

"Yes please. And some fresh fruit and vegetables. That's all I will eat. I can drink most things, water, soda, that sort of thing."

"Fruit and vegetables? What, you think this five-star hotel?"

"You asked what I can eat…" Yael said in a pathetic Nena voice.

The woman grunted. "Okay. I see what we have. I am not going shopping today. What we have, is what you get." Her footsteps receded.

A little later she reentered the room and Yael heard the clink of a spoon against a dish.

"Here. Cereal and milk. And apple. And banana. Banana a bit brown but still okay inside. You eat." It was an order.

The woman walked behind Yael and untied her hands. Yael

rubbed her wrists to get the circulation back into them. She lifted her hands to her blindfolded eyes.

"If you try and remove blindfold, you no get any more food," the woman said sternly. Yael as Yael would have thought it worth the risk to get a look at her kidnapper, but Yael as Nena would have played it safe, so she did.

The woman took her hands and placed them around the bowl, which had been placed on a table close to the chair she was tied to. The spoon was put into her right hand.

"Eat," the woman said again. Cautiously, Yael smelled the contents of the bowl, more to elucidate what cereal it was for *berachah* purposes than anything else, but the woman sounded angry.

"Why you smell? We not poison you. We still need to take you to prison."

The cereal smelled like Weetabix, and when she tapped it with her spoon she could tell that it was. She made the *mezonos berachah* and took a bite. Weetabix was not Yael's favorite cereal but she was hungry and she ate the bowlful quickly. Then the woman put the apple into her hand, and the banana close by.

"I take bowl," she said. "You eat fruit. I stand here until you finished. Then I take you to toilet. Then I tie your hands again. Understand?"

Yael-the-wuss nodded meekly even though the real Yael was dying to say something outrageous and cheeky. She remembered her training. *Don't try and do anything clever that deviates from the plan.*

When she was left alone again, she sat there, contemplating what the future would bring. She experimented with her bonds, wriggling and wriggling her wrists. They loosened ever so slightly, but not nearly enough for her to get her hands out. Yael had deceptively slim hands and wrists and it was just possible that the woman had not taken this into account when she tied her up.

Hm, she thought, *this might be worth carrying on with…*

The police had trained her how to behave if she was blindfolded and tied up. *Try to get free but if you do manage, don't let your captors know you're free until the moment is right. If you can't get free use your other senses to help you. Your other senses will be heightened if you are blindfolded. Smell your surroundings. Anything unusual that could be used to trace the place? Listen carefully. Any clues that we might be able to use later?*

Yael listened. They were definitely not on a busy road as there was no traffic noise. She couldn't hear the ocean either, and despite listening for what seemed like a long time, she heard no evidence of a railway line.

But then she heard something. It sounded like dogs. Lots and lots and lots of dogs. All barking at once.

CHAPTER THIRTY-FIVE

The fast had begun at six in the morning and now it was ten. Most of the girls were stalwart about it, but some were already whining about being parched and starving. Breakfast had been offered in the school dining room at five so if anyone preferred sleeping to eating, it was their own fault if they were hungry now. Rosie, Nena, and Shuli had all gotten up for breakfast, much to the annoyance of the seniors whose sleep had been disturbed.

"Come and have breakfast!" Rosie had said to Kaylah.

"If I sleep, the fast will be shorter," Kaylah had groaned and pulled the duvet over her head.

It had been weird eating breakfast at five — rather like when they had an early flight to catch. But even then, Rosie surmised, she'd always taken breakfast along to eat later, not feeling hungry that early in the morning. But now, knowing the day ahead, she forced herself to swallow a bowl of cereal and milk and drink a cup of hot tea even though she really didn't feel like it.

"We can go back to bed now," Nena yawned sleepily, putting her bowl, spoon, and cup into the dishwasher. All the girls who had chosen to rise at this unearthly hour were still in pajamas, hair tousled and uncombed.

"Yeah, we don't have to get up for at least an hour and a half. Let's grab some more sleep," Shuli agreed.

Rosie wasn't sure she *could* sleep. She hadn't been sleeping much at all since the awful news broke of the whole mission going so badly wrong, and she didn't want to waste this day.

"You go back to bed," she told the others. "I'm going to get dressed and daven, and say *Tehillim* before class."

The others looked at her for a while, deciding if they could manage to emulate her, but sleepiness overcame them and they trundled drowsily back to bed murmuring about "catching up with the davening and *Tehillim* at a civilized hour later…"

Rosie got dressed quietly in the darkened bedroom, the humped figures of her sleeping roommates her only company. She closed the door silently and went to the school's *beis medrash*, where she sat in the *ezras nashim* and davened her heart out. Tears poured down her cheeks as she thought of the feisty, courageous Yael, so willing to risk everything to help Nena. *I was born to do this!* she had said, and the intensity had burned from her eyes as she danced along the path. But now, would she *die* because she did this?

"Please, Hashem," Rosie prayed with bitter tears, "look after

Yael, guard her and keep her from harm…"

Yael was lying down on a bed of some kind. She was still blindfolded. The woman had wiped her face and allowed her to brush her teeth with something. The woman had maneuvered her around until she was relatively comfortable, on her side, with her arms not too compressed. She had lain there, davening what she could from memory, and thinking about what she could do. Then for some reason, she had fallen asleep.

She had no idea how long she had slept or whether it was day or night. She listened. All was quiet. No dogs barking. No traffic. So she presumed it was night.

Then she remembered — she was wearing an earpiece. The police could hear her! Her heart pounded with excitement; how could she possibly have forgotten about that?

"Hello?" she whispered quietly. "Can you hear me? Hello? Are you there?"

Nothing. The police couldn't be sleeping, could they? Not when they were meant to be looking for her. She wriggled her head around on the pillow, moving it this way and that, trying to feel the earpiece.

It wasn't there. She had felt it before, like something annoying deep in her ear that she had been trying to ignore. Now, either it had fallen out, or her captors had removed it. The second option was worse, as it meant her captors would be more suspicious as well as angrier, than if she had lost the piece accidentally.

Yael wriggled her head on the pillow a few more times to make sure, but there was nothing there. She grunted in frustration. She was lost, alone, frightened, and disconnected too. This wasn't meant to happen!

Furious, she struck her head again and again on the pillow, twisting her head this way and that, and then she noticed something.

The blindfold was getting looser.

With each bash it loosened a little. Invigorated now, she threw all her energies into wriggling her head against the pillow in all possible directions until she had to stop, breathless and panting, scared she would literally knock herself out. She rested a while, and when her heart slowed, she listened for outside sounds. Nothing. So she presumed it was still nighttime outside. She decided to have another try at loosening the blindfold before daybreak when it would be too late.

After a full ten minutes, the blindfold shifted slightly. She saw a narrow band of dim light at the top half of the blindfold. With the greatest difficulty, she turned onto her stomach, and slowly, painfully, rubbed her face into the bed, up and down, up and down until she was moaning in pain. But she didn't give up. She eventually moved the blindfold down so that it almost covered her mouth, but her eyes were largely clear for vision. For the first time since her capture, Yael Reed looked around her prison.

What she had imagined to be a cavernous dungeon was a small suburban bedroom. There was a window, a door, some basic furniture, and a sink against one wall. She eased herself off the bed, her hands still firmly tied behind her back, and looked for something sharp to cut those bonds. There was nothing. She went to the window and eased the curtains back with her teeth to look out.

A suburban street, but up the road was a building that didn't look like a residential house. It had high gates and wire mesh fences. She presumed that was where all the barking had been coming from.

The street lights afforded a low light, but looking at the dark sky, she assumed dawn wouldn't be any time soon. Unless of course, the window faced west and dawn was indeed beginning to blush in the eastern skies. She couldn't tell from this vantage point. There was no time to lose. She had to find something to cut her bonds.

Then she saw it. The window ledge was raw and unfinished at one corner, and provided a sharp edge on which an unwary person could cut himself quite nastily. She maneuvered herself so her back was to the window ledge and tried to lift her bound hands to the level of the sharp part. Darn! It was too high! Desperately, she looked around the room for something to stand on. There was a night table. How was she going to get the night table over to the window if her hands were bound? Crying with frustration, she just knew she had to try.

Pushing the night table with her knees, she got it to the window. She thanked Hashem for her flexibility that enabled her to wriggle up onto it with her hands tied behind her back. Then she crouched so that her bonds were directly in contact with the sharp corner, and started the slow, painful process of rubbing her tied hands up and down against the jagged edge.

CHAPTER THIRTY-SIX

Nesbit crashed his fist again and again against his desk.

"The earpiece!!! It's gone!"

"What do you mean it's gone?" asked his sergeant.

"I can't communicate with Yael. That means somewhere along the line either it's fallen out of her ear or it's been removed. How could this have happened? I thought those things were foolproof."

"Nothing's foolproof, sir," the tech officer commented from his desk. "It wasn't deeply wedged into the ear canal in the first place — that would've been dangerous for her. So if she'd been roughed up even a little or shaken about, it could have fallen out fairly easily. For the girl's sake, sir, I hope it fell out accidentally. If they found it and removed it, it won't be good news for her, for us, or for the whole case."

"That poor kid," Nesbit said. "Put herself forward, a real courageous little girl, to help her friend, and this had to happen to her! She's really on her own now!" A few more well-chosen explosive words came out of his mouth in pure frustration.

"Maybe not entirely on her own, sir," the tech officer said, pointing to his computer. "We've been tracing the CCTV camera footage of the car they took her away in."

His spirits boosted a little, Nesbit went over to look at the computer screen. It was split into about eight sections, each one showing a different photo or video.

The officer pointed at the screen, moving his finger left to right from the top. "Here…is where the car passed this camera yesterday at nine fifty in the morning. That was the first sighting, just after they pulled out of the Little Cook parking lot. This next one," he said, pointing at the next scene, "is on the main road about two miles to the east. After that it all starts getting confusing."

"Why?" Nesbit asked.

"Because they dumped the car *here*…" The tech officer pointed at the third screen along. The car was clearly shown on the shoulder of the road, with three figures leaving — a tall man, a short woman, and a girl who was being pulled along by the woman.

"They *walked* from there?"

"No…not for long, anyway. Look at this next image." He pointed. "There's the three of them getting into a car at this junction." The car seemed to be a small, green jeep, the kind that does very well off-road. The man was in the driver's seat, the woman and girl sat at the back.

"Then, we lose them." The officer sighed and spread his hands, palms up, in a gesture of defeat. "They went into an area of low scrubland that's part of the New Forest. Them and the New Forest ponies. Both equally hard to track out there."

The New Forest is a well-known national park in the area.

Covering 220 square miles, it includes the largest remaining tracts of unenclosed pasture land, heathland, and forest in England's heavily populated southeast. It provides natural habitat to many species, including the famous miniature ponies.

"Once they're in the forest, they're off the radar," the officer said with another hand gesture. "They could simply be anywhere."

"But if they don't change the green jeep for another vehicle, we have a chance of picking it up on camera elsewhere, right?" Nesbit was desperate. He was wondering what on earth he was going to tell them back at the school.

"Well, yes…" the officer said somewhat doubtfully. "We have it on our computer database, so wherever it shows up on CCTV, we'll be notified immediately."

Clutching at straws, Nesbit thought. What an apt description of a drowning man. He was drowning in the failure of this whole operation, and terrified to tell them back at the school what an almighty mess he had made of it all. Yael…if she was still alive…was in the gravest danger. The criminals were bound to find out sooner or later that she wasn't Nena and then, well, he didn't like to think what would happen to her.

Yael looked down at her bleeding hands. They were in front of her, and free from bonds. It had taken her a long, painful twenty minutes of rubbing against the jagged window edge but she was free and unencumbered. She looked out the window. It was still completely dark outside. *I have to get out of here before they come for me*, she thought urgently. She looked at the door, but remembering the creaking noises it had made whenever her captors had opened or closed it, she decided not to risk it.

The room was on the first floor; there was a ten-foot drop to the street outside. Inch by inch, pausing to listen each time, she pushed the window open. It didn't creak or whine on its hinges; it opened as silently as a puff of smoke. Once the window opened, Yael looked outside for a foothold, a ledge, anything to give her feet something to grip on to. The ledge was too narrow…but there was a drainpipe nearby.

Shinning down drainpipes had been a favorite pastime of Yael's when she was in the children's home. She was as agile as a monkey, and the effort didn't bother her in the least. The only thing that troubled her now was her clothing. She was wearing some kind of pajamas that her captors had provided her with, and her feet were bare. One last desperate look around the room revealed her clothes in a corner — the clothes in which she had been captured — and her shoes and tights on the floor beneath.

Panicking, she wondered if she had time to dress — or would the extra time this took mean her captors would awaken? In a second she decided. She found a plastic bag in another corner, stuffed her clothes and shoes into it, and climbed out onto the ledge. Her plan was that once she felt safe, she would find a quiet place to dress. She didn't dare waste a minute of her precious "alone time" now.

Sliding down the drainpipe took all of twenty seconds and Yael found herself standing in a street. Without stopping to consider what kind of street or in which direction she should best flee, she turned her face towards the right, and ran.

Barefoot and in pajamas, she ran and ran until she reached the end of the road. It was not, as she had thought from looking out of the window, a town, but some kind of tiny village on the edge of what looked like an uncultivated moor or forest. On her way down the street she had passed the source of the dogs barking with barely a glance, but she had registered a name in the periphery of her mind: "New Forest Dog Kennels."

She looked right and left, but the village ended right here. She had two choices. Either to run back the way she had come and turn left instead of right, hoping to find some kind of civilization — a friendly shop, or maybe a police station, to which she could turn for help. Although at this hour of the night nothing was likely to be open. But that choice would mean running past the house she was held in, and there were no other streets she could use as an alternative route.

Or, she could run into the forest, and completely unknown territory.

Panting, she looked up at the sky, and saw the first gray glimmerings of dawn — which meant she was facing east, or rather southeast. She didn't have much time left before her captors would awake and find she had gone.

She made her decision. Sending up a prayer to Hashem to the slowly lightening heavens, she ran barefoot and vulnerable, into the New Forest.

CHAPTER THIRTY-SEVEN

Yael ran through the low scrubland of the New Forest until she reached the cover of some trees. She ran into the copse and then collapsed, panting, looking around her to ensure she was alone, that no one was pursuing her. Once reasonably certain, she quickly dressed.

Her feet were bleeding like her hands, from all the barefoot running, but she couldn't do anything about that now. She just hoped she wouldn't get an infection, and resolved to stop at any place she could to get some antiseptic cream. She remembered someone in the children's home who hadn't bothered taking care of a small graze obtained on some wild parkland, and later the kid developed septicemia, a nasty infection that made her very sick.

Once dressed and feeling more like herself again, Yael turned her attention to the pajamas she had been provided with. Her first instinct was to toss them as far away as possible, deep into the forest, like some loathsome insect that had found its way into her possession. But then her innate survival instinct took over. Much as she wanted to discard them, she knew that if her captors pursued her into the forest and found the pajamas, they would know they were on the right track.

So, disgusting as those garments were to her, she realized she had to take them along. With the slightest of shudders, she put them into the plastic bag and pushed them down as far as they would go, so she couldn't see them. Ready, she looked around again. Dawn had spread over the entire sky; it was gray rather than navy blue, and the gray was lightening. She could see more of her surroundings now.

She was at the edge of a deep copse of trees. Outside the copse was open scrubland, and in the distance she could see animals grazing. Deer or possibly small horses; she couldn't tell. Even though she liked the idea of going up close to the animals to see them, she thought she'd better stay in the safety of the trees. They were better than the exposed area of low scrub beyond. The copse hid her like a giant friend, spreading its branches around her like a hug, keeping her from sight.

Turning her back on the open landscape, she ran into the security of the forest's open arms. She had no idea where she was heading, but knew she had to keep going. She was still worried about her bleeding wounds and prayed she would find some help. But for now, she just had to try and ignore them and keep running.

At seven o'clock Svetlana, her spiky hair tousled and her face pink with sleep, rose and stumbled towards the room where Yael was being held. She dreaded today. Today was the day Alexander planned to get rid of the girl. Despite Svetlana's hard appearance, she had a touch of a soft heart deep down somewhere. Even though she knew it had to be done, she wasn't looking forward to it. She knew the end justified the means but still preferred not to think about it.

So when she opened the door to the girl's room and found it empty — with the window open and curtains fluttering — Svetlana had two conflicting thoughts. First was that she must run and tell the snoring Alexander that the girl had somehow, brilliantly, managed to escape. She had managed to get her blindfold off; there it was on the floor…then managed to get her hands unbound…and lastly, had obviously shinned down the drainpipe outside the window. Svetlana looked carefully at the window ledge and saw the bonds lying on the floor beneath it.

And then she saw the blood on the sharpened part of the ledge, and understood at least how she had gotten free of her bonds.

"Girl," Svetlana said to herself in Russian, "you are brave. You deserve to escape. You have gone through so much…I don't want you to die." It wasn't a thought created out of any deep compassion for the girl, more one of silent admiration for a lamb that had escaped the abattoir.

And then came her second thought. *Let Alexander sleep a while longer. He's so tired. I might go back to bed myself, in fact.* Svetlana turned, carefully avoiding touching anything that might incriminate her and lead Alexander to know she had been in the room. She tiptoed back to her bedroom.

She knew that once Alexander woke up, all hell would break loose. He would blame her for not having been vigilant in guarding the girl. Then, when she batted her eyes at him in feigned innocence, he would shout and scream a lot, swear at her in Russian, and make his pursuit with all intention not to stop until the girl was recaptured.

Meanwhile, Svetlana had given the little lamb the gift of a head start from the abattoir. How long the head start would last she couldn't tell, but she guessed the girl was running for her life, and every second was precious.

As she lay down in bed and covered herself against the chill of the gray dawn, Svetlana was smiling. She remembered herself at about that age, feisty and determined to get her own way. Her father was a drunk, and had come home most nights roaring with the rage of the alcohol, and laid into her mother and siblings with an iron fist. But she, Svetlana, the youngest, had found a way out of the top floor apartment through a small hole in the roof. The hole in the roof let pigeons, mice, and bats into the roof space, but it also let a small, skinny girl out.

Once on the roof, she had an ingenious escape route — jumping roof to roof onto her neighbor's apartment block, then the neighbor after that, and from that third neighbor. She climbed in through a small skylight, and into a roof space that had been turned into a bedroom for another small girl, who just happened to be her best friend. Her friend greeted her with a smile, turned back her covers, and little Svetlana climbed in. Her father was too drunk to even notice she was missing.

Now Svetlana, for the first time since her childhood, thought she had found a kindred spirit. A girl like the girl she had once been. And she desperately wanted that girl to live.

CHAPTER THIRTY-EIGHT

The previous night the fast had ended. The girls had trooped into the dining room, having spent the day in *tefillah*, *Tehillim*, *cheshbon hanefesh*, and a great deal of tears. Now weak, tired, and drained, they sat down to bowls of hot, thick, vegetable soup; shredded cheese and croutons to put in it; fresh rolls baked in the school's own kitchens; spreads; and as much tea or coffee as they wanted.

"The cook has outdone herself," Shuli commented on the soup.

"This is the best vegetable soup I've ever tasted. Look at all these chunky bits — beans! And she's put pasta in too!"

"Well," came a voice. The cook came out of the kitchen with a flushed face and a smile. "I thought, all you girls been fasting for poor Yael Reed, you deserve a decent supper after that. So I got out my minestrone recipe and I put my heart and soul into it."

"Your heart? I hope that doesn't make it *fleishig*, 'cause there's cheese in the soup!" joked the school clown, a girl named Shira. The whole hall burst out laughing and it raised everyone's spirits just a little. The cook had a good laugh too, flushed even redder, and retreated to her kitchen.

"So," Rosie said conversationally to the others as they tucked into the delicious soup, sprinkling more cheese and croutons onto their portions. "What do you think is happening with Yael?"

The girls frowned at her and shook their heads. Rosie flushed, realizing she had spoken without thinking.

"I dread to think, to be honest," Nena said. "It's tearing me apart, knowing she did this for me, and how it all went wrong."

"I'm sorry," Rosie said sincerely. "It was stupid of me to ask it like that. I don't know what I was thinking…"

"You were thinking what we were all thinking, that's what you were thinking," Shuli said with a reassuring pat. "Maybe it's best we talk about it rather than pretend it isn't happening." The others nodded.

"Look, Nena," Shuli said. "If anyone can get through this, Yael can. She's like a cat, which always lands on its feet."

The others nodded gamely at this but none of them looked as if they believed it. "We must just daven and daven," Rosie said resolutely. "Hashem is the only One who can help Yael."

"I bet Yael could use some of this soup," Nena said miserably. "She must be starved."

"No," said Rosie firmly. "Her captors will want her strong at least while they find out what she knows. It's not in their interest to starve her."

"But once they find out she's not me..." Nena said in a doom-laden voice.

The other girls went silent. There was nothing to say to that scenario. The soup had lost its appeal and they all pushed their bowls away.

Yael had been running, it seemed to her, for hours. On and on through the forest, keeping the cover of the trees around her, and yet keeping the open scrubland always in view so she could see the distance. She was looking for a house, a village, a shop, something, somewhere, she could seek refuge.

Every now and then she stopped, gasping, and sat down a while, making sure she had a tree at her back so no one could sneak up behind her. She looked out at the open land, searching. The sun was up now. It was actually a lovely day. A lovely autumn day, providing you had a nice picnic with you, and a water bottle to drink from. But Yael had nothing. She was thirsty, so thirsty. And the Weetabix of the night before had long since been digested and absorbed. She was getting hungry. She saw many of the miniature New Forest ponies the area was famous for, and lots of deer too. But no humans. At least, not yet.

"SHE WHAT??????"

Alexander was awake. And furious. Just as Svetlana had known he would be.

"She escaped, Alex. I told you. She's much cleverer than we gave her credit for. Somehow she got the blindfold off, no idea how, and then she rubbed her hands against this place until the rope got cut through…"

"Why didn't you check on her, you stupid Russian peasant?" roared Alexander.

Svetlana bristled. "Why didn't *you*?"

He snorted. "I was sleeping."

She sniffed in retort. "Yes, I heard you. Could hardly miss the snoring even from a few rooms away."

"I don't snore!"

"Of course you don't," Svetlana said in a conciliatory tone that just served to make him even angrier. He started pacing the room, rubbing his hands on his shiny bald head and across his rough, stubbled cheeks.

"How could this happen? We had everything worked out so perfectly! She couldn't identify us due to the blindfold! How do we know she wasn't peeping out of it much earlier?"

"I doubt that," Svetlana said. It was so much easier having a whole conversation in Russian instead of breaking her teeth in English. "It was firmly in place when I gave her supper and put her to bed. I checked. Everything that happened, happened after that."

"I don't understand one thing," Alexander said in a low, measured tone. "Ivan said the girl who witnessed him was a meek little thing. Scared of her own shadow. He said she shouldn't present any problems or an escape risk, she was too scared and nervous. Doesn't sound like the same girl at all…does it?"

He stopped pacing and stared at Svetlana.

"No," she said slowly, "it doesn't."

"They've duped us!" he said. "This isn't the witness at all! It's a police plant! Probably that cop's daughter or something!!"

"You're probably right," Svetlana said. If he believed this, as she was beginning to also, it made her life a lot easier. He would stop blaming her for the escape and put it down to the fact that this was no ordinary schoolgirl but a highly trained operative from MI5. "So if this isn't the witness, what are we going to do?"

"What are we going to do?" Alexander said, picking up pace again, and getting redder in the face. "We're going to search for her. She can't have gone far. She was in pajamas and bare feet, wasn't she?"

Svetlana didn't have the heart to tell him her clothes and shoes had gone too, along with a plastic bag. She just nodded.

"So, let's go!" he said, pulling on his shoes.

"But which direction? To the village or to the forest?"

"Look," Alexander said with an air of patronizing superiority. "She's obviously a highly trained operative. She's going to go where it's safest. An amateur would run into the forest, thinking it's safer there. But there's no food or shelter, and where would she go? An expert like her will try and hide out in one of the houses until the heat's off her, or borrow a car or something."

"Borrow a car?" protested Svetlana. "She's only a child!"

"She may look like a child," said Alexander knowingly, "which is why she's so useful to MI5. She's probably really about twenty, with a full driver's license."

"So how do we find her?"

"We put on disguises again, and go house to house in the village. There aren't that many houses; it shouldn't take us too long to find someone who knows something. Then we can track her down. And when we find her, we are going to get out of her everything she knows. Including where the real schoolgirl witness is."

CHAPTER THIRTY-NINE

The sun was fairly high in the sky. Yael had no watch; someone had taken it from her during her capture, so she had to gauge approximately what time it was by the sun. *Like explorers in the olden days*, she thought to herself. She looked up, saw the position of the sun, and guessed it was about eleven in the morning. Just as she watched the sun, a massive, dark cloud came out of nowhere and covered it. Other black clouds followed, and within minutes the whole sky was overcast and threatening.

Oh no, it's going to pour, she thought in dismay. Here she was, out in the open, unprotected and unsheltered, and the heavens were about to open. She really had to find a roof somewhere. This was besides the fact that her wounds were beginning to throb and she was getting seriously scared about them.

"Hashem!" she whispered. "I know I don't deserve Your help, but please help me anyway!" She remembered she hadn't davened *Shacharis* yet. She didn't have a siddur, but sat down under a tree and said what she could remember. Then she stood up, faced east, and said as much of *Shemonei Esrei* as she could.

"I hope that'll do," she said. "Sorry I couldn't remember any more."

She held out her hands to the skies in supplication and apology, and in reply, the heavens parted and rain started falling, gently at first, and then more heavily. She took shelter under the broad branches of the tree but the water soon dripped down from the branches and down the back of her neck.

She was wet. She was chilled to the bone. And she was getting hungrier by the minute. Yael Reed had had enough. She started to cry.

"Okay!" shouted Alexander in Russian. "You start on that side of the road and I'll do this side."

Their disguises this time, an ingenious hotchpotch of things slung together, had the effect of making them look either like slightly rumpled Social Services personnel, or possibly private detectives. Svetlana wore a baseball cap pulled low over her hair so no one could see what color it was. She wore jeans, a battered-looking tweed jacket, and cowboy-type boots.

Alexander too wore a hat. His was an equally battered-looking trilby, horn-rimmed spectacles, and a trench coat. The rain served only to improve their image of looking like tired, overworked officers of the law.

Alexander had downloaded and printed out two fake warrant cards. These, slipped into plastic sleeves, looked genuine enough on casual glance. Besides, who in a tiny village like this was going to make more than a cursory examination of their IDs? He reckoned they were quite secure in their new roles.

"Excuse me, lady," Alexander said to the first person who opened the door to him, an elderly woman with a tightly set white head of hair. He stuck the fake ID card in her face. "We are looking for young woman, about *this* high, who have gone missing. Her parents are so worried."

The old woman peered at him through thick spectacles, then looked at the warrant card, which held a picture of him neatly photoshopped into place.

"Oh, Detective! How exciting to meet a real detective! Hardly anything exciting happens around these parts! Why don't you come in and have a cup of tea and we can have a chat?"

Alexander felt alarmed. "Sorry, I don't have time for tea. Have you seen the girl or not?"

The old woman looked mortally offended. "Round here, *everyone* has time for a cup of tea, Detective. No, I haven't seen any girl. Good day." The door slammed in his face.

Alexander's first instinct was to kick the door down and do something very unpleasant to the old woman. But he reined himself in, thinking that might blow his cover. "Stupid English," he muttered, and went on to the next house.

There, a younger woman, probably in her fifties, and with what seemed like a houseful of dogs and cats, took the warrant card and looked at it closely. All this close inspection was making Alexander nervous. He had fondly imagined people wouldn't examine it too closely, but he was mistaken. However, he must have done a reasonable job because no one seemed to question its authenticity.

"Good day, nice lady," said Alexander, smiling broadly — which was not a good look for him, as he had a mouthful of gold teeth. "We are doing house-to-house search of area looking for a girl age about fifteen to eighteen, who is missing. Have you seen such a girl? Curly hair." He fluffed an imaginary head of curls around his hat to demonstrate.

The woman was bottle blonde, very well dressed, and looked intelligent.

"No, Detective, I can't say I've seen any such girl. Sorry."

"Maybe she come looking for shelter or something?" he pressed.

"Why would she do that? Why wouldn't she just go home?"

Alexander decided the less he said the better. "If you see girl, please let me know." He was halfway down the road to the next house before he realized he hadn't given the woman any means of letting him know. She stood at the doorway, staring after him.

Across the street, Svetlana was having little success. Nobody on that side of the street seemed to be home. Which was just as well because her English was worse than Alexander's. Then she came to the New Forest Kennels.

Svetlana hated dogs. All dogs. Big, aggressive ones; small, yappy ones; even medium-sized, fluffy ones that looked like a hearth rug with legs. There were several concrete blocks that looked like they could be army barracks, but the wire mesh enclosures on the outside told a different story. Svetlana had to steel herself to enter.

The kennel girl was young, with hair as curly as Yael's, and strong, brown, capable-looking hands. She approached Svetlana with a huge dog on a leash attached to each hand. Svetlana cringed but held her ground. She showed the girl the ID. As the girl could hardly let go of either leash for a closer look, she just gave it a cursory glance and nodded.

"We have missing girl," Svetlana said. "Maybe you see her sometime last night? Her parents so worried."

"Sometime last night, you say," the kennel girl mused. "Actually, I was up working here last night, and I did see something. I couldn't go to sleep because I was attending a dog who was about to have puppies. I took a break and was standing by the front gate, hidden by the post over there." She pointed. "At about five in the morning I saw a girl running by on the other side of the road. She was barefoot and in pajamas…"

Svetlana could hardly contain her excitement. She forced herself to remain calm. "Which way she run?"

The girl pointed. "Into the forest. But Detective, if she was running away from home, why would she be in pajamas and barefoot? Doesn't make sense to me…"

Svetlana swallowed hard, then smiled a charming smile and shrugged. "Who knows? Kids, eh! Thank you."

She could hardly wait to tell Alexander. She signaled to him from across the road. He caught her eye, understood the signal, and grinned at her. They made their way across the road towards each other.

Inside the house with the cats and dogs, the blonde woman made a phone call.

"Is that the Criminal Investigation Department, the CID? Listen, I know this country is letting immigrants come here to work — but I just wanted to know why you'd employ a detective who can barely speak English. Yes, that's right, he just came to my door. Spoke in a very strong Russian accent…"

CHAPTER FORTY

Yael stopped crying. Realizing no one was coming to her aid, no one had heard her, and it was up to her to get herself out of this predicament, she wiped her eyes and nose.

"Yael Reed," she told herself sternly. "Stop being such a wuss. You've had your moment of self-pity. Now get on with it. Find civilization. Find help. You won't find it sitting under this tree getting wet."

The rain was easing off a little. She could see the black clouds parting up ahead and a glimpse of blue peeping out between the dark curtains, like hope. Turning her tearstained face towards the source of that blue, she started walking again. This time she had a good look around her, and saw no one coming after her in the clearing, so she had confidence to walk across the open land.

In the very distance was a shape. It could have been another pony or a deer, but as she grew closer to it, her spirits lifted. It was a house. No, a clutch of houses — a tiny hamlet, nestling in a hollow about a mile ahead. With renewed vigor, she started running towards it.

Alexander and Svetlana gloated over Svetlana's successful news. "She went into the forest!" Svetlana told him triumphantly, standing there in the rain, her wet baseball cap drooping like a dead flower over her face. Alexander grinned at her, his joy only slightly tempered by the fact that it hadn't been him who had found out this prize nugget of information.

"Let's go! Quickly, before she gets too far!" he ordered her. Dripping, they started briskly off down the road towards the edge of the forest.

The blonde woman in the house with the cats and dogs opened her door. She thought about calling after the pair, but then she thought better of it. If they weren't genuine detectives, then who were they? It wouldn't be prudent of her to try and find out. So she quietly closed her door again, and after another moment's thought secured it with all the locks the door possessed.

Yael moved fast across open country towards the hamlet. Her hands and feet were throbbing but she ignored the pain in her determination to reach help as soon as possible. The rain had stopped fully now, and that tiny split of blue had torn the dark sky wide open and released the sun from its black coat. Yael almost laughed aloud in delight at the sudden warming sunshine that lit up the countryside. It also shone a beam directly on the hamlet, as if calling to her.

Nesbit put down the phone and turned to Jim, his eyes alight.

"That was CID. They just got a call from a woman in a small village near the New Forest…"

Jim's attention was sharpened. "Go on." He looked intently at Nesbit.

"Seems a 'detective,'" Nesbit made quotation marks in the air with his fingers, "called at her house as part of what appeared to be a house-to-house investigation looking for a missing girl. Missing girl fits the description of Yael."

"What made her call the cops?"

"She wondered why CID would employ a detective whose English was so poor and who had a strong Russian accent."

"Bingo!" Jim shouted, and thumped the desk with his fist. "Had the woman seen the girl?"

"No, but as the detective left her house, the woman saw what appeared to be his partner crossing the road in her direction looking as if she had some good news."

"Which means bad news for Yael," said Jim grimly, pulling on his jacket at the same time Nesbit pulled on his own. They both moved quickly out of the office towards the car. Nesbit was on the phone to the local police as they set off for the New Forest, only a few miles down the road.

"I've told the local police to go into the area and look for her," Nesbit said as they drove, slapping on their police siren and blue light and breaking all the speed limits. "But between you and me, they sound as dozy as a nest full of dormice on hibernation. I don't think they have the least idea how critical this is."

"You'd think they'd appreciate a bit of excitement in their lives," Jim agreed, shaking his head, and growling in frustration at a minor traffic holdup they couldn't bypass.

"Nah," Nesbit said. "That's the reason they choose to stay down there in the sticks instead of moving to a city. They just want a quiet life. I think they aren't going to move off their chairs until they absolutely have to. So I'm afraid it's up to us."

"How much further?" Jim asked impatiently, looking at his watch, the traffic, and Nesbit with alternating panic and frustration.

"Not long," Nesbit said, finally swerving past the holdup. "The question is, how quickly can the Russians move on this one, and where has Yael got to?"

"She's a resourceful girl, I could tell that when I had her in my car," Jim assured him. "If anyone can outsmart those two criminals, she can."

"She's still only a fourteen-year-old," Nesbit replied. He bit his lip. "We'd better get there fast."

Yael reached the hamlet finally. It had looked closer than it was, and with her bleeding, infected feet the run had cost her dearly in pain. Her feet had lost all feeling by then, even in her shoes. Her hands were throbbing as bad as ever.

Panting, and starting to cry again, more out of relief than distress, she looked around the hamlet for signs of life. A shop? A restaurant? Half a dozen houses were grouped together but there were no stores or amenities nearby. She ran to the nearest house and rang the doorbell. And rang and rang it. She could hear it echoing inside, but no one answered.

Crying harder now, she ran to the next house and rang the doorbell. Again, the house seemed deserted. She stood looking at the remaining four houses, desperately seeking some signs of occupation, but all seemed equally dark and empty. She ran from house to house ringing doorbells and crying.

At one of them, she had a glimmer of hope when she heard a dog barking inside the house at the sound of the doorbell. She rang and rang, and the dog barked and barked. Too regular, too rhythmic to be a real dog. One of those dog-barking alarms triggered by doorbells, to scare off unwanted visitors. She sat down on the wall outside the house, sobbing and defeated.

And then, in the distance, she heard a sound.

A tractor, rumbling across the countryside. Laughing through her tears, she ran towards the sound of the tractor. Then two things hit her at once: the realization that the sound of the tractor was rumbling from the direction she had come, that is, the direction of the village where she had been held prisoner.

And the second thing: There were two figures; one tall and burly, one short and petite, running across the countryside towards her.

CHAPTER FORTY-ONE

When Svetlana crossed the road to speak to Alexander, her eyes were not shining so much with excitement as with fear. She was about to lie to Alexander, right in his face, and she wasn't sure how he would take it.

He looked at her expectantly. "Well? What did that girl over there say? I saw her point towards the forest."

"I don't know," she said at last. She put on her most appealing, and at the same time unsure, expression she could muster. "She said she saw something in the middle of the night; she was up with a sick dog. But it was so dark, it was just a shape. It went towards the forest but then disappeared into a gap between the houses halfway down. Probably just a farm worker."

"Let's go towards the forest anyway," Alexander decided. "It has to be the most likely direction she'd have taken."

Heart sinking, Svetlana nodded. She had tried, and she had failed to turn him off the scent. But any more deflection and he'd have become suspicious of her.

Yael assessed the situation, summing up the components in a heartbeat. Tractor rumbling across farmland meant hope. That was the good news. The bad news was that the tractor was coming from the same direction as the kidnappers. She would have to outsmart them somehow and reach help.

She screwed up her eyes and looked at the two figures running towards her. As far as she could assess, they hadn't spotted her. They didn't have that sense of purpose that pursuers have when they see their quarry. She hoped she was right about that.

She looked around her. There was plenty of cover in the shape of the forest to the left of her. The hamlet, once the beacon of hope, lay behind her in open country, and now signaled only despair. No one was home. She would have to take a chance and keep to the cover of the trees.

She ran back the way she had come, but this time did not risk being seen in the open. As soon as she hit the trees, she ducked into them. Here, she didn't exactly feel safe, but a little safer than when she was so easily visible out in the open. She thought about climbing a tree until they had passed her by, and decided she would leave that option for a last resort, as climbing the tree meant she was stuck up there and couldn't reach the tractor.

Yael could almost feel the neurons in her brain working overtime to metabolize her thoughts. She had never felt so alive before, and yet she knew she was probably closer to death than she had ever been. Those kidnappers, once they reached her, would show her no mercy, of that she was pretty certain. She had led them a merry dance and they were probably sick and tired of it by now.

She ran through the trees, keeping to the edge so she could keep the kidnappers in her sights. They had slowed somewhat now. The larger one, the man, was overweight and burly and probably not very fit. The woman was slight and fleet on her feet. Her only glimmer of hope from this duo was that the woman seemed slightly more merciful and much more reluctant to put an end to her than her male companion. Maybe she could play on this?

The kidnappers were so close now that Yael could hear them shouting to each other in Russian. Shouting was hardly the operative word. They were so out of breath that their voices came in short painful gasps. As she didn't understand Russian it made very little difference to her what they were saying but all she knew was, this was not the time to make more noise. Once they could hear her crashing through the undergrowth, they'd be onto her.

They stopped running, obviously needing a breather. Panting, the man pointed into the trees. The woman shrugged and said something that Yael guessed meant, "If we go in there we'll never find her."

Yael almost smiled to herself despite her panic. This was her proof that the woman wanted her to have a fighting chance to escape. It made no logical sense for them not to enter the forest, even though she would be harder to find in there. But for some reason the man listened to the woman and they skirted around the edge of the trees, looking deep into the forest.

They were walking now instead of running, both badly winded. The man kept bending over, his hands on his knees, to catch his breath. He was really unfit, Yael thought. A big belly overhung his pants.

Yael was standing behind a huge oak that afforded a small girl like her complete cover from her position. Unless they actually came around it to look, they would never spot her there. She stood silently, hardly daring to breathe.

They were now so close that she could see the design on their clothing. They looked ridiculous. Dressed up like Purim, in some kind of pseudodetective outfits pulled together from a child's dressing up box. She davened silently under her breath.

And then, miraculously, they passed her by. As silently as she could, Yael moved around the oak so that it protected her from view from the new angle.

The man sounded angry as he continually peered into the thick covering of trees and low-lying shrubland. Then the woman pointed ahead.

They had spotted the hamlet.

Their voices sounded triumphant. She was obviously there! Shouting and pointing, they turned away from the forest and walked as quickly as they could manage, towards the silent cluster of houses in the distance.

Yael waited as silently as she could until she thought they were out of earshot, and then slowly, painstakingly, watching them at every step to see if they turned around, she started moving again, towards the tractor. She had at least a few minutes grace before the two of them discovered the hamlet was deserted.

She walked as if the ground wasn't beneath her feet, heel-toe, heel-toe, to reduce the cracking and crunching of undergrowth beneath her. She continued towards the sound of the tractor.

Nesbit and Jim pulled up outside the blonde woman's house, ran up to the door, and rang the bell. After a painfully long time during which they heard locks being drawn back and undone, a woman answered.

"How do I know you're genuine?" she said doubtfully, looking at their IDs. "The last lot had genuine-looking IDs, at least at first glance."

"Well, we're not speaking Russian, for a start," Jim said cheerfully. "And we came straight to you. We didn't stumble onto your house by chance."

"That's true," the woman conceded, and opened the door to them.

"There's not much time," Nesbit said urgently. "The girl they're looking for is in extreme danger. Please, tell us which way they went."

The woman pointed. "Into the forest. It's probably the safest place for the girl to be, actually. If my grandchildren go to play in there, I'm always terrified that I won't ever find them again. I have devised this method whereby…"

She launched into an enjoyable explanation of how she kept in touch with her grandchildren, but the two policemen were already back in their car. They obviously decided it would be quicker to drive into the forest than to walk.

"Oh, you can't drive into there!" she called after them. "There's no road and your car will get stuck in the mud, especially after all this rain we've been having."

"She's right, you know," Jim said as they reached the edge of the forest. "Our car isn't designed for terrain like this. We're going to have to make a run for it."

They parked the car at the very edge. At least they wouldn't have far to go to get back to it.

"I should've worn running shoes," Jim said, looking at his highly polished police shoes.

"Yeah, so should I. But we haven't, so let's get on with it," Nesbit said angrily. "I'm sure poor Yael isn't wearing running shoes. If she's wearing any shoes at all."

The two cops, barely fitter than the two kidnappers, started running into the forest.

There was the tractor! It had stopped though. Yael looked at it doubtfully. She hoped against hope that the driver hadn't left it there in the middle of the field and gone off for his lunch or something. *Well, I don't have a choice*, she thought to herself, and ran across the field towards it.

CHAPTER FORTY-TWO

The tractor driver was about twenty years old, and, to Yael's intense astonishment, female. She was as guilty as the next person of assuming tractor driving was a male occupation. There was no reason why it should be.

The girl was wearing a checked shirt and jeans. She was sitting in the tractor, eating a sandwich. She looked curiously at the disheveled girl limping towards her.

"You're the girl that detective woman is looking for, aren't you?"

she said at once. "I'm afraid I saw you running into the forest in your pj's and I pointed the way for her. Here, get up."

Yael was puzzled as she gratefully climbed up into the tractor.

"I work part-time at the kennels," the girl said, jerking her thumb back towards the village, "and part-time at my Uncle Jack's farm. I might have rather given the game away for you. I'm sorry."

"That detective," Yael said. "Was she English?"

"Funny you should mention that," the girl said. "It did strike me as funny at the time. She had a very strong foreign accent. Couldn't place it, myself. I've never been abroad. Furthest I've ever been is the Isle of Wight. I've only heard foreign accents on the telly."

"It's Russian." Yael sighed and the girl nodded her recognition. "And she isn't a detective. She's a criminal, and she and her partner kidnapped me. They think I'm someone else and they want to kill me to prevent me from testifying against someone in jail. I'm running away to escape them."

The girl looked at her with narrowed eyes. "Sounds like a bit of a tall story to me," she said suspiciously.

Yael started crying. "It's true! If I saw real policemen I would jump into their arms, believe me!"

"Okay. I think I believe you. It's too exciting not to believe anyway… Nothing like that ever happens down here." The girl stuck out her hand. "Casey Donald."

"Yael Reed." They shook hands.

"Yael? What sort of name is that?" Casey was having difficulty pronouncing it.

"It's Hebrew. I'm Jewish." Yael hoped she hadn't stumbled upon a secret enclave of anti-Semites. But the girl grinned.

"Never met anyone Jewish before."

"Look," Yael said urgently before this turned into too much of a cozy little chat. "Those kidnappers are after me. They went into the hamlet and it won't take them very long to find out no one is living there. Then they'll come back looking for me."

Casey fired up the engine of the tractor. "No problem." They started rumbling across country. "You'd better duck down into the footwell of the tractor so no one can see you," she added. "By the way, that hamlet is not uninhabited. It's just uninhabited during the day, that's all. Everyone is out at work. It hardly gets lively in the evening, but at least people are living there."

"Is that where we're going?" Yael said, alarmed to think they were going in the same direction as her pursuers.

"Don't be silly," Casey said. "I'm taking you back to the kennels. You can hide out with the rottweilers. They're big enough and scary enough to keep any old kidnapper away."

Yael looked worried. Like many religious Jewish girls, she had grown up unfamiliar with dogs, especially large ones. "I'm a bit… er…scared of dogs," she confessed.

"You have kidnappers running after you threatening to kill you, and you're scared of a few dogs?" Casey threw her head back and laughed.

"Well, the dogs can kill me too…" Yael said uncertainly.

"Nah, don't worry. I'll be there to protect you. If I tell the dogs you're a friend, they won't touch you. If I say 'attack,' like if your kidnappers turn up, well, I wouldn't like to be in their shoes, you get what I'm saying, girlfriend?"

Yael smiled weakly, wanting to believe her new friend had that much control after the big, fierce dogs, but not quite achieving it.

"Hey, want some of my sandwich?" Casey held out a meat-filled roll.

"No thanks," Yael said politely.

"Why not?" Casey looked mildly offended.

"I'm sorry, I only eat kosher food," Yael explained.

Casey made a big *O* with her mouth as if she definitely understood all about it. "I don't get it," she said at last. "But no time to explain it to me now. Let's get there, shall we? You can tell me all about kosher food while we're with the dogs."

"Which house is she hiding in?" growled Alexander to Svetlana in Russian. They had rung the bells of all four houses, and, aside from the barking-dog alarm, which had momentarily startled them both, they had no response.

"Whichever house it is, that's why they aren't answering," Svetlana suggested, secretly hoping no such thing was happening and that the girl was safe somewhere far away.

"Shall we break in to each one and look?"

"We could get into trouble if we do that," Svetlana replied, seemingly unaware of the irony of her remark.

Alexander grunted, thinking anyway it wouldn't be so easy to break in; those little houses looked quite solid. "Maybe she also couldn't get in," he concluded after a few minutes of musing. Then they saw two other figures moving swiftly across the open country in their direction.

"Police!" Alexander said in alarm. "Come on, let's go!"

"I think that's them," Nesbit said, pointing. They started running in the direction of the two figures outside the cluster of houses.

"Police! Freeze or we'll shoot!" Jim shouted when he caught a glimpse of them.

The two villains did not freeze; they kept right on moving.

"That went well," Nesbit commented to Jim on his threat.

"I didn't honestly expect them to freeze," Jim admitted, "but we don't have weapons anyway."

British police are not routinely armed and have to be specially issued with guns for specific missions. The two of them had been in too much of a hurry to wait for weapon authorization, and had just belted off after Yael when they had heard where she was and in how much danger she was likely to be.

"I can call in for backup, get some armed cops here," Nesbit said. "I think we might need it."

As if to confirm this, there was a loud bang, and something whistled past their heads.

"Look out!" Jim shouted, dropping to the ground.

"Haha!" Alexander shouted back from around the houses. "You British police are so stupid! You come after us without guns! Well now we have you, and you won't get out of this one alive!"

Once Yael had explained a little about kosher food to Casey, she had been given some fruit to eat. The bananas were delicious, and she ate three of them, plus a pear and a glass of water, before she admitted feeling full.

The rottweilers were temporarily quiet and docile, probably under Casey's control. The other cages however, were full of yapping smaller dogs, but Yael felt as long as the big guys were quiet, she could cope with being up close and personal with them.

During a lull in the yapping, they both heard it.

Fireworks?

Gunfire.

"You have fireworks here?"

"Not at lunchtime," Casey said worriedly. "Not that we have many fireworks here anyway, but certainly not at lunchtime."

"Oh my gosh, they're shooting," Yael said. "But at whom? I'm here. Who are they shooting at?"

CHAPTER FORTY-THREE

Back at the school, the three other girls only had an inkling of what was going on. They saw Rabbi Moslovsky looking sicker and paler than ever, doing a lot of pacing around, puffing on his heart meds inhaler. There were constant *Tehillim* sessions called in the school hall.

The girl who took it the hardest was Nena. Her guilt was threatening to overwhelm her.

"I can't do this anymore," she told Shuli finally. "I'm going to give myself up to the kidnappers. They're doing heavens-knows-what to Yael and she isn't even the right girl! It's up to me to put that right." She looked like she was going to go to the school office and ask to be put in touch with the police.

"No you don't!" Shuli admonished sternly, putting a restraining hand on her arm. "If you do, you're handing the bad guys victory on a plate. Yael is an amazing girl. If anyone can get herself out of this, she can. I know you feel horribly guilty letting her take the fall for all of this, but take it from me — she's better at it than all of us put together. Leave it to the police and Yael, and you do your *hishtadlus* by davening."

Nena accepted this piece of wisdom grudgingly but pushed on. "Yael might be the one to end up dead," she said worriedly. "I don't think I could live with myself if that happened."

"Hashem will decide what happens. We can only do the best we can and Yael is our best shot, not you."

Rosie nodded her agreement with this. "I know it's hard to wait and imagine what she's going through…but I don't think we have a choice."

Every time they saw Rabbi Moslovsky, the three girls crowded around him for news. He just shrugged sadly and said there wasn't any.

"The Rav doesn't look so good," Rosie said to him in a concerned tone.

"The Rav doesn't feel so good either," he replied with a weak smile. "But all I can say is, boy-oh-boy am I glad Jim took over the exchange mission and left me out of it. If I'm like this without doing anything, imagine what I'd have been like if I had!"

"Sometimes waiting on the sidelines is worse than being in the action," Nena said meaningfully.

Rabbi Moslovsky looked at her firmly. "You must *not* blame yourself. Those guys were cleverer than we had anticipated, that's all. You, and certainly I, could not have done better than the team who undertook it. Probably a *lot* worse, actually. Probably would have gotten Miss Colton, you, and myself killed, and what good would that have done anyone?"

Casey was, after all, a kennel worker and a farmer, and she knew about infections. With gentle swabs of a disinfectant-diluted water bath, she kneeled in front of Yael, cleaned her poor, bleeding feet and hands, and applied cream and plasters where they were needed.

"There. I think that should protect you against getting septicemia." She smiled up at the girl.

"Oh, thank you! I was so worried! I've seen people get *so* sick from just a tiny, little cut from a twig in the countryside. That scared me more than the kidnappers, if I want to be honest."

"How on earth did you come by those wounds?" Casey wanted to know as Yael pulled on her tights and shoes again, feeling much more comfortable.

Yael explained how she rubbed her hands against the sharp window ledge, and wriggled out of her blindfold before making her escape.

Casey's jaw dropped. "I know you said you were captured by kidnappers, but you never explained much about it… Maybe now's a good time to tell me?" she said.

"It's a long story," Yael said, "but basically I'm trying to help my friend Nena, who was a witness to a crime. The kidnappers think I'm her." She sighed.

"Why on earth would you put yourself forward as a decoy? Do you have a death wish or something?"

Yael was going to answer, "No, of course not!" but something stopped her. Hadn't she told the other girls that she didn't really care if she lived or died, which made her a perfect candidate for this mission?

And yet…and yet…when it came down to it, she knew she wanted to live more than anything in the world. And she had fought to survive with the instincts of all survivors.

"I was considered a better risk, that's all," she said finally. "I'm known for being a bit of a risk taker."

Casey stared at her in openmouthed admiration. "You're something else, you know that?"

"If it hadn't been for you," Yael said with a smile, hugging the other girl and not finishing the sentence. "I owe you my life, Casey Donald."

"Nah," the kennel girl said with a dismissive wave. "I was just in the right place at the right time, that's all. Coincidence."

"We don't believe in coincidence," Yael said. "G-d orchestrated you being there."

"I'm not really much into G-d," Casey confessed, "but I'll take your word for it."

Alexander and Svetlana crouched behind the third house, peering out. It afforded them near perfect cover. The problem was that the two cops crouching in front of the house, were also almost perfectly protected. A situation of stalemate had arisen, with no one being able to outwit the other. If both pairs stayed put, they could be like that forever.

The only difference was that Nesbit had called for armed backup. And the SWAT team, freshly unsedated after their encounter with Svetlana's needle the previous day, was on its way. So all Nesbit and

Jim had to do was wait it out and they were home free.

After about fifteen minutes with no gunfire, Jim turned to Nesbit and said, "Are you sure they're still there?"

"Mm," Nesbit agreed. "But it's probably what they want us to think. Keep quiet and they'll think we've gone, so they'll come to look for us and *blam*!"

"So we just sit here?" Jim asked. "What if they *have* gone, and we're giving them an endless start by just waiting it out?"

"Can't see where they'd get to, myself," Nesbit said. "What's behind those houses? More open country? Surely we'd spot them running away?"

"Not if they're cleverer than the stupid British police and sneak up behind them, no?" came a gruff voice in their ears and the two cops froze. With guns pressed firmly into the base of both their necks, they realized that once again, the two Russians had outsmarted them, and they were probably in the worst place they could possibly have been.

CHAPTER FORTY-FOUR

"So what now?" Nesbit said at last.

"Now, my stupid policeman," the Russian captor growled into his ear, and his bad breath swept over Nesbit's nose and made him want to gag, "you are going to lead us straight to the girl."

"How can we do that?" Jim asked. "We don't have a clue where she is either."

"Maybe not," the captor said gruffly. "But if you call out and tell her who you are, she will come running towards you, no?"

Silence from the two cops as they realized the truth in this.

"So, you and I are going to work out where she is, find her, and then you are going to call her. Simple but genius, no?"

"And if we don't?"

The gun clicked in his ear. "I know you are stupid and ignorant, but even you can work that one out," the captor hissed.

The two cops remained silent.

"So," he said in a conversational tone, "are we sure she isn't in one of these houses?"

"How can you be sure about anything?" Jim asked.

"If you ring the bell and call out 'Police!' — if someone is home they will answer, yes?"

"I would imagine so," Nesbit said.

"I would imagine so!" mimicked the captor in a silly voice and laughed. Then he grew serious in a flash. "So do it. Now."

The guns continued to press firmly into their necks.

"You need to let us get up," Nesbit said, "I can hardly ring bells lying on the ground here."

The pressure from the guns eased off, and Nesbit and Jim could hear the two behind them getting up. Without daring to turn around, they got to their feet.

"Oh, you can look at us, it doesn't matter now," the voice said, "since you won't be around to identify us anyway." Another nasty laugh.

They turned around and for the first time, looked properly at the two kidnappers.

"Alexander Kadnikov," Nesbit said with recognition. "One of the big players in the Moscow Mafia. What brings you to the UK? No…wait a minute, of course I know why you're here. Because your friend is in our jail, right? Rodchenko. Ivan Rodchenko. Currently locked up without bail and awaiting trial for murder, as I recall, yes?"

Alexander's eyes narrowed. "A crime that has only one witness. Your little girl. Who is stupidly testifying for the prosecution. So you see why we have to silence her."

"Yes, I see. It could be rather inconvenient, having an eye witness. How was it that she witnessed the killing?"

The two Russians exchanged glances, then Alexander shrugged and said something to Svetlana.

"No matter; you will die anyway," he said to Nesbit. "There was a chase. The Russian Ivan killed was meant to be killed in a quiet alley but he got away. Ivan chased him through the streets and into a park. It looked empty but she was there. Reading a book, studying, something. If Ivan had let him go, he'd have never caught him again, so he took his chance and shot, thinking he'd get the girl right after. Only when he looked around, she had gone.

"So now he was chasing her. This was a very Jewish area of London. I don't know the name. She disappeared into a synagogue or something, so Ivan calmed down and pretended to be a relation of hers. Luckily he always wears hats so he could pass for Jewish. He asked a child who was the girl who had just run into the building and the child said her name was…well…I can't remember but whatever the girl is called.

"'Ah, my niece!' Ivan said. 'I have come all the way from Russia to visit! Where does she live?' The child pointed at a street but didn't know the exact house. Ivan figured out the rest just before the police caught up with him, but the girl had been taken into safekeeping somewhere. We've been searching for her ever since."

"Touching," Nesbit said.

"And now you are here to help us!" Alexander finished with a flourish and a grin of triumph.

Nesbit looked at Svetlana.

"And who are you?"

Svetlana opened her mouth but Alexander jumped in.

"My little sister," he said. Svetlana closed her mouth again. Nesbit looked from one to the other and decided he didn't believe a word of that. He couldn't see them being in a relationship either. He could almost feel the resentment coming off the woman in waves, like heat. He guessed; human trafficking. It was rife throughout Eastern Europe.

He looked at Svetlana to see if she was trying to send him any subliminal signals but her eyes were blank, cold, and reptilian as she looked back at him. Either she was brainwashed, too terrified of Alexander to send the cop signals, or had really moved over to the dark side.

"So. We wasting time. Go ring bells."

Inwardly sighing, Jim and Nesbit set about the task of ringing doorbells and calling out, "CID! Open up!"

They got the automated dog alarm, which gave them all a start, but nothing else.

"Okay," said Alexander. "So, I think we go back to the village, yes? I think she must be there somewhere. But on the way, you keep on calling her name."

This was a problem. If they called out Yael, the Russians would know it was the wrong girl. Nesbit hesitated.

"Oh, we guessed this girl is a plant," Alexander said airily, reading Nesbit's thoughts. "The girl who witnessed, was not as brave or clever at escape. She was just what you English call a 'scaredy-cat.' This one, she's like a real cat. Throw her off a roof, she'll land on her feet." He laughed loudly.

"So what do you want her for if she's not the right girl anyway?" Jim asked, not bothering to confirm or deny Alexander's summation of events.

"That's none of your business. We will find out from her who the real girl is and where she is."

This was a horrible thought. However brave and resourceful Yael was, Nesbit and Jim had little doubt she would crack under torture. A grown man would, let alone a fourteen-year-old girl.

The situation seemed insoluble. Try as they might, the two cops couldn't think of a way out. They felt the guns at the smalls of their backs now, goading them forwards.

"Come on," Alexander said with a gourmand's appreciation of the plan ahead. "We walk, you call."

"But if she sees you behind us, she won't come out," Jim pointed out reasonably.

"We will stay hidden," Alexander said impatiently. "Not right behind you. But believe me, we'll be able to hear every word you say, and if you make one false move…"

The cops had no doubt of this.

"When she comes out to you, make sure she's close enough that we can get to her," Alexander said.

CHAPTER FORTY-FIVE

"How exactly do you suggest we get out of *this* one?" growled Jim to Nesbit out of the corner of his mouth.

"Dunno," Nesbit growled back, "I'm just hoping something will turn up. A miracle, maybe? Aren't miracles supposed to happen to the Jews? Like the parting of the sea or feeding thousands with manna from Heaven?"

"Yeah, but those miracles happened a bit before our time," Jim said, unable to suppress a grin, even in the seriousness of their situation.

The two cops were being frog-marched along the path back through the forest towards the village.

"You start calling her name!" Alexander ordered. They had reached the edge of the forest and were approaching where the policemen had parked their car. The Russians' green jeep was parked slightly further down; the two cops recognized it from the CCTV pictures and they jerked an eyebrow at each other to show they had seen it.

Okay… Nesbit thought. *If I call Nena rather than Yael, they'll know the name of the real witness. Why hand it to them on a plate?*

"Yael!! Are you there? It's Inspector Nesbit! Are you safe?" he called.

They all stopped walking so they could listen to any sounds bouncing back at them.

Dogs barked in some undisclosed location. Birds twittered in the dripping trees. No girl's voice.

"Keep walking and keep calling!" Alexander snapped.

Casey sat bold upright. "Yael, I think I hear something. Someone calling your name!"

Yael jumped up. "The kidnappers! They're coming to get me! Oh!"

"I thought you said they didn't know your real name. That they thought you were someone else."

Yael stared at her, trying to sort out her jumbled thoughts. "They don't know me as Yael or as Nena, just as the girl."

"So maybe someone has come to rescue you?!" Casey was excited now.

Then they both heard it. "Yael!! It's Inspector Nesbit!! Are you there?"

Yael's face lit up with joy. "It's the police!" She started to move towards the entrance but Casey put a restraining hand on her arm.

"Wait…let me check before you take any chances."

"But I recognize his voice!" Yael was beside herself with excitement.

"Let. Me. Check," Casey said firmly and pushed her back down on the seat.

Slowly and cautiously, Casey made her way to the gate, leaving Yael safely ensconced with the rottweilers. She kept close to the wall, and peeked around to see who was calling.

She saw the two cops followed by the two Russians who had been looking for Yael. Even though their guns were hidden she guessed they weren't just following the cops for the fun of it.

Unfortunately, by the time she had the whole picture, they had seen her too.

A shot rang out. Screaming, Casey fell to the ground. Pandemonium broke out.

"It's not the right girl!" shouted Svetlana. "It's the girl from the kennels!"

They all rushed up to the prone Casey, who was lying unconscious on the ground. Nesbit crouched down and felt her pulse. "She's alive, but no thanks to you!" he snarled at Alexander. For once Alexander was unable to summon up the aggressive repartee in response. He was so shocked that he had shot at random and at the wrong person.

"Where's she been shot?" asked Jim.

"In the leg. Luckily it missed the big artery but it's a nasty wound nonetheless." He looked up at Alexander angrily. "Another inch to the left and she could have bled out in minutes!" he snapped at the Russian.

Alexander recovered himself and his fierce expression was back. "You in no position to tell me what I did wrong!" he growled, pointing the gun threateningly at Nesbit.

"Let me at least call her an ambulance," Jim pleaded.

"No. No ambulance. You said it was not a dangerous wound. She will recover, right?"

"She will recover if she gets medical attention quickly," Nesbit said angrily. "She could easily get an infection if she's just left here. The ground is dirty and no doubt so are her clothes. You cannot just leave her!"

"I am the boss here," Alexander reminded him. "She stays. One of the neighbors can call an ambulance."

He looked towards the kennels. "I think we look in there," Alexander said. He jerked the gun into Nesbit's back. "Up. Start walking. Now."

They all walked into the gate of the kennels. "You call," he ordered Nesbit again.

"Yael! Are you in there?"

Dogs started barking madly.

"I no like dogs," Svetlana said worriedly.

"Shut up, "Alexander said. They walked on. "Jewish girls also no like dogs," Svetlana pressed on. "I never meet a religious Jewish girl who likes dogs. She not in there. She too scared."

Nesbit wondered how many religious Jewish girls Svetlana knew, but decided to keep quiet. There was something decidedly unusual about Svetlana's assertion; he couldn't quite put his finger on what it was.

The barking turned to growling. Deep-throated, menacing growling.

As they neared the first lot of cages, a couple of huge, black dogs jumped up, flinging themselves at the bars of the cage, growling and baring their huge, yellow teeth.

Alexander wiped some sweat from his forehead. Then he glanced in the direction of a cage up ahead that was open. Both he and Nesbit heard low growling coming from that direction. The dogs were loose!

Nesbit saw Alexander shoot Svetlana a quick glance.

"Let's go. You're right. The girl is not here."

They wheeled around and walked briskly away from the terrifying noise. Nesbit wondered briefly why no dogs were chasing them, but with a gun at his back he didn't want to turn around and find out.

The four of them walked off down the street, with Nesbit ordered to call out Yael's name every few yards.

When she could no longer hear their voices, Yael got up from the seat in the rottweiler enclosure, still holding tightly onto the chain leashes of the four dogs. She left the cage, closing it securely behind her. Only when she was outside and they were inside, safe, did she let go of the leashes and let them slide back through the wire mesh.

She looked through the mesh at the dogs. They whined at her and tried to lick her hand through the mesh. She had made four canine friends. "Thank you, thank you," she said softly to them. "You probably saved my life. No, you definitely saved my life." They whined at her again, showing their affection.

By leaving the door to their enclosure open, and making sure they were growling menacingly at the advancing enemies, she had misled her pursuers into thinking the dogs would attack. She had overcome her innate nervousness of the dogs and had sat amongst them quietly, allowing them to deflect the search party from her.

But what about Casey? Yael didn't dare go out into the street where she lay. But there was Casey's cell phone, lying where she had left it, and so she quickly made an emergency call for an ambulance, leaving herself anonymous. In a few minutes, she heard the ambulance siren in the distance, as she made her way to the back of the kennels, looking for an alternative escape route.

The sounds of the ambulance came ever nearer, and then the four in the street saw it screech down the street and stop where Casey lay, still unconscious.

Alexander grinned at Jim and Nesbit. "You see?" he said. "Such good neighbors you English people have. Your little kennel maid will be well looked after. Now you, walk and keep calling! She has to be here somewhere!"

Nesbit turned his head just a little, and caught Svetlana's expression. She was smiling to herself.

CHAPTER FORTY-SIX

Y*ael is in there,* Nesbit thought. *In the kennels. And Svetlana knew it too. That's why she did the whole thing about being scared of dogs. She was protecting Yael.*

It took a lot of getting his head around the concept that Svetlana wasn't entirely in cahoots with Alexander and his plans for Yael. *What was her hidden agenda?* he wondered. But whatever it was, he had to act upon it. It occurred to him that the villains had had the upper hand for most of this episode and were mocking the "stupid British police" at every opportunity. It was time to turn that on its head.

Somehow, he had to deflect his captors and gain control of the situation. The Russians could not be allowed to win, even though it seemed that they knew every move of the chess game before the cops had even come to the table. It was time for things to change.

He knew he couldn't do it without Jim, and in order to do it, he had to somehow let Jim know his intentions. If they acted together... Nesbit wished as he had never wished before, that there was a language he and Jim knew that the Russians didn't.

Then he remembered. When Jim was being tutored on acting Jewish, to take the rabbi's place in the exchange, he had been taught a few words of Hebrew and Yiddish to make him sound convincing. Nesbit had helped him practice them, and in so doing had learned them himself. It wasn't nearly enough to make conversation, but maybe a word or two to Jim could alert him somehow, some way... What had he learned?

Oy vey (Oh dear). Not too useful, he feared.

Die meidel (The girl). Now *that*...

Ich ken nisht (I can't). Hmm...

He was very worried that if he started spouting a foreign tongue to Jim, Alexander would realize that they were sending each other a signal. He seemed to be very much on the ball, our Alexander, mused Nesbit, and gave up the idea of speaking Yiddish. It would have to be subliminal messaging. No idea how that worked, but he'd have to try it.

The gun jabbed him painfully in the lower back. "You aren't shouting," Alexander growled.

At that very moment there was a burst of furious barking from the kennels behind them. Alexander looked back nervously, and Nesbit took the opportunity to kick Jim on the shin, and with various impressive expression techniques, send him a signal that he hoped read: "The girl is back there... Work with me..."

Jim nodded almost imperceptibly. The message had been passed, and the dogs had once again served a valuable purpose.

"I no like dogs," said Svetlana conversationally, just as the two cops did a synchronized 360 that would have put an Olympic swimming team to shame, and with force, knocked the guns out of the Russians' hands. They had taken them so much by surprise that it wasn't that difficult a maneuver. There was a tight and anguished scuffle that morphed into a frantic struggle for power. Punches flew but the two cops were fit and both were purple belts at martial arts.

Even though they hadn't come out armed, they were now. They both had handcuffs on them, which they skillfully used to snap onto the Russians' wrists. They were sitting on the Russians, who were facedown in the dirt, when the most welcome sound in the world hit their eardrums.

Police sirens, coming closer. The backup they had requested was finally here.

Once the two criminals were in the police van, and the two cops were busy dusting themselves down and congratulating each other on a job well done, Jim commented to Nesbit, "The woman didn't put up much of a fight. It's as if she wanted it over and done with."

Nesbit nodded. "I honestly think that's true. For some reason I haven't yet fathomed, the woman protected Yael. She knew that Yael was probably in the kennels and deflected Alexander by all that 'scared of dogs' talk. It was a brilliant move and I've no doubt it saved Yael's life."

"Hopefully that will be used in her favor in court," Jim commented as the van drove away. They watched Svetlana's face in the rear window. She was watching them, and smiling, as if she was pleased with how things had turned out.

"What do you reckon?" Nesbit asked.

"She's been trafficked here," Jim replied as they walked back towards the kennels, "probably promised England was the land where the streets were paved with gold and all that rubbish. Comes here, finds herself at the mercy of that bully Alexander."

"Ah, so this is her way out. Even if it means a spell in jail."

Jim nodded. "Indeed. A spell in a British jail is going to be heaven to someone bound hand and foot to a man like Alexander. Especially if she gets off relatively lightly compared to him. That way she can skip the country, maybe go back to Russia, do whatever she wants in safety and he can't catch up with her."

They walked up the side passageway into the kennels. On the way in they noticed a dark patch on the pavement where Casey had fallen and bled.

"I hope she's all right," said Nesbit.

"I saw her being taken into the ambulance," said a girlish voice, and Yael appeared cautiously from behind some enclosures. "And she seems fine, *baruch Hashem*. She wasn't unconscious anymore; I heard her talking to the ambulance people."

"Yael!" Jim said, grinning broadly as he recognized his charge. "How did you know it was safe to come out?"

"I watched the whole thing," she said, grinning back. "I had wanted to escape from the back of the kennels, but there isn't another way out, so I just waited it out with the dogs. There's a kind of gap just over there where I can see the street through quite clearly, and I saw what was happening. I saw him nudging you and I thought, if I can just distract him for a second, you might be able to do something. So I startled the rottweilers and they started barking."

The two cops stared at her in open admiration. "*You* did that? Wow."

She smiled. "I was right, wasn't I? You did do something."

"That was pretty awesome," Nesbit admitted. "Good, clear thinking, action planning. I told you, you'll make a spy one day."

"I'm not sure I want to be a spy," Yael said. "It was all pretty scary."

"Coming home?" Jim said.

"Home? I don't have a home. School is the only home I know."

"Then let's take you back to school. I'm sure you'll get a hero's welcome there."

"I don't want any hero's welcome," Yael said. "I'd just like a long, hot shower, something to eat, and to be with my friends."

They all started back towards the police car waiting at the edge of the forest.

"Aren't we forgetting something?" Jim reminded Nesbit darkly, as they walked. "Alexander and Svetlana aren't the head honchos in this matter. Ivan Rodchenko is. And he's still in jail, and he still wants Nena silenced. If Alexander and Svetlana failed to do it, he'll find someone else who will. This isn't over yet. Not by a long shot."

CHAPTER FORTY-SEVEN

The whole school came out to greet Yael when she arrived. There wasn't a girl, or a teacher, or a cleaner, or a gardener, who wasn't suffused with joy at the girl's safe return. The school choir stood outside in the chilly afternoon, and sang as her car drew up. Everyone cheered and clapped.

Nesbit and Jim stopped the car and got out, and then opened the back door to allow the overwhelmed young girl to step out to the welcome she neither wanted nor felt she deserved.

Shuli, Rosie, and Nena ran forward to hug her. The four stood there, crying and hugging, and hugging and crying, as the school choir sang a rousing rendition of *"Chasdei Hashem ki lo samnu, ki lo samnu chasadav"* from Miami Boys. Yael stood there, watching and listening, her gaze passing over all the cheering girls and applauding female teachers and auxiliary staff, and just allowed the tears to run unchecked down her cheeks.

Once the singing was over, the male teachers, including Rabbi Moslovsky, joined the crowds outside. The *rav* held up his hand for silence. The noise gradually faded.

"Chasdei Hashem! Chasdei Hashem!" he cried out and the cheering rose again. He held up his hand and it died away.

"I know that Yael Reed does not want to be considered a heroine, but this school would be failing in its duty if we did not recognize the immense danger she has been in, and the innovative and daring ways she found to overcome it. Yael fought back bravely, used intuition and immense courage, and escaped from her captors who had only her worst interests at heart.

"When the police were at the point of no return, and there seemed no way out for them, Yael created a diversion that enabled them to turn the tables on the villains. Whatever she says to the contrary, she *is* a heroine, and heroism deserves acknowledgment."

A huge cheer and applause rang out. The *rav* waited until it had died down and then continued.

"I would also like to thank and acknowledge the fantastic efforts put in by the members of this school, who fasted diligently, and davened and said *Tehillim* for her safe return. Hashem listens to the prayers of the pure hearts. Thank you."

More cheering and clapping. Those among the teachers who were either non-Jewish or not so *frum*, shuffled a bit and looked uncomfortable, but the *rav* then went on.

"G-d listens to everyone's prayers if they are meant sincerely. And tonight, in honor of the safe return of Yael Reed, we are having a *seudas hodaah*. The cooks are already hard at work preparing a feast to be remembered. In the school hall, at seven thirty! Now, all of you, back to class! And thanks to the school choir."

The crowd dispersed, and Yael walked slowly back to the school with her friends close around her, like a protective shield.

"We want to hear all about it!" Shuli said.

Yael frowned. "I'm not sure…"

"Leave her be…" Nena said, worriedly. "She's been through enough."

As if to confirm this, Nesbit and Jim joined the little group and took the girls aside, away from the curious gazes of the others.

"I just want to stress to you, enjoy this, but be aware, it isn't over. Alexander and Svetlana are in custody, so they no longer present a threat. But they were only worker bees for the head honcho. He is still in prison and he still wants to prevent Nena from testifying. He will, repeat *will* try again."

Nena burst into tears.

"I thought this was over!" she sobbed. "When will it ever be over? Even if I testify and he is convicted, he will try and get me, won't he?"

"Yes, he probably will," admitted Nesbit. "And since he has found you here, I think the only thing to do is to move you again to another safe place."

Yael glared at him. "What do you mean *another* safe place?? *This* was meant to be a safe place! Why wasn't it? How did he find her?"

"Someone, somehow, somewhere, must have blabbed," Nesbit said with a shrug, turning his palms up. "I can't think of another answer."

"There isn't a safe place in the entire world!" sobbed Nena. "I'll be running my whole life! He'll find me wherever I am!! Oh, I wish I hadn't seen him killing that person!! I don't want to move from here. I like it here!"

The other girls closed ranks and hugged her.

"By staying here you're putting others at risk too," Jim pointed out.

"We'll take that chance," Shuli said with bravado. "We want Nena to stay." She wasn't at all sure she meant what she said. Yael might be a superhero but she, Shuli, didn't feel like one.

Nesbit sighed. He really hadn't wanted to pour cold water on what was, after all, a huge celebration. Maybe he should have timed this conversation for after their festive meal.

"We'll talk later," he said. "You go, enjoy having Yael back, and enjoy all the celebrations."

The girls were very happy to comply with this suggestion, and put his doom-laden words out of their minds as they joined the rest of the school.

Only Yael retained some level of gravitas. She had been the one who had experienced the closest contact with the "baddies" and as such, she knew what they were capable of. She had no doubt at all that this was not over. But for now she just wanted to enjoy being back, being with her friends, and not think about anything else.

"What do you want to do first?" Rosie asked her excitedly when they were back in their rooms.

"I'd like to phone the hospital and find out how Casey Donald is," Yael said firmly. "After all, she's probably saved my life not once, but twice. Once, when she took care of my infected hands and feet. And second, when she confronted the gunmen and got herself shot in the process. And after that…take a long, hot shower! Been waiting to do that for days now!"

"I'll run it for you!" Shuli said.

"I'll get your towel!" Nena added.

"You can use my new shower gel!" Rosie said.

Yael held up both her hands to stop them.

"Look guys," she said seriously. "I know you're happy to have me back, and believe me, you're not half as happy as I am to *be* back. But I don't really want all this fuss made over me. I just wanna be one of the gang again, you know?"

The trio all nodded and stopped their dancing around her. "Sorry, Yael...you go right ahead and get your own shower."

"I'll accept the shower gel though, please, Rosie," giggled Yael. "You always get the nicest smelling ones!"

Yael made the phone call to the hospital. She was put through to Casey's room, and spoke to her directly.

"It's so nice of you to call," Casey said. "I'm doing well. They stopped the bleeding and saw that the bullet had gone straight through my leg so there wasn't anything to remove. I'm on antibiotics but they said I can go home tomorrow, all being well."

"You saved my life. Twice." Yael said, almost crying on the phone. "You're a very special girl, Casey Donald. Thank you. I hope we meet again someday."

They said their good-byes, promising to keep in touch, but even as they did, Yael knew it would be unlikely that they would. Their lives had touched briefly and significantly, but they were from two different worlds.

Yael was so tired, she fell asleep at her own *seudas hodaah*. The meal had been so delicious, and she was full for the first time since her capture. Someone up on the podium was making a speech, she didn't know who, and she didn't really care. She was back at school, with her friends, safe and sound, and in one piece. She sent up a prayer of thanks of her own to Hashem, and fell fast asleep, right there in her chair.

Her friends nudged her, but she was out cold. When Moslovsky noticed, he called for early *bentching*. Her friends half walked her, half carried her, back to her bed, where she fell straight back to sleep without even getting undressed.

Alexander and Svetlana were in police custody, and were shortly to be moved to jail, where they would await trial. There was no question of them getting bail; they were both far too much of a flight risk.

Nesbit went in to see the pair of them, in cells as far away from each other as possible in that small station. Svetlana was lying on the hard bed, facing the wall, and refused to look at or talk to him. But Alexander was up for a bit of interaction.

"You know you have achieved nothing," Alexander hissed at him through the bars. "Ivan will just find someone else to do the job. We are only…how you say…the drones? He will get more. There are always more. Stupid British police…"

CHAPTER FORTY-EIGHT

"I. Do. Not. Want. To. Move. Schools. Again," Nena said. "End. Of. Story."

The four girls were sitting on Rosie's bed, their favorite perch, the afternoon after the *seudas hodaah*. Yael was somewhat recovered now, although still looking pale and shaky. She kept zoning in and out of the conversation, as if keeping up with it was too much of an effort. It almost seemed as if she went to sleep for a few seconds every few minutes, but with her eyes open. Rosie looked at her worriedly.

"I think you need to go to the hospital," she told Yael. "You're obviously not well."

Yael zoned in and blinked at Rosie. "I'll be fine," she said. "The cops have sent me their best trauma counselor. She's great. I spoke to her this morning just to say hi, and I'm seeing her again later today for a proper session. Apparently even the cops get a trauma counselor if they've been in very dangerous situations, so how much more so me, a kid."

"Well, is she medically trained enough to know if you're suffering from something physical as well as trauma?" Rosie persisted.

"Yes, she is. Please don't worry. I really will be fine." Yael insisted. They turned their attention back to Nena.

"Look," Shuli said sternly to Nena, "I know you don't want to move schools, and we don't want to lose you either. But you've heard what these guys are capable of. This isn't a game, Nena. They were ready to kill Yael and they'll kill you. Whoever this Ivan guy sends next will be twice as bad as Alexander and Svetlana."

Nena said nothing, but picked at the bed sheet until a tiny thread unraveled.

"This is awful," Yael said. "I just don't know what to tell you, Nena. However reckless and brave I might have been before this mission, I've discovered one thing I didn't know about myself before. I have a survival instinct far stronger than I ever imagined I had. And if I'm the one with nothing to lose — or so I thought — how much more so do *you* not want to die? What's more important to you, three friends you can always catch up with at some point in your life, or actually living that life? Being able to grow up, get married, have a family, and a future?"

The other two girls nodded their agreement of Yael's assessment and Nena sighed.

"I don't think I'll ever be safe, that's the worst part of it. I'll spend my entire life looking over my shoulder."

The other three girls had nothing comforting to say to this. Especially

Yael, who had been at the sharp end of Ivan's drones and knew what they were capable of. The four of them sat in silence for a while, each thinking of what they could say to make it all better.

Then Nena said with a huge effort and forced cheerfulness, "Well guys, as you say, I'll always be able to catch up with you later in life. When we each have six kids, we'll meet up and talk about the past, huh?"

There was an unenthusiastic chorus of "yeah's" and "sure's." No one had any confidence in Nena's future, if she had one, and all were thinking the same thing. *I sure hope I never witness a crime by a heartless killer like Ivan…*

Rabbi Moslovsky was in his office, but not at ease. He had so many issues burning up inside his head. Should Nena be sent away to another safe place? If so, how could anyone guarantee it would be safe? This school, in its remote location hadn't proved to be safe, had it? He felt responsible for the child, and felt that if he sent her away again, it would be like absolving himself of that responsibility.

Who had blabbed? How had Nena been traced? That could remain a mystery forever. It might have been careless talk by a gardener or workman who had overheard the girls talking… It could've been anyone. It hardly mattered anymore. What mattered now was how to keep Nena safe.

And what about Yael? Who was to say Ivan wouldn't come after her too, knowing that she had duped his people and led them a merry dance?

The *rav* put his head in his hands and groaned. Miss Colton safely back. Yael, safely back. And yet…it was all far from over. When would it ever feel safe?

Miss Colton had been through a lot in her fifty years of life. She could have just shoved her parents in an old-age home and got on with her life; she knew lots of people who had done that. But she didn't, couldn't have, wouldn't have ever. She had missed out on so much by being a good daughter.

Ner Miriam had seemed so very prosaic when she had first joined it. What excitement could there possibly be in a secondary school full of religious Jewish girls? These girls had been well brought up and were all pretty mainstream. There would not be a great deal of rebellion, truancy (nowhere to go anyway!) and other inappropriate behavior so common in less genteel schools.

She had sighed to herself and hoped that, if there was a G-d somewhere up there, He had made a note of her martyrdom for her parents and would save her a specially nice cloud to sit on up in heaven.

Maybe Miss Colton had misinterpreted the phrase "pretty mainstream." After all, there was little about Nena and Yael, to name but two girls, that could be called mainstream. Nena had witnessed a terrible crime and was now in a Witness Protection Program at the school. And Yael was the religious Jewish girl's answer to Batman, Superman, and Spiderman, all rolled into one, some daredevil who had come along to rescue Nena from possible harm.

Miss Colton sat there, thinking about everything that had happened to her in recent days. She wasn't nearly ready to just hang that part of her life up on a clothes peg, and shove it into the back of her closet. No, she had experienced the adrenalin rush to end all adrenalin rushes, and she wanted more of it.

And she was going to make it happen.

CHAPTER FORTY-NINE

Miss Colton was trying to bring back the feeling of excitement and the thrill of danger of her capture, but like a puff of cloud, it was eluding her, slowly slipping between her fingers. The exchange with Yael-Nena itself had been a knife-edge experience.

On enforced compassionate leave for two weeks to recover from this "ordeal," she smiled to herself. Miss Colton had spent enough of her life wishing for things that could never happen. All the time her parents were alive and she was caring for them dutifully and lovingly, she had wished a Prince Charming, preferably on a white horse, would ride up to her modest suburban home, and rescue her from her life. He would marry her of course, and take her and her parents away to his palace.

This had not happened. Now her parents had both died and it was too late for her to marry. She couldn't see any Prince Charming, even a balding, aging one, wanting her now.

She had another whole week of enforced "rest" from school before she had to go back, and she decided to make the most of it. She had to do something to recreate that aura of excitement, whilst at the same time help Nena out of her continued predicament. She wasn't sure how she would achieve that, but she had heard that the Russian who had put a price on Nena's head was still seeking her permanent silencing, and the girl, the real Nena, was absolutely terrified. Maybe she, Miss Colton the Brave, could do something about that.

It didn't take her five seconds to elicit where Alexander and Svetlana were being held. And so, calling a cab, as she had never learned to drive, she made her way to it that morning with a new spring in her step.

She wasn't exactly sure what she was going to say to either of them if she got the chance to speak to them. All she knew was, no one duped Barbara Colton the way those two had with their disguises, and got away with it. She had been sorely mocked by the two of them and she was going to confront them about it. That was the first step, and then she'd play it by ear to see if there was any way round it for Nena.

The policeman on duty recognized her from the news photos of the exchange and botched rescue attempt, but was dubious about allowing her in.

She drew herself up to her full height, which wasn't much, and glared at him.

"Young man!" she said in her best schoolmarm voice. "I have been held prisoner by these two. They mistreated me and duped me with disguises. I think I have the right to speak to them now. You needn't worry, I have no weapons with me."

The policeman had been worried of exactly that. He called a female colleague to give her a proper body search, and ordered her to leave her coat and handbag at the front desk. She was even told to remove her shoes.

"I can hardly batter anyone to death with these sensible shoes," she said, irritated, but took them off all the same and handed them to the cop at the desk.

When she saw Alexander and Svetlana in cells not too far from each other, but too far to communicate, she looked at the policeman to signal to him that she'd like some time alone with them. The policeman nodded and stood back a bit, unwilling to completely leave her on her own.

She approached Alexander first. He looked so different now without all the bushy hair, moustache, and eyebrows. He looked startled when he saw her.

"It's the fat old woman!" he exclaimed with a grin. At least his teeth hadn't been altered for the disguise, so his smile was the same.

"You can stop calling me names now. I am no longer your captive," she ordered him, and her tone of voice brooked no arguments. She had always possessed the makings of a teacher and a devastating tone had always been enough for discipline. Even with Alexander, it seemed to work. He glared at her.

"Did you know the girl they sent wasn't right girl?" he asked.

She hadn't the slightest idea until she saw Yael when they changed places in the parking lot, but she wasn't going to confess that. She looked at him archly.

"Maybe," she said.

He looked nonplussed. Obviously processing the fact that she had possibly outsmarted them all the time. He couldn't think of a single thing to say in reply.

She smiled, tossed her head with its tight bun of gray hair, and moved on to Svetlana's cell. Svetlana was lying on the bed facing away from her. Miss Colton called her name.

"It's me, Miss Colton!" she said in a stage whisper. Svetlana turned and a slight smile touched the very corners of her mouth.

"Is girl okay?" she asked quietly.

Miss Colton was surprised. "Yes, she's fine…" She faltered.

Svetlana got up from the bed and came to the bars of the cell, putting her face close.

"I wanted her to be safe. I didn't want her to die. Even if she the right girl."

"She isn't," Miss Colton said.

"I know. How is the real girl?"

"Terrified. Everyone feels that this isn't over. It's an unsafe feeling."

Svetlana put her mouth close to Miss Colton's ear through the bars. "You are all right. It isn't over… Not at all…but there's something I really need to do…something very important…I need your help…"

Miss Colton looked around her covertly. The guard was checking his iPhone for e-mails. *Thank heavens for the addictive properties of the Smartphone,* she thought.

"Yes, Svetlana," she whispered back. "I will do whatever I can to help… What is it you need me to do?"

CHAPTER FIFTY

Miss Colton and Svetlana were standing very close, just the metal bars of the cell separating them. She listened as Svetlana spoke a few words. Then the guard looked up from his iPhone. Presumably he had finished checking his messages, or he had lost the signal, but either way, the spell was broken. His gaze had been rather unfocused, but now it sharpened as he saw them, heads bent together at the bars.

"No whispering to the prisoners!" he shouted, stepping forward, trying to salvage the situation. "All conversation must be clearly audible!" It was like shutting the prison gates after everyone had escaped. Just. Too. Late.

"Sorry!" Miss Colton said ever so politely, and withdrew. She had heard what Svetlana had wanted to tell her, and she nodded ever so slightly to the Russian girl to signify it.

"What was she talking to you about?" the guard asked aggressively, trying to make up for his lack of awareness. If something had passed between those two women and he hadn't noticed it, there would be more than just disciplining; his job would most likely be on the line.

"It's a…woman thing," Miss Colton said. She winked at Svetlana, who winked back, and she walked out of the cell area. She was subjected to another body search by a female guard, just to ensure Svetlana hadn't passed her a note or something tangible, but everything that had passed between them was invisibly stored in her head and wouldn't show up on the most stringent of searches.

Safely outside the police station, Miss Colton sat on a bench in the autumn sunshine and thought about what she had been asked to do.

Back at the school, Nena was still in a state of agonizing flux. It didn't seem to matter which way she dealt the cards of her life, it came out the same. Ivan Rodchenko was still out to get her, he now knew exactly *where* she was — if not exactly *who* she was, but that wouldn't take him long to elicit — and he would be pursuing her until she was no longer any risk to him. Or to anything on this planet, for that matter.

But she so didn't want to leave this school, and the wonderful new friends she had made here. She had had problems her entire life with friends and fitting in to a social group, and now, for the first time, she felt at home, and accepted. She was fighting an internal battle between her innate survival instincts, and wanting things to stay exactly how they were right now, surrounded by her loving friends in a school she adored.

All the adults around her, who cared about her surviving beyond the age of fourteen, strongly persuaded her that she had to put personal issues aside, and move on from Ner Miriam. Probably go abroad, and probably somewhere totally alien and distant, where Rodchenko would have a job and a half catching up with her. Even her lovely friends were coming around to this way of thinking.

"How could we ever live with ourselves if we persuaded you to stay and something happened to you?" Rosie explained. And it was true. Was Nena being selfish by not caring about the effect some disastrous incident could have on other people?

Now the talk was of sending her to a school in a suburb of Melbourne, Australia. That could hardly be further away if it tried. Unless there were schools on Mars.

"Or Jo'burg," Rabbi Moslovsky, originally of that town in South Africa, suggested.

This was not met with enthusiasm or agreement from anyone, not even other South African expats.

"There's enough crime already in Johannesburg without this poor girl importing her own," another teacher said, and there were nods all around. So that idea was discarded as unworkable.

The undercover workers in the school had left now that the exchange was over. Even though Nena was still on the Witness Protection Program, she did not need half a dozen or so people pretending to be teachers, hovering around her. She just needed…well, she just wanted…to be left alone to get on with her life, although that didn't look like it was going to happen.

There were meetings in the staff room almost every day on the subject of Nena and what should be done with her. She was never allowed to attend these meetings. It was as if her entire future was to be taken out of her hands and she just had to do what she was told.

Australia remained a firm favorite. One of the women teachers was originally from Melbourne and still had a lot of connections there. She took it upon herself to find out about schools and foster homes that would take Nena in.

When Nena heard about this she shut herself in her room and sobbed for hours. To be shipped off to the other side of the globe and lodged with foster parents when she had a wonderful loving family, and a school where she felt at home, right here in the UK, was her idea of a draconian punishment. Yes, that was it. She was being punished for having been a loyal citizen and having done her civil duty, when she identified Ivan Rodchenko.

Endless, endless times, she went over that scenario in the park when she saw him shoot that man, and endless, endless times in her mind, she gave it a different ending. One where she just hid until it was safe to come out, and then she just went back to school and said nothing to anyone. No one need ever have known what she had witnessed. What a different life she would have had!

But then as she watched the story play out, she knew that, had she said nothing, she would still be back in her home town, unhappy at school, friendless and unpopular. Yes, she would have her family to support her, but no one else. Here, at Ner Miriam, she knew she still had her family's backing even though they weren't allowed to keep in touch. And she had made the most wonderful friends in the world. So life wasn't all bad. If only she could just stay here!

But as plans were rumbling relentlessly forwards, plans to ship her away to Melbourne, she knew the dream of staying here had as much substance as a puff of smoke. So she cried bitter tears, and resigned herself to her fate, resolving to spend as much time as she had left, with her friends.

"There's always the phone," Shuli said.

The four of them were sitting on Nena's bed, hugging and wiping their eyes as they contemplated the future. Nena sighed.

The idea of her sitting on the other side of the world, with a twenty-three-hour time difference, trying to find a common time to talk to her old friends, was sad and impractical and she knew it would never last. Once she got on that plane, she would probably never see Rosie, Shuli, and Yael again.

"It's the end of my life as I know it. I might as well accept it. I'm going to Australia and that's it," Nena wept, hugging the others.

Miss Colton, however, now back at school after her enforced rest, sat in her office, staring out of the window at the crashing waves on the rocks below, a grim expression on her face.

CHAPTER FIFTY-ONE

It was the worst possible week for Nena. She was going to leave for Australia in about ten days, after she had testified at Rodchenko's trial via video link. The video link would be set up from the school to keep her as safe as possible, but in the meantime she wasn't even allowed to say good-bye to her parents. As part of the Witness Protection Program, no one could be sure if she did meet up with them, that someone might not have followed her to the venue, possibly placing her parents' and siblings' lives in danger.

However, Nesbit took pity on the poor girl, and arranged for a phone call between them on a secure line that could not be tapped into or monitored. This was a highly technical operation and involved MI5. Nena's family had to go to their headquarters in the center of London to receive the call.

Nena was handed the secure phone in Rabbi Moslovsky's office. It was a cell phone and looked like any other, but apparently it wasn't. She held it like it was going to explode in her hand, and looked at Nesbit and Rabbi Moslovsky. They nodded at her as a signal to begin speaking. Despite her obvious wish for privacy at this most awful time, they didn't dare leave her alone in case she gave a clue as to her whereabouts now and where she was going.

The phone was on a special seven-second delay, so that if she did slip up and say something she shouldn't have, it could be deleted before her parents ever heard it. The phone engineer stood by with a small machine, his finger poised on the button. It was all totally surreal.

"I don't know if I can do this…" Nena said, looking appealingly at Rabbi Moslovsky, tears pouring down her face.

He was uncharacteristically crying too. "Go on, Nena," the *rav* said. "This could be your last chance to speak to them."

Nena stood there a few seconds, thinking of that life-changing moment in the park and wished, as she had wished countless times before, that she could press the back button on her life and then delete that episode.

"Hello?" she said, her voice choking with emotion. The call had begun. Nesbit and the *rav* stood by, anxiously watching the phone engineer's finger, hoping it wouldn't move to the Delete button. And so it was, that an anonymous telephone techie from MI5 was the only person in Nena's new life to hear her real name, because it was this name that her parents sobbed on the phone. No one else heard their side of the call.

Nena did a lot of crying and a lot of reminiscing, and some more crying, going over her past life. By clips of what she said, the listeners in the room were able to piece together what her parents might be saying to her.

"I know, Mummy," Nena sobbed, "but one day I'm sure I'll be able to see you again. After all, he can't live forever... I know you're older than he is but...I feel sure that somehow we'll meet again... I just know it... Oh, Mummy, I don't want to go away again! I like it here; I've made so many good friends..." The techie's finger twitched over the delete button but she didn't give away any more clues.

She sobbed and sobbed, clutching that small, black oblong as if it was her mother's arms. At length the call ended. Nena handed back a rather wet cell phone to Nesbit, and fled from the room, head averted, not wanting to see or speak to anyone, just wanting to hide herself away in her room like a wounded animal waiting to die alone.

The day dawned of Ivan Rodchenko's trial for murder. The video link had been set up at the school, in a quiet room away from everyone else, and again technicians abounded, with cameras, microphones, computers, and recording devices.

Nena was in a catatonic state; somewhere between caring about life and not caring about anything. She just went through the motions of her life like a robot. She had been prepared by the lawyers and she knew what she had to say. She also knew how she might be attacked through the video link in cross examination, and she had been prepared for that too. Now there was nothing to do but wait for it all to begin.

Her three friends were with Nena every step of the way. They didn't want to spend a moment away from her, knowing that this day was one of her last at the school. Their support, their love and admiration, was the greatest boost of all, and yet made her realize with even more pain, what she would be leaving behind.

Shuli, Rosie, and Yael didn't want to keep crying because they knew it wouldn't help Nena if they did. They were determined to keep stoic, but every now and then events caught up with them and they would excuse themselves — never all at once, just one at a time, and go somewhere to cry about the unfairness of it all.

The rest of the school had not been informed about the trial or that Nena was giving evidence. After the initial leak back to Ivan, the police decided not to trust anyone except the people in immediate proximity to Nena. So no other girls, no teachers, no assistant and general workers at the school had any idea what was going on today.

"We traced the original leak," Nesbit said grimly to Moslovsky, as they waited for the trial to begin. "It was one of the gardeners. He was Eastern European and had, without the school's knowledge, connections to Rodchenko. Not that he was criminally involved, no. Just a man scared for his life so willing to pass knowledge back in return for safety."

"How did you find this out?" the *rav* asked, impressed with the detective's acumen.

"His body was washed up on the rocks below the school yesterday," Nesbit said with a sigh, "and was eventually identified as one of the school gardeners. Who killed him we don't yet know."

Moslovsky shuddered as the full impact of Rodchenko's dark power reached him.

"It seems indeed that anyone who crosses Rodchenko is never safe, no matter what he or she does to save himself," said Nesbit. And both men looked towards the room where Nena sat, silently waiting.

All Nena really wanted to do was run away as far from this room as possible, but there was no way out of this. The trial was beginning this morning, and after she had given her evidence and presumably been grilled in cross examination, she would pack up and disappear from the school forever. It was a one-way ticket to oblivion.

CHAPTER FIFTY-TWO

Nena didn't even allow herself to think because thinking hurt too much. She had to go through the motions. There was no choice. She had been promised that the girls in her new school in Australia were nice and friendly, but she would take on yet another identity; she would no longer be Nena there. She had become so used to being Nena that she had almost forgotten it wasn't even her real name.

Miss Colton, back at school but on a day off, was determined to see this thing through. She had done something so against her nature that she could hardly believe it of herself, but she believed, if there was a G-d up there, He would understand. She couldn't really pray; she never had done so. No one had ever been religious at home, but she decided to have a chat with G-d, tell him why she had done it, and hope He would forgive her.

She sat in the back of a cab going to the courthouse, closed the dividing window between herself and the driver, and looked up at the ceiling of the cab.

"If you're there, G-d," she said quietly, but with feeling, "I want you to know that the reason I did it was to save Nena. I don't know much about the Russian Mafia, and until they kidnapped me, our paths had never crossed. So I bore the indignity of my incarceration with as much stoicism as I could, because of that girl. And in the end, poor Nena was no better off than she'd been in the beginning." Miss Colton sighed and wiped away a tear.

The driver watched his passenger in his rearview mirror, puzzled to see her talking to herself. But as a London cabbie, he'd seen all sorts.

"So this girl would be at the mercy of this horrible, horrible criminal her entire life. So I decided I had to do this, even though I know it's against Your laws. I really hope you'll accept mitigation when it comes to the Day of Judgment…if there is such a thing."

Outside, the gloomy autumn day brightened as a shaft of sunlight suddenly parted the clouds and shone directly into her cab window. She took it as a sign, and sat back, satisfied, never once considering that as a G-dless person, she might not quite be deserving of such signs from above.

"The courts are just over there, missus," the cabbie said through the intercom. "I can't really get to the front of the building. Is it okay if I drop you off 'ere?"

"Quite all right, thank you," Miss Colton said. "And it's miss, not missus." She reached into her bag for the fare and drew back the glass partition.

"Who was you talking to back there?" the cabbie asked, unable to contain his curiosity.

"I…really have no idea," she replied with an enigmatic smile as she got out of the cab. She walked off, leaving him sitting there, rubbing his flat cap against his skull, puzzled.

Barbara Colton crossed the road carefully, and went up the steps to the courthouse.

In the cells below the courthouse, a new guard presented himself for a shift change. He had all the right credentials, his details checked out to the last degree. So the suspicious British guard was relieved of duty, and Bill Wayman of Croydon, Surrey, took his place.

Bill Wayman, aka Grigor Ivanov, previously of Moscow, was now a fully integrated and trained member of the Prison Officers Union. His Russian accent was undetectable now. He had fought hard to conquer it, even going to voice lessons for actors, until he spoke in a mixture of Croydon and Essex cockney that fitted right in to the job in hand.

But Grigor had a history with Ivan Rodchenko — one that involved his parents and sister mysteriously disappearing under unexplained circumstances — and he had been waiting a very long time for payback. When he heard Rodchenko was in the UK, he had made it his business to go there too.

Once there, he had bided his time, working in the prison service, first just for money to stay alive. But later, when he heard Rodchenko was under arrest, Grigor finally saw an opportunity to avenge his parents' and sister's deaths.

So no, Miss Colton had not slipped a weapon into Svetlana's hand while they talked. Nor had she smuggled some poison into the prison. She was not clever enough to work out a way of doing that without detection anyway and the guards were watching her like hawks. All Svetlana had whispered to her was to get ahold of Bill Wayman, a prison guard currently at Belmarsh Prison. She had explained nothing else but had intimated that once Wayman knew what was going on, he may show a sudden interest in switching duty rosters for a while.

So Miss Colton had done her homework and had found Wayman/Ivanov. When she told him about Rodchenko and the girl, he moved heaven and earth to be the one to accompany Rodchenko from his prison cell to the courtroom. That's all she had done, but she was fully aware of the presumed outcome of her actions.

Nena sat in the quiet room in a daze. She was waiting for it to be time to give her statement. Time was dragging. Surely by now?

A noise and flurry occurred outside the door to the quiet room, and Nesbit and Jim came in looking pale and shocked. They told her the news.

On the way to the courtroom from the cells below, Ivan Rodchenko had suffered a massive heart attack. It was totally unexpected; he had seemed very healthy only a few moments before. Indeed he had been fired up for the occasion, and could hardly wait to inflict fear and terror on Nena, even by video link. He had collapsed and been pronounced dead at the scene.

The attending officer, a new man called Bill Wayman, had

administered CPR. Court medics had been called, but no one could save him. The officer was being treated for shock and post-traumatic stress in a side room at the court.

Nena couldn't believe her ears. She sat there stunned. It was too much to take in.

"So how…what…?" she managed.

Rabbi Moslovsky ran into the room. He was exultant.

"It's over, Nena. Nothing more to fear. He can never get to you, never hurt you again."

"So…what about Australia?" she asked dumbly.

"No need for Australia," Nesbit grinned at her. "You are off the Witness Protection Program. You can stay here at Ner Miriam, or you can go back to your previous life and previous school."

There was no hesitation in Nena's voice. "I want to stay here. But I want to be me, not Nena Sheinfeld. And I want my parents and family."

At that moment the door opened and Shuli, Rosie, and Yael came rushing into the room.

"Is it true, Nena? Is he dead? Is it really all over?"

"It's true, and I'm staying here, with you guys! I don't have to go to Australia! Group hug, everyone?"

The girls hugged and sobbed their hearts out in relief and joy. Then Nena said, "Of course, I can now tell you my real name. It's…"

"Shhh," Rosie said. "We don't want to know. Not yet. For now, this is enough. More than enough."

ABOUT THE AUTHOR

Ruthie Pearlman is a well-known writer of many decades. Her earliest books were the *Rifki Nesher* trilogy, *Working It Out*, *Getting It Right*, and *Making It Last*. She then wrote *Daniel My Son*, based on her experiences as a foster parent. After a gap of almost ten years, Ruthie completed a crime-thriller trilogy featuring the popular detective couple Colin and Leora Summers: *Dark Tapestry*, *The Movement*, and *Carers, Ltd*. This series was followed by *Against the Wall*, a groundbreaking novel on at-risk youth. After another long hiatus, Ruthie began writing serials for *Ami* magazine, with *School of Secrets* being the first to be turned into a book.

Ruthie lives in Golders Green, North West London. Her children are all married and she has many grandchildren and great-grandchildren. She also works for the National Childbirth Trust as a prenatal teacher and helps new mothers with nursing difficulties.

MENUCHA PUBLISHERS

More great reads from MENUCHA PUBLISHERS!

PRISMS
by Riva Pomerantz

"The more I write, the more I see how the themes that bind us bring us even closer when explored. That is the driving force behind this collection."

Riva Pomerantz, celebrated author of *Green Fences* and *Breaking Point*, has outdone herself in this book. Like a prism reflecting beams of light, this colorful and illuminating collection will infuse your imagination with sparkle and light. Read and shine!

TRAPPED IN CYBERSPACE
by Ayala Stimler

"Get real! No one normal could possibly fall into the Internet trap."

Michal never meant to get trapped in the sticky strands of the Web. But once she started, she found it hard to stop.

Ayala Stimler expertly weaves together the threads of Michal's story in a groundbreaking novel that will shatter our complacency and open our eyes to the alarming world of addiction.

"Chillingly real... An incredible message."
— Tamar Ansh, author of *Riding the Waves* and *Pesach — Anything's Possible!*

Available wherever Jewish books are sold or at www.menuchapublishers.com

MENUCHA PUBLISHERS

Sit back and relax with these terrific titles!

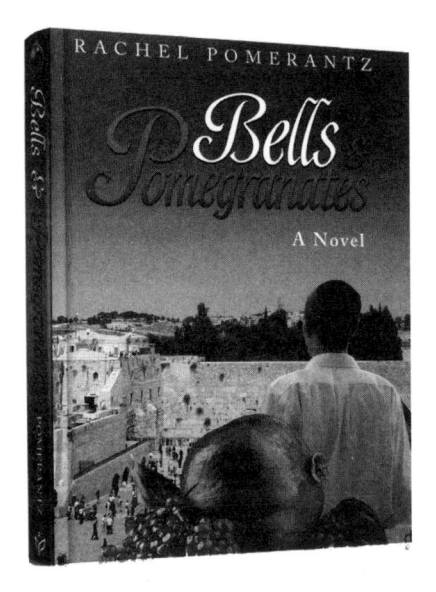

Bells & Pomegranates

by Rachel Pomerantz

In this brand-new novel by celebrated author Rachel Pomerantz, four young people and their families confront daunting lawsuits, life-threatening diagnoses, and menacing thugs, forcing them to acknowledge their deepest fears and overcome them. Building new relationships and repairing old ones, they're determined not to be felled by the faults society finds in them and in their less-than-conventional backgrounds.

DIAMONDS FROM THE Past

by Ruth Benjamin

When Moshe Sher takes a massive loan to avoid bankruptcy, he plunges headlong into an international web of intrigue and deception. When all seems desperate, only his wit and faith can save him.

In *Diamonds from the Past*, popular writer Ruth Benjamin spins a tale that is magnificent in its scope and endless in its implications. Each page is filled with spine-tilling adventure, and each line infused with insight and faith.

Available wherever Jewish books are sold or at www.menuchapublishers.com